PSALM
SPRINGS

by Dane G. Kroll

BOOKS BY DANE G. KROLL

Science fiction:

Realm of Goryo: Prelude- Japan vs Mankind
Realm of Goryo: The Four Pillars
Realm of Goryo: The Culling

Fantasy:

Eluan Falls: The Inheritors of the World
Eluan Falls: The Tides of Utter Undoing

Dedicated to
Josh and Susan
for their support
during every incarnation of this project

Special Thanks to
Joe, Mallory, John, and Kelly

PSALM
SPRINGS

Deuteronomy 21:18-21

If a man has a stubborn and rebellious son who will not obey the voice of his father or the voice of his mother, and though they discipline him, will not listen to them, then his father and his mother shall take hold of him and bring him out to the elders of his city at the gate of the place where he lives, and they shall say to the elders of his city, 'This our son is stubborn and rebellious; he will not obey our voice; he is a glutton and a drunkard.' Then all the men of the city shall stone him to death with stones. So you shall purge the evil from your midst, and all Israel shall hear, and fear.

Welcome to Psalm Springs

It was now the official start of summer for many teens and children. School was out and the days were getting hotter. All across the country summer camps opened their doors. They offered activities and new experiences for the youth of America. For many parents, summer camps were considered a blessing.

Tucked away in the mid-west, the heartland of America, there was one summer camp that stood above the rest, Psalm Springs. Troubled youth and honor students mixed together under the guidance of their Lord and Savior. It was praised as being the only true way to save the future generations of the world. In a society where sin runs rampant and many people have turned away from God, Psalm Springs brought God to the children. They are shown the awesome power of the Lord Almighty.

After three months away many of the campers returned spiritually stronger than ever. Their faith and fear in God was restored. The society that surrounded them could no longer taint their souls with sin. They all followed in the footsteps of Jesus Christ and his Father.

Every year the word spread of the amazing transformations that many of the teens were going through. Boys came back tamed and girls returned obedient. And every year the attendance grew larger.

The first day of camp began right as the schools ended. There was no time to waste. The devil makes work for idol hands. Several cars were parked along the road that served as the entrance to the camp. The gate was wide open. A sign saying PSALM SPRINGS welcomed each and every visitor. Parents were saying their final good-byes to their children. Many parents cried as they left their child for the summer. Prayers and blessings were offered.

One mother could not let go of her daughter. She held her arms tightly around the young girl. The daughter looked away in annoyance and embarrassment. Her hair was colored blonde on one side and red on the other. Piercings shined up the side of her ear. The father had to break his wife's hands free while she cried. She did not want to let her little girl go.

"She has to stay," the husband said to console his

wife. "It's the best thing for her. She will learn."

Along with the cars, white indistinguishable vans parked near the entrance. Each one had several teenagers inside. None of them had parents with them. They were escorted outside by the drivers and handed off to counselors of Psalm Springs.

The expressions on the teenagers' faces ranged from confused to angry. Some of them were half dressed in pajamas; others were formally dressed as if for a school dance. Without a word they were shown to their bunks while families looked on.

Once the morning was over and the families were gone all of the children, teens, and young adults were left on their own. This was their chance to prove to the world and to God that they would make the right decisions.

Each camper was given shirts and shorts to wear for the duration of their stay. There would be no distractions at Psalm Springs. The shirts were bright yellow with a logo of the camp's name and a silhouette of people raising their hands to God. The shirt was accompanied by blue shorts that felt like swim trunks. Every camper was given the same dress.

As the day rolled on all of the campers made their way to the community hall. Empty seats were waiting for them. The counselors stood in the back. They wore a similar shirt only the color was green.

Pastor Samuel Robbins walked onto the stage after all of the campers had arrived. He stood silent for a moment as he looked down at all of the new faces. He was happy to see that the turnout was even better than last year. The good word was spreading.

"Welcome," Robbins said with a smile. "Welcome to another great summer at Psalm Springs. The Lord has blessed us with yet another wonderful year." Half of the crowd cheered, already anticipating Pastor Robbins' opening line.

"Thank you," he said. "I am so pleased to see so many of you here this year. There are a lot of faces I recognize and many I do not. It is truly a wonderful thing when families put their faith in the Lord and their trust in your choices.

"While you are here your time will be spent devoted to God and living the life that He has offered you. Follow in His guidance. His way is the way of the world and only through Him can the world find peace like that of Heaven.

"Our camp is a sanctuary. It needs to be free from the outside influence of sin. This is the Lord's home. You will follow His rules. I know at this moment you bring with you sin in your heart. I do not blame you for that. I do not judge you for that. That is the corruption that the devil has spread across our world. You know nothing else.

"But now is the time to change. To you newcomers here, you will be seeing the resolve of God for the first time. That is a mighty responsibility. It means the duties of our Heavenly Father are now on your shoulders. When this summer is over it will be your privilege to continue to spread the word of God.

"And for the rest of you, welcome back. This summer will be another step in the grace of God. You have been at Heaven's door before and you were welcomed to continue to spread the good word. Acts 19:20, *so the word of the Lord continued to increase and prevail mightily.*

"Now, do not be fooled. This is a warning to everybody. I have seen many of our best return to only falter in the eyes of God. This summer will not be easy. Many of you have sin in your souls. When you leave this sermon I want you to say a prayer as you exit through those doors. Look up to the sky, open those arms wide, and say to God, 'I am ready.'

"That's all you need to do. Prayers do not have to be complicated. They just have to be truthful. God does not want sin in His house, and He doesn't want it here. Tell yourself that you don't want it either.

"You have to find it in your heart to let sin go. It weighs you down and when God cuts your ties you will fall fast into Hell. I see the sin in your heart. Many of you wear it like a badge of honor. That is your mistake.

"Sin will not hold you up above the pits of Hell. Only God can do that.

"You have lasted long in life going on the path of temptation. Many of you may be doing well for yourself, but in the end your life will amount to an eternity in Hell. God is your only salvation.

"Whatever troubles you have had in the past, God will carry them for you. You just have to offer yourself to Him. He will welcome you with open arms as long as you are humble before Him.

"God is the solution and this summer you will see that. Take your predispositions and leave them back in that sinful society.

"God holds no grudge against you. He is not neglectful. He is not dismissive. He is not inattentive. No. God is patient. Do not think for a second God does not know what you are doing. What you are thinking. He may not act, but He is aware. There are ways off of the path to damnation. He waits for you. You have to come to him. That's how it works. He will carry you over damnation and bring you into salvation. But it is up to you.

"You must make the choice to brush away the sin your soul is carrying. Fill the void of temptation with the love of Christ.

"This summer your days of judgment are at hand. Give God your soul or He will rid the world of your sinful ways. He will save this world one sinner at a time

"Romans 1: 29-32, *they have become filled with every kind of wickedness, evil, greed and depravity. They are gossips, slanderers, God-haters, insolent, arrogant, and boastful; they invent ways of doing evil; they disobey their parents; they are senseless, faithless, heartless, ruthless. Although they know of God's righteous decree that those who do such things deserve death, they not only continue to do these very things, but also approve of those who practice them.*

"I say to you all, do not go down this road. Embrace our Lord and Savior.

"Thanks be to God. Amen."

Greed

Mindy wanted to get the most out of her summer.

After the welcoming sermon was over, Mindy was even more passionate about her time at Psalm Springs. Her nerves went away the moment Pastor Robbins began to speak. She was confident that Psalm Springs was going to bring her into a greater relationship with God.

Back in the winter, her congregation, Church of Modern Day Christ, had received flyers and messages from Psalm Springs promoting the summer camp. The papers described the camp as being all inclusive. Any and all were welcome to participate.

Mindy found the idea refreshing. There were so many groups that excluded others for being different. Psalm Springs looked like an opportunity for something new. The camp offered the chance to become closer to God like no other.

Mindy believed the more you knew the better off

you were. She did not want to stay at home and surround herself with the people she already knew. She wanted to meet new people and learn about other people. It was what God wanted. They were all God's children.

When Mindy first brought up the idea of going to the camp, her parents, her friends, and her pastor were all hesitant about wanting her to go. They said she was not ready for this experience. Three months was a long time to be away, and there were dangers of going to the summer camp. Mindy argued for her independence. She believed she was strong enough to handle the time on her own, and she knew that God would watch over her. After several more days of back and forth between her and her parents they finally made the decision to let her attend for the summer. She wanted the chance to experience God one on one. Psalm Spring was the way to go.

First, Mindy had to drop off her suitcases. She had a big suitcase in each hand and a book bag strapped to her back. They contained clothes and keepsakes from back home. Mindy worried she was going to be homesick and without realizing it she packed up many of her pictures to remind herself of home.

As Mindy walked to her cabin she noticed several of the other campers looking her way. They watched her walk by with all of her things. Mindy smiled back only to have an exaggerated grin returned. It wasn't unusual for Mindy. She knew her weight put off several people. She was not overweight or unhealthy, but she was never going to be one of the glamour girls you see in magazines. It always took her extra emphasis to get people to talk to her and get to know her.

The first day had a number of meet and greets for the campers. There were several ice cream socials and various games being held all around the camp. Mindy planned on attending all that she could.

This summer she was going to be away from everybody she knew. It meant Mindy had to start from scratch and introduce herself to as many people as possible. The more friends the better.

She first stopped by a game of volleyball being played down by the lake. It was a mud pit. Campers surrounded the court while the games were going on. Everybody was friendly. People cheered for both teams. Players rotated in and out of the game in order to give everyone a chance to participate. When Mindy was in she was able to score three points for her team. She wanted to stay in but her rotation was up and she knew she had to go.

Then Mindy was off to a cabin that was holding an arts and crafts workshop. The counselor, Alex, was showing the campers how to work the pottery wheels.

All of the girls swooned over Alex. He was in his early twenties. His brown hair lifted gently above his head every time he moved. Every now and then he would have to flick his head back to get his hair out of his eyes. The girls smiled every time he did it.

Mindy tried to stay focused on the class, but her eyes kept wandering around the room. She wanted to see who was all there. Mindy needed new friends for the summer.

As she panned the room one guy caught Mindy's attention. He was looking as intently at Alex as the girls were. Mindy smiled. She was happy to see a gay guy at the camp with no issue.

When the session was over, Mindy made a bee line toward the guy she had noticed earlier. She wanted to know who he was.

"Hi," she said once she approached him. "My name is Mindy."

"Hi," he answered hesitantly. "I'm Gabe."

"Did you like the class?" Mindy asked. She tried to keep her conversation casual. Gabe looked a little nervous.

"It was alright, I guess," said Gabe. "I've never done it before. I was kind of just brought here."

"You should try the volleyball," suggested Mindy.

"It was really fun."

"I don't know. I kind of just want to go back to my cabin. I hate this kind of stuff."

"But you'll miss out on all the fun activities," said Mindy. "I'm sure there is something you want to do. Come with me. We can do something together."

Gabe looked at Mindy in awkward silence. He shifted on his feet several times, unable to give her a proper excuse.

"Please," she said. "I want you to come with me. I need a friend. I don't know anybody here. Do you?"

"No," muttered Gabe.

"Then it's perfect. You'll join me. I think there is swimming going on the other side of the lake. Let's go do that!"

"Fine," gave in Gabe.

With the final surrender to Mindy's demands, they were off. Mindy walked with a hop in her step. She had a new friend.

The first night at Psalm Springs many of the girls stayed up late passing along gossip about the people they met earlier. The cabin Mindy was in had a dozen girls bunked together. Their beds were all nicely made and they were expected to have them just as nice the next day.

The curfew for the camp was nine o'clock. Every camper was supposed to be in their cabin at that time. Then they were all to be in their beds one hour later. Instead, all the girls in the cabin were huddled together. Mindy wanted to go to sleep. Her day had been long, but she did not want to miss out on what the girls were saying. She did not want to miss out on anything.

They were not talking about the boy's looks or the other girls' attitudes. Mindy's bunkmates were discussing how long many of the other campers would last at Psalm Springs.

"When do you think the first judgment will be?" asked Chrissy. Her hair was always tied in a ponytail. She was quickly becoming the leader of the cabin. Not coincidently, several girls started wearing their hair back that day.

"The first week. It's always the first week," said Rose.

Mindy leaned in closer. The girls started to talk at a whisper. She wanted to hear what they were saying.

Rose was a veteran of the camp. She had been going for the past three years. Mindy tried hard to learn more about her, but Rose never boasted about herself. Never afraid to talk, but she was very closed off.

"Who do you think it is going to be?" asked Chrissy. "Are they save-able?"

"They are all save-able," said Rose. "That is the point. God doesn't want you to fail judgment."

"What happens to them?" Chrissy asked.

"They're taken away," said Rose. "God takes care of it."

"What do you mean God takes care of it?" Mindy cut in. She was growing curious about the conversation. The brochure for the camp never mentioned any judgments or leaving early.

Rose looked over to Mindy. She did not look annoyed at her questions. Her expression never changed from a humble smile.

"God passes judgments on all of us every summer," said Rose. "If sin is in your heart then he will send you to Hell. It's why we're here. Some are here to reaffirm our faith. Others are here to have it made clear they need to follow in God's path or else Hell awaits them."

"God wants us in Heaven," said Mindy. "He loves us. Judgment every summer seems a little harsh."

"He does want you in Heaven," agreed Rose. "He just doesn't want sin there. We were not created to automatically go to Heaven. We have to earn that. Psalm Springs shows us why."

"You shouldn't have anything to worry about," said Chrissy. Her eyes elevated up and down Mindy's body. "I'm sure you're still a virgin, after all. That's one thing you have going for yourself."

Mindy tightened up. She crossed her arms to hide her frame. Some of the girls chuckled at Chrissy's joke. Rose rolled her eyes.

"It's not that simple," said Rose to Chrissy. "You have to not only obey the laws given by God; you have to help spread the word. God would love nothing more than to see all of His children earn their spots in the Kingdom of Heaven, but many of them do not listen. Many of them do not care, or are blinded by the teachings of false gods."

"Is that what you're doing?" Mindy asked.

"Yes!" Rose delighted. "I've seen the power of God. It is inspiring. It's what makes our time at Psalm Springs incredibly important. We have the chance to see God's work in plain sight. I know of his strength and of his resolve. So will all of you soon enough. It is our responsibility to continue to spread the message when the summer is over. We know of the one true power."

"So," said Chrissy. "Who do you think it will be?"

Rose looked back and forth several times. She was scoping out the cabin. When she saw the coast was clear she leaned in even closer.

"I've noticed several people that we will need to help," said Rose. "There is one girl in the cabin. She's not here right now. She's gone to the medical ward."

Mindy looked around the room. She counted eleven girls in the room. She had not noticed the missing girl until Rose brought her up.

"Her name is Cora," continued Rose. "She was brought here on one of the vans. She has several tattoos on her body. I tried talking to her earlier. She seemed out of it. I think she is going through withdrawal. She might have been hungover. She will need our strength if she is going to get through this summer."

All the girls nodded in acknowledgement. Cora was their bunkmate. They did not want to see her judged to Hell.

Mindy wanted the same thing. Cora could be saved. They could all be saved. Mindy believed that.

The next couple of days the campers kept busy. The construction of a new cabin began. All of the campers had a part in putting it together.

Mindy stayed by Gabe's side. They roamed the camp together. She would show him off to the others they would meet.

"This is my friend, Gabe," she would introduce him. "He likes guys, but that is totally cool."

Most of the campers would nod their heads at Mindy's introduction. Some of the guys would take a step back. Mindy never faltered. She was proud of the new friend she had.

On Thursday, Gabe was nowhere to be found. Mindy went to go meet him near his cabin, but he never showed. His bunkmates said he left earlier. Mindy was irritated. Gabe said they would go back to the lake for more swimming. She wondered where he could have gone, but she did not want to dwell on it. There were other things Mindy could be doing. She could have fun without Gabe.

There were still plenty of activities and socials that helped introduce campers to each other. Mindy decided to try out some more of those. One meeting in particular caught her eye. The pamphlet schedule called it Shinning Light.

It was described as a group that helped the more troubled teens view better examples set by their own peers. Mindy was excited about it. She was proud to keep a large range of friends. She never wanted to be looked at as fitting into only one group. She wanted to be seen in all of them. Mindy believed everybody was great just the way they were.

She arrived at the shelter house earlier than most everyone else. A counselor was putting together a number of chairs in a circle. Some refreshments were set out on a table to the side. There were several bottles of water and some cookies.

"Hi," Mindy announced. "I'm here for the meeting."

The counselor looked up from her duties of setting up for her campers. She beamed a generous smile back at Mindy.

"Hi," she said. "I'm Jennifer. I'm so glad you came."

"Do you need any help?" Mindy asked. Without waiting for a reply she grabbed two of the chairs in the stack and carried them over to the slowly forming circle.

"Thank you," said Jennifer.

As they set up for the rest of the meeting the two girls talked about where Mindy was from and what brought her to Psalm Springs. Jennifer then told her that she had been going to Psalm Springs for five years now. She was a counselor for two of them.

"This place is really great," said Jennifer. "I was having a lot of issues before I came here. It's actually why I started this group. I wanted to show people that you do have a chance at changing."

Mindy did not say anything, but Jennifer continued to explain her story.

"It's rough. Sometimes you have to leave everything that you thought you loved. My life seemed great, but really it went against God.

"Friends of mine were starting to get high a lot. They started drinking. A couple of them got into serious relationships, or so they thought. I started seeing less and less of them. When I did see them all they talked about was getting high. I rarely ever said anything in our conversations because I had nothing to say.

"Then I started to slip in to their way of life. They were my friends. They wanted me around, so I thought I had to participate.

"I went to some parties with them. I drank a little. I tried to smoke a bowl with them. I didn't like it, but this was what my friends were doing.

"Eventually, I lost myself. I didn't realize it then, but I became a nobody. I stopped going to church with my family because I was too tired from partying with my friends the night before. Meanwhile, I was still cut off from conversations with my friends because I was still mostly reluctant to join in all of their activities.

"It took me to a sad place. It made me lash out at people. I hated being anywhere because I didn't fit in. I didn't have any friends that understood me.

"Then I came here to Psalm Springs. It opened my eyes. There is only one thing I should be devoting my life to. God. Everything else is second string."

"That's amazing," said Mindy. "This camp did that for you?"

"Yes," said Jennifer. "I am blessed that I got to see the true power of God. It's enlightening, but it can also be intimidating. That's why I keep coming back. I want to show people that it's going to be okay. You may be hurt now, but there is a way to get out."

"I hope to have that moment," said Mindy. "I try to show the love of God, but sometimes I feel like it doesn't get through."

"Not everybody will want to listen. It's a difficult thing to realize," said Jennifer. "Thank you for coming though. I'm sure you'll be a wonderful example for others in the group."

A few minutes later more campers started to roll into the shelter house for the meeting. Several of them were accompanied by counselors of their own. Those particular campers did not look thrilled to be there. They sulked in their chairs and kept their heads down as Jennifer introduced herself. Then she started on her left and had the campers say hello and tell everybody their name.

Mindy enthusiastically stood up and introduced herself. The others did not share her passion. Many of the campers that were forced to attend simply grumbled their name and let the attention move on to the next one.

After the introductions were finished Jennifer moved on and wanted to open the group to open topics. She wanted to hear from them.

Mindy raised her hand to speak. All eyes turned to her.

"Hi, I'm Mindy," she introduced herself again. "I am so excited to be here. I was really nervous on the first day. All of my friends stayed back home. I just wanted to say that I hope to make a lot of new friends with all of you.

"And I guess what I kind of want to talk about is what brought you all here? I came here because I want to get closer to God. His love is so strong. He loves and accepts everybody. That is how life should be. We should take everything and embrace it with love and understanding, no matter what. I was happy to see Psalm Springs welcome that."

A boy to Mindy's right raised his hand. Jennifer called on him and he stood up to talk to the rest of the group.

"Steven," he proclaimed to the group again. "I'm thinking about joining seminary school. I was told Psalm Springs would help with that."

"That's great," said Jennifer. "Anybody else?"

More of the campers started to raise their hands and speak out. They attended Psalm Springs because they wanted to enjoy the summer and experience God first hand. Some wanted to experience something new. Some were returning campers.

Then the group grew silent again. Jennifer looked over at the other half of her circle of campers. There were still four campers that had not spoken yet. They were the ones that were joined by their counselors.

"Let's hear from somebody else?" said Jennifer. "How about Erika?"

The campers turned to look at Erika. She sat slumped in her chair. Her face was at a forever rest of annoyance.

"What brought you here?" Jennifer asked.

"My parents," fumed Erika.

"They mean well," said Jennifer. "There is no need to get angry at them."

"They forced me to a place I did not want to go. I think I have the right to be angry," argued Erika.

"Psalm Springs is here to help," said Jennifer. "If

there is anything you need to talk about then this is the place. We will listen. God is listening."

Erika scoffed at what Jennifer said. "God is not listening."

Jennifer sat straight up in her chair. She was not amused with Erika's words.

"God is always listening," said Jennifer.

"Then He does not care," said Erika.

"He cares," spoke up Mindy. "He loves all living things."

"Bullshit," said Erika. "If He loves us so much then why is there so much suffering in the world? Why does He have so many fucking rules about how to live your life? This is good. This is bad. Unless I say it's good. Everything happens for a reason. There is a grand master plan. That is all bullshit."

The group of campers went quiet and wide eyed as they listened to Erika's rant.

"God is cruel. We're His fucking toys and He is a child setting up a car wreck. Oh sure, here you go, a nice convertible. Drive slowly. That's nice. Oh no, here comes a drunk driver! Aaaaaahhhhhh! You're dead. They live. I planned that out. Ha ha!

"Then what? Just accept the plan. That's the plan. Just keep loving God though. He knows what He's doing. It doesn't matter if He just tore your life apart.

He is far more important than you, and His happiness is all that matters."

"Erika, I don't think you understand," said Jennifer. Erika did not let her finish.

"No, you don't understand!" Erika yelled. She stood up from her seat. "You're devoting your lives to a charade. God will damn any sinner, but as long as He says He loves you it's all good. He'll never do that to you… unless you sin. Then you deserve it."

"Erika, please settle down," said Jennifer.

"No!" screamed Erika. "I've had it with this place. I've had it with everything."

Erika turned and dashed away. The counselors were too slow to grab her.

"This whole camp is crazy!" Erika yelled as she reached the door. Then she ran outside and continued yelling obscenities and proclaimed her anger at God. Several of the counselors went after her. They would have to catch her and try to calm her down.

Jennifer was left with the rest of the campers in the now very quiet shelter house. Jennifer was at a loss for words. She looked over at her table of refreshments.

"Have some snacks. I think we're done for the day," said Jennifer.

The end of the first week was approaching. Mindy

was excited because it meant a small rotation through the cabins. New girls would be coming over as a way to further integrate all of the campers. Mindy could not wait to meet even more people, and make more friends. She went to two more meetings with Jennifer. Erika never returned. Mindy heard they caught up to her on the baseball field.

The rest of the meetings went smoothly. Several of the other campers that were forced to attend went willingly. They were encouraged to talk about their lives and Jennifer offered advice on what to do and how they could return to God's good graces.

Sunday was the day of rest. There were no scheduled activities on that day. Church was held in the morning. In the afternoon, the campers were told to enjoy the camp and enjoy their Bible.

Gabe was still missing. Mindy wandered the camp looking for him in their usual spots, but he was nowhere to be found. She wanted him to join her for the meeting sometime. Suddenly, she felt all alone again. Without Gabe she realized her circle of friends was gone. The last couple of days were fruitless in making new friends that wanted to stick around. Whenever one of Jennifer's meetings was over the campers went their separate ways. They never wanted to hang out afterward. What happened to all those people she met earlier? She met so many people in the past week. Certainly she could go join any of them.

There was a group of campers sitting on the patio. She recognized two of them, Amy and Mike. Mindy decided to hustle over to the table and join their group.

"Hi," she said, "I'm Mindy. Mike and Amy right? We were in prayer together."

"Hi," said both Amy and Mike meekly. Mindy could feel the elevator eyes coming from the three others at the group.

"How has your morning been?" Mindy asked rhetorically. She sat down at the table in one of the empty seats.

Shuffling of stuff occurred when Mindy sat down. Amy reached for her books to pull them away from Mindy. "Let me get those out of your way," she said with a smile. The others at the table brought their books and bags in closer to give Mindy more space.

"Have you guys gotten far on your readings yet?" Mindy asked. "I haven't started yet, but I can start where you guys left off. I'll catch up later."

"Oh," said Mike. "We've already assigned the readings around the group." Everybody mumbled in agreement with Mike. "We weren't anticipating anybody else joining us."

"Well, I can take some off your guys' hands," suggested Mindy. "It's no problem."

"I really like my readings," said Amy.

"Me too," said Patrick. The two other campers, Clare and Jane, stayed quiet.

"I think Neil is looking for somebody to partner with," said Mike. He pointed with his thumb directly behind him. Mindy leaned over to see who he was pointing at.

In the distance at another table, a boy in his mid-teens was walking alone and kicking rocks. He wore knee high socks. His left sock had already fallen and was scrunched up by his ankle. He kept his hair nicely combed and parted to the side. His glasses along with the rest of his clothes looked just a bit too big for him.

Mindy stared at Neil for several more moments. She knew she was not welcomed at the table. Sadly, it was not unusual. She met a lot of people that did not want to talk to her. That was their loss she felt.

She stood up from her chair with her book in her arms. "Thanks," she said. "He looks cool."

Mindy walked off to go talk to the outcast, Neil. If they did not want him around then Mindy would. She would take anybody.

Neil noticed Mindy approaching him. He did a little scramble when she kept getting closer. It was almost like a dance performed out of fear.

"I'm Mindy," she said.

"Hi, I'm Neil," he answered. His voice held a hint of embarrassment in every word.

"Would you like to do some readings together?" she asked.

Neil bobbed his head as if contemplating the answer while he looked down at his feet.

"Sure," he finally got out.

"Where's your Bible?" Mindy asked. She just noticed that Neil was empty handed.

"I gave it to my friend, Morgan," said Neil. "He said he lost his and really needed one. He asked me for mine because he knew I didn't need it as much."

"Why don't you need it as much?" Mindy asked.

"Morgan quizzed me on the Bible. I passed. I know it better than him."

"That was very nice of you," said Mindy. "I have a couple of Bibles back in my bunk that I brought with me. I can lend you out one until Morgan gives yours back."

"Thanks!" said Neil.

The rest of the day was filled with the teachings from the Bible. Mindy and Neil retreated to her cabin to fetch another Bible for Neil. Mindy wanted to read outside, but Neil insisted on staying indoors.

Eventually, Neil gave in and Mindy escorted them to the tree line surrounding the camp. They sat comfortably in the shade the rest of the day.

Sunday evening was approaching. Earlier in the day there was an announcement that everybody was to gather at the sermon hill.

The sermon hill was essentially a church set up outside. It sat on a hill just at the edge of the entire camp. Stone seats were arranged on the hill allowing visibility to the stage for everyone. It was a natural auditorium.

At the foot of the hill was placed the altar, and just a few yards past the altar was a grand gate. Then there was nothing but woods. The woods circled the entire camp. They were a natural barrier from the outside world.

While dusk approached, the campers made their way to the hill. Mindy and Neil walked together. She had yet to find Gabe that day. Neil was not the greatest company. He often times would try to flirt with Mindy, but ended up only leaving the conversation at an awkward point. Mindy grew used to it quickly and started to shrug it off. She wanted a friend to talk to.

The two of them found a seat high up on the hill.

The crowd of campers was filing in. After only a few minutes the entire auditorium hill was packed. Despite the fullness of the area, Mindy and Neil still found themselves with empty seats on either side of them.

Mindy looked around at everybody in the area. She picked through all of the faces. Then she finally saw him across the hill. Gabe was sitting next to a guy she did not recognize. They were sitting really close together. Their arms were almost one. Gabe laughed at something the guy said.

Mindy tried to wave for his attention, but he did not notice. She shouted his name a couple of times. Gabe was not paying attention. Mindy gave up. She tried to hide her anger at Gabe's disappearance but her emotions could be easily seen on her face.

"What's wrong?" Neil asked.

"Nothing," said Mindy.

"You just look really angry."

"I'm not angry," said Mindy. "My friend isn't paying attention to me."

Neil looked over toward the sea of yellow and blue. He could not tell which person she was talking about.

"Was he your boyfriend? Did he break up with you? Are you okay? Do you want a new boyfriend?" Neil asked.

"No," said Mindy. "He is gay."

Neil sighed in shock. "He has sex with guys?"

"It's no big deal," she defended.

"It's a sin," said Neil. "God does not like that."

"God loves all of us," said Mindy.

"He won't get into Heaven. You shouldn't be friends with him."

"I am friends with him, and he will get into Heaven. We all will as long as we are good people. God wants us in Heaven."

"That's not what others say," said Neil.

"Then they're wrong," Mindy scolded.

Neil shut up after that. He did not want to anger Mindy any further. She was thankful. Gabe ignoring her was more irritating than she cared to admit.

After all of the campers and counselors had arrived on the hill Pastor Robbins made his appearance behind the altar. He approached the podium slowly. His walk held the sense of solemn.

He did not need a microphone. His voice carried from the foot of the hill to the sky above it.

"This day saddens me," Pastor Robbins began. "There are so many wonderful children here at Psalm Springs; it breaks my heart when one of them strays. Sin is a vile act. It cannot be tolerated. As the children of God it is our duty to help eradicate this world of sin. I say to all of you, if you see someone in the acts of sin please come to me. There is no worse thing than letting sin continue.

"Galatians 5:19-21, *the acts of sinful nature are obvious; sexual immorality, impurity and debauchery, idolatry and witchcraft; hatred, discord, jealousy, fits of rage, selfish ambition, dissensions, factions and envy; drunkenness, orgies, and the like. I warn you, as I did before, that those who live like this will not inherit the kingdom of God."*

Then Pastor Robbins gestured with his hand. He waved his fingers for somebody to come on stage. Erika was brought on to the stage by two men that were counselors at the camp. She was being held tightly by her escorts. Erika was their captive.

Mindy looked on at the situation in shock. What had she done? She was just an angry girl. That was all. The noise of the crowd rose. All of them were asking the same thing. The speculation had begun.

"Please, settle down," said Robbins. He waited for the crowd to hush before he started again. "This young girl, Erika, speaks out against our Lord. She calls Him vile names, and disrespects His sacred laws. She does not kneel before God."

"Fuck you!" Erika yelled. She tried to break free from her captors, but they were too strong. Their grip only tightened, hurting her arm.

"Hold your tongue," Pastor Robbins ordered. Then he turned back to continue to address the rest of the campers.

"We gave her the chance to repent. We told her to quell her anger and accept the ways of the Lord. She cursed us. She wished to see us all in Hell. Now, because of her actions, Erika must deal with the consequences. She will be alone in Hell. I trust the rest of you will be free of sin. Consider this an eye opener.

"Erika is no longer welcomed within the gates of Psalm Springs. Her sins are a danger to the rest of you. Her day of judgment has arrived."

The two counselors holding Erika began to carry her toward the opening gate behind the altar. Erika continued to struggle to break free with no use.

"Please, help me," she cried out. "Please. They are going to kill me."

"Hush child," said Pastor Robins. "We are not going to kill you."

Mindy froze in terror. She had no idea what to do, if she could do anything.

"You pieces of shit!" Erika yelled as she was taken away. "You are all crazy. God is a monster!"

When the counselors arrived at the gate they

dumped Erika to the ground outside the perimeter of the camp. She hit the ground hard. Before she could recover the two counselors retreated back toward the altar. They shut the gate behind them.

Mindy heard the locking of the fence. It echoed up the hill for all the audience to hear. She was on the edge of her seat. The entire field grew quiet. The sound of Erika's feet rustling through the fallen leaves and foliage could be heard as she stood up.

Quickly, Erika ran back to the gate. She tried to pry the gate open, but it would not budge. Then she started to shake the fence violently. "Let me in! Let me in!"

"You made your choice, Erika," said Pastor Robbins. "You chose the path of sin. You chose to turn your back on the Lord. You became His enemy. Just because you do not understand His actions or do not agree with them, it does not make His decisions unjust. He is our Maker. He is our Teacher. He is our Fate."

Silently from the shadows of the woods emerged a massive figure. The man-monster towered nearly seven feet in the air. A grubby old mask covered its head. It was the face of an old man with thinning long hair and a long beard. Layers of dirt and grime covered a once light brown shawl and robe. In its hand was the blade of a spearhead. It had lost its shine years ago. Dirt and blood were caked over it.

"Numbers 35: 26-27, *but if the accused ever goes outside the limits of the city of refuge to which he has fled and the Avenger of Blood finds him outside the city, the Avenger of Blood may kill the accused without being guilty of murder.*"

The crowd of campers gasped. Many of them had never seen such a sight. They held their breath afraid the killer might notice them.

Erika slowly turned around. The goliath continued to walk toward her. Each step echoed in the hearts of the campers.

Erika started to beg. She begged for mercy from the monster approaching her. She begged to Pastor Robbins. He turned away from her. The situation was out of his hands.

"Please, help me!" Erika cried. "Anybody! Please, help me!"

Mindy could not move. None of the other campers were willing to go down there and save her.

"You are all garbage!" Erika began to yell at the audience. "Goddamn all of you! Go to Hell!"

Pastor Robbins shook his head at her words. Erika continued to yell obscenities to the crowd.

Then the Avenger of Blood grabbed Erika around

the waist. The other arm wrapped around her head. She could no longer scream.

Erika kicked and punched. The monster was unfazed. She would not stop fighting. Then the blade of the spearhead went diving into her thigh. Even with her mouth covered people could hear Erika's scream.

Mindy clenched her hands as she heard Erika panic. She would never forget that scream.

Erika gave up. Her body went limp in the arms of her judger. The Avenger of Blood tossed Erika to the ground. With the struggle over, the Avenger of Blood had no further trouble. The angel of death grabbed Erika by her hair and began to drag her away from the sermon hill and into the heart of the woods.

Pastor Robbins waited until Erika was gone. There were no further cries.

"Ladies and gentlemen," said Pastor Robbins, "That is the reason you have all come here. God is at our doorstep. These gates are now the only thing that protects the sinners from the almighty power of God. He has you all in His sights. Your days of judgment have arrived. Through the Avenger of Blood, God will rid this world of the sin that contaminates it. Use your time here to free yourself of your sin or you will be sent to Hell."

Over the next several nights, Mindy could not sleep. She kept replaying the event over and over in her head. What was that thing that came out of the woods? It looked like a man, but why would anybody do such an act? She remembered the horror in the eyes of Erika. Her rage turned into panic and desperation the instant the monster appeared from the woods.

Mindy was starting to understand why so many people told her not to go to Psalm Springs. Had they known?

Jennifer's meetings dwindled down. Less and less campers willingly attended each day. More counselors came by with disobedient campers to attend. Eventually, Mindy was the only one who volunteered to come to the meetings.

Others wondered why Mindy still attended. They knew about the other campers. They were troublemakers. Several of them came from the white vans in the beginning of the summer. They were deemed unclean and unworthy for God's acceptance into Heaven.

That was why Mindy was going. She still loved them. She still accepted them. She believed God had a place for them.

Every night Mindy prayed to God. She prayed for the campers in her meetings. She prayed that God would watch over her. She prayed that she would be protected from the killer in the woods. She was a good girl. She was a Christian. She went to church every Sunday. She loved everyone she met. She accepted everyone. As she prayed she told herself there was nothing to fear. She was not a sinner.

May turned into June. Psalm Springs occurred without incident. There were no further gatherings at the sermon hill. The routines of the camp continued normally. Every Sunday was offered for church and rest. The rest of the week was filled with activities and Bible study.

The counselors never mentioned the Avenger of Blood. They continued their teachings as if nothing had happened the first week of the summer. Mindy tried to make sense of it all. Gabe had disappeared from Mindy's side completely. She heard word about him once from Chrissy and her sidekick, Alissa. Gabe was seen in a fight with another boy. Word was the two guys were hooking up. The counselors took Gabe away to another part of the camp.

Mindy wanted to learn more, but she did not know who to ask. Rose was the most helpful. She explained that Psalm Springs offered more than just a summer camp.

"There are all kinds of programs here," said Rose. "We take care of the elderly, the sick. There are programs for the more troubled teens, and rehabilitation centers for gays and lesbians. It's all to help people see the grace of God."

"Do they help?" Mindy asked.

"Yes," said Rose. "It all helps. People get confused. That's all. It's easy to lose sight of things. They have good counselors there. They will set your friend straight. There is nothing to worry about. He's in good hands."

There was little else Mindy could do. She went to the rehabilitation building once. They were allowed no visitors and said that they already had all the volunteers they needed for the moment. Even Mindy's help in Jennifer's group did not give her enough credentials to get inside.

One day Mindy took a walk around the building that was the rehabilitation center. There was a fenced in area around the back. As she walked along the line she noticed several campers inside. They were in little bunches of groups. Each one was talking and laughing. They weren't in pain or distraught. Rose was right. Psalm Springs was a good place for them.

She continued her walk around the perimeter in order to try to catch a glance of Gabe. She could not see him in the group, but she was not going to give up until she was all the way around.

The fence reached out toward the tree line. There was only a small open space between the perimeter fence and the actually gated fence of the entire camp. Mindy walked along its wild grown path to get to the other side.

It was quiet. Nobody walked along this small pathway between the fences. Not even the campers in the rehabilitation center were near her.

Suddenly, she felt like she was being watched. It was a feeling like never before. Powerful eyes were on top of her. Mindy turned in a circle. There was nobody around. There was nobody to see her, but she could still feel an ominous glare bearing down on her.

It made Mindy uncomfortable. Despite her clothes she felt naked. She could not handle it for any longer. Her mission to see Gabe again came to an end. She had to retreat.

Her feet carried her faster than ever before back toward the main campground. She tried to forget about the feeling she had while at the fence. There were people around her again. She was safe.

But the anxiety never went away. Over the next few days, wherever she went the eyes followed. They watched her every waking move. Dread followed her like the plague. She no longer participated in any of the activities or meetings. Nobody came to invite her to their groups. She was alone.

Then the day came that Mindy needed answers. The girls rarely spoke to her again. All Mindy ever did was hide in her cabin most of the day. They ignored her presence in the cabin and chatted like she was not even there. The only book she was given was the Bible. She had read it from cover to cover. It was the first time she had ever really done that. In the past, she had always picked through the Bible. Mindy discovered there was so much she was missing.

She waited until all of the girls were gone for the day. After an hour of being alone, Mindy built up the courage to make her move.

Mindy finally came to the administrations office. It was also the office and home of Pastor Robbins. The secretary at the front desk let Mindy right in. She was more than gracious, but Mindy noticed that the older woman never touched her. The secretary offered her hand, but she was always careful to take it away as she guided Mindy to a seat in a private room.

Mindy waited for several minutes before Pastor Robbins finally appeared. Before Mindy could say anything Robbins greeted her and told her to remain seated. He quickly walked to the other side of the desk in the room and sat down on the leather chair that complimented the desk perfectly.

"Mindy, how are you doing?" Pastor Robbins greeted. His interest was genuine.

"I want to go home," said Mindy. "I need to get out of here. I can't stand it anymore."

"I'm sorry," said Robbins. "There is no going home. Not yet. At least it is not advised."

"It's like I've been black listed! Nobody will talk to me. Nobody will even come near me. That thing that took Erika away, I think it is watching me, now. I can feel it. I need to get away from here."

Pastor Robbins let out a small sigh. He looked at Mindy with a solemn face. "That thing is the hand of God. Just as God watches over all of us at once; the Avenger of Blood watches over the few. There is sin in your heart, Mindy. The Avenger of Blood is here to take that away."

"No," cried Mindy. "No, there is not. I have done nothing wrong. Please, you have to believe me. I am a good girl. God would not do this to me."

"Why is that?" Pastor Robbins asked.

"Because God loves me. He loves everybody and everything. God is love. He would not kill people just because they did something wrong."

"Are you sure about that?" Robbins questioned.

"…Yes," hesitated Mindy.

"Let me guess for a moment," said Robbins. "You go to church every Sunday. You welcome all guests. You do not judge. You volunteer around Thanksgiving, Christmas, sometime during the summer. You love just as God loves."

"Yes," said Mindy.

"Then you are a child that needs to grow up," said Pastor Robbins.

"Excuse me?" Mindy said.

"You say you love someone. You mean you love their time in the now, and all their quirks and weaknesses. God on the other hand does not just love you. He loves your soul. Your eternal soul.

"He created mankind in His image. That includes their souls. God created us with the potential to experience the universe just as He does. Heaven is open to us because of that.

"But Heaven was not created specifically for mankind. It is not a right. Heaven is the Lord's home and we are His guests. He does not welcome the corruption and sin that freewill can latch on to.

"Do you see? You cling to this ideal that everybody can get into Heaven; that everybody can have everything they want. That is not true. If you want to get into Heaven then you must do what God asks. That means you must worship Him. You must obey Him. He has given us the instructions to get into Heaven. There is no excuse for not following them."

"I do follow them," interrupted Mindy.

"Yes, I'm sure you do," continued Robbins. "But what about the people that you have brought into your circle? You do not judge them, which is wonderful, but you do not help them either. You tell yourself that they will get into Heaven along with you. You are lying to yourself whether you know it or not."

"They can all get into Heaven," argued Mindy. "God welcomes all."

"No," said Robbins. "He does not. He cannot if Heaven is to remain pure. There are people that choose to sin. They cannot be welcomed through the gates of Heaven."

"That does not mean that people have to die," said Mindy. "Erika was dragged away screaming. Nobody helped her."

"We tried to help her. She refused to accept the Lord. God is patient, but there comes a time when everybody must finally be judged. It was Erika's time. She was not going to make it into Heaven. Then there is no point in living further. Her soul was destined for Hell."

Mindy sat quietly taking in all that Pastor Robbins was saying. Had she been wrong her entire life? Was everything she was building toward the wrong thing to do in the eyes of God?

"Am I going to Hell?" Mindy asked.

"That is for you to decide," said Robbins. "You are being watched right now. It means you are at a crossroads. God is pushing you towards the right decisions. He wants you to make it into Heaven."

"And if I decide to leave?" asked Mindy. "What If I leave right now? I can go far away from this place. I need more time. I can do this for God. Just not here. Not now. Please. Let me go."

"You are free to leave whenever," revealed Pastor Robbins. "I warn you though; past the gates of the camp you are no longer safe."

"I am not safe here," said Mindy.

"You are safer than you think. Leaving early violates the covenant that you made with God. Breaking that vow will send you straight to Hell with no further judgment."

"When can I leave?"

"At the end of the summer," said Robbins. "There is one final night, the Night of the Tenth. The Lord will make his final judgments on all of the campers here.

"You still have time, Mindy, to rid yourself of the sin in your soul. You are so close. That is why God is watching you now. He has faith in you. Let go of your old way of thinking. Your old life was corrupted by society. This is your time to free yourself from those shackles. The only thing you should possess is the love of Christ. He will provide you with the rest."

Mindy nodded her head. She left Pastor Robbins office feeling more scared than ever. She could still feel eyes watching her, only this time they were feeling disappointed.

It was July. Mindy returned to her bunk one evening. She had been out walking alone for hours. She had to keep moving. It kept the eyes off of her.

When Mindy returned she could see out of the corner of her eyes all of the girls staring at her. They quieted down when she entered the room. Mindy paid them no mind. They had not talked to her in weeks. She could already hear the whispers. The other girls were talking about her. They called her a sinner. Mindy knew that was not true, but she could not shake the feeling that she was being judged.

Mindy arrived at her bed to discover it had been moved. Her bed now sat on the other side of the cabin all alone. Rocks completely surrounded it on the floor.

They were each the size of a fist. Mindy looked at the gaping hole that was once her spot. All of her stuff was still there. None of the girls bothered to move them with her bed. Her home away from home was now nothing. She stood staring on the outside of the circle looking in at her bed.

Some of the girls started giggling behind her. Mindy turned around. Chrissy was standing up. She hugged a Bible close to her heart. Her confident smile scared Mindy. Rose had left their cabin weeks ago. Chrissy became the de-facto leader soon afterward.

"Aren't you going to lie down?" Chrissy asked.

"What is going on?" asked Mindy.

"We know," said Chrissy.

"Know what?"

"That you are unclean," said Chrissy. "You're being judged right now. God is watching all of us, but he is looking at you in particular. He sees something in you that he wants to eradicate. It would have been nice if you told us sooner."

"I'm not unclean," Mindy pleaded. "I haven't done anything wrong. God loves me. He loves us all."

"Then why are we praying for you?" asked Chrissy.

Mindy was growing short of breath. Her heart was racing. All of the girls were staring at her. They waited for her to say something.

"What did you do to my bed?" Mindy finally got out.

"It's your quarantine," said Chrissy. She opened the Bible in her hand. It was bookmarked to a specific page. "The purity of the cabin must be maintained. We ask that you use the backdoor of the cabin from now on. 2 Corinthians 6:17-18, *therefore go out from their midst, and be separate from them, says the Lord, and touch no unclean thing; then I will welcome you, and I will be father to you, and you shall be sons and daughters to me, says the Lord Almighty*."

Mindy turned back to her bed. She eyed the quarantine line of rocks. Then she looked back at her bunkmates. Their stern glares urged her forward. Chrissy scowled at Mindy.

The pressure was becoming too much. Mindy could still feel the eyes of God on her. Her foot began to move. Mindy did not even feel as if it was under her control. She stepped over the line of rocks. Then like a weight was lifted off she brought over her other foot.

Mindy was inside the quarantine zone of the cabin. Her spiritual filth would remain away from the others' pure souls. Chrissy and the others girls smiled. They were all so proud of Mindy for making the right decision.

"See?" said Chrissy. "Doesn't that feel so much better? You're going to be saved, Mindy. I promise."

Mindy stayed in the quarantine zone most of the time from then on. Meals were brought to her. All of the counselors understood the situation and forgave her absence. She was not allowed to pass into the other part of the cabin. Her books were on the other side. Pictures of her friends and family smiled at her from a distance. Whenever Mindy thought about crossing the line she could feel the daggers across her neck. Goosebumps would race down her arm. In her heart, Mindy felt that she was never going to get her little corner of life back.

Every now and then she would go on walks to try to shake the feeling that she was being watched. If Mindy moved she felt like she could run away.

Nobody bothered her. It was horrible. Mindy liked being social. She liked talking to people and becoming friends with them. She had over a thousand friends online. Some of them she had never actually met, but she knew so much about them because of their pictures they'd post. It made Mindy feel like she was a part of something.

At Psalm Springs, she was a part of nothing. She was becoming a pariah for the only reason that she felt like she was being judged. Whatever it was Mindy could not shake it and her fellow campers could tell.

Her walks never lasted long. The feeling of impending judgment became too much for her and Mindy would retreat back to the cabin and her quarantine zone.

Then she started seeing Gabe again.

At first it was from a distance. His hair was cut short. Mindy almost didn't recognize him. She spotted him crouched against a wall. He kept his head down. He never stayed in one place for very long. When Mindy went on approach Gabe ran off.

This continued for days. Mindy wanted to find Gabe again. Maybe he would understand what she was going through. He was viewed as an outsider at the camp. Mindy had to know if he was going through the same things.

One day Mindy tried to chase Gabe down. She caught sight of him outside of the boy's bathhouse. He was faster than she was. Her stamina slowed her down. Before she knew it Gabe was gaining ground as he made his way to the outer perimeter of the camp. Mindy thought she knew where Gabe was going, but when she turned a corner he was gone.

Generators hummed in front of her. The tree line was yards away. The fence hid in the bushes. Metal spikes stuck out from the top of the leaves. All the she could see past the fence were the trees.

The days only got worse. The girls in the cabin continued on with their lives like she wasn't there. Mindy would overhear them talk and whenever she tried to come in to the conversation she was ignored.

The talk of the camp became about her bunkmate Cora. Cora was rarely at the cabin. After she returned from the medical ward she would go off during the day doing who knows what. Many people said she was doing drugs with other campers, but nobody said who. Only at night did Cora return. Then by morning she was gone again.

Now, the story going around was that Cora had been caught by the counselors having sex in one of the boys' cabins. Chrissy and Alissa called Cora a whore. Cora was not going to last much longer at Psalm Springs.

Mindy silently worried for her. She did not want to see a repeat of Erika.

As the days rolled on Mindy stayed back in her cabin and began to rethink what she was doing with her life. She wanted to include everybody in her circle, but that resulted in her being abandoned by everybody she knew. Her friends and family did not want to join her to Psalm Springs. Many of the campers here wanted nothing to do with her because Mindy believed everybody could go to Heaven no matter what.

Mindy was worried that maybe she had gone too far. Maybe she shouldn't have hung around many of the campers that were considered unclean. Then Mindy shook that idea away.

Mindy believed what she did was right. Everybody could get to Heaven. It just meant they would have to be shown how to change for the better. She could do that. She could have all of her friends with her. They just had to listen.

She stepped quietly toward the back exit of the cabin. Her steps were silent as she walked on the balls of her feet. As Mindy approached the door her hand grew heavy. It took several deep breaths to calm her down. God would protect her, she kept saying over and over again in her head. What she was doing was right.

The sun blinded her as the door opened. It felt like forever since she stepped outside midday. The heat from the summer day brought sweat down her face in an instant. At least that was what she blamed it on.

There was a solution. Mindy believed that. Pastor Robbins told her that she could still be saved. She did not have to die and go to Hell. She just had to change her ways. Robbins told her that she was selfish. She believed that everybody could be saved the way they were. She wanted to love everybody.

That morning, Mindy cleaned herself up. She looked herself over for the first time since the incident at the sermon hill. She combed her hair and put on a fresh outfit offered by the camp. The clothes fit nicely. They showed off her curves in all the right places.

She rushed through the camp. No longer did she mind the onlookers and avoidances that the rest of the campers displayed. After nearly half an hour of wandering through the camp she found who she was looking for.

Gabe was walking quickly through a group of campers. He kept his head down in an attempt to not be noticed. Mindy zeroed in on him. She kept him in his sights as he made his escape from the group of people.

Before Gabe could disappear once again Mindy was able to catch up with him. She grabbed hold of his shoulder. He jumped at her slightest touch.

"It's okay," she said. "It's just me."

Gabe stared at Mindy with wide eyes. His head darted in either direction. He was never satisfied looking in one spot for more than several seconds.

"What's wrong?" Mindy asked.

"Nothing," said Gabe. "I just have to be going."

"No," said Mindy. "I want to talk to you."

"I don't have time."

"Yes, you do," demanded Mindy. "This is important."

"Fine," said Gabe. He started to bounce on his toes. The second Mindy stopped talking he would bolt.

"I want to help you," said Mindy. "We can get through this together."

"I do not need help," said Gabe.

"Yes, you do," said Mindy again. "You are going to Hell, Gabe."

"Shut up," scolded Gabe. "You don't know that."

"I've spoken with Pastor Robins. I've read the Bible. You saw what happened to Erika. You're not going to make it to the end of the summer."

"Not if I stay here," said Gabe. He was ready to run.

"You're a good guy, Gabe. You can still be saved. So can I," said Mindy. "I know what we have to do."

Gabe turned away from Mindy. He took a couple of steps before Mindy grabbed him again. She had a hold of his arm and pulled him back toward her.

Before he could tell her to let go, Mindy lifted herself up and kissed Gabe. She forced her tongue into his mouth. Caught off guard, he let the kiss happen for a moment.

Mindy let go of Gabe. She pulled back to look at Gabe. There was no hiding the joy in her smile.

"Don't you see," said Mindy, starry eyed. "We can be together. You can renounce your homosexuality and I can support you. This way we can save each other."

Gabe shoved her back several steps. He looked at Mindy with disgust.

"Are you crazy?"

"I want to be with you. I want to help you. You'll learn to like me. Like this. It's what God wants."

"I am not attracted to you," said Gabe. The words stung for Mindy. She had heard those words several times in the past few years.

"What's wrong with me?"

"Nothing," said Gabe.

"Then be with me."

"It does not work like that," said Gabe.

"It can," said Mindy. "We can use our love of God for each other. I like you Gabe. I don't want to see you go to Hell."

"This isn't the way, Mindy," said Gabe. "You can't

just kiss me, hold my hand, and say I am saved! I am not attracted to you! I will not love you."

Mindy could not speak. She was using all her strength to hold back her tears. Gabe was breaking her heart.

"I have to go," said Gabe. "Keep your head down. You still might survive this."

Then Gabe was gone. Mindy did not have the energy to chase him down again. She never wanted to see Gabe again.

The rejection from Gabe destroyed Mindy. She returned to her bunk and was worse than ever. It did not take long for word to spread about her attempt to get with Gabe. Somebody had overheard their conversation and was spreading the story.

Chrissy was the first to question Mindy about the whole thing. She did not wait for a good time. As soon as Chrissy entered the cabin and saw Mindy lying in her bed in the quarantine she pounced.

"I heard you were rejected by a gay guy. Is it true?" Chrissy asked.

Mindy turned over in her bed. She did not want to look at Chrissy or the other girls.

"Oh, you poor thing," said Chrissy. "Did you offer him anal? It's the same thing whether you're a guy or a girl for the pitcher."

"I heard that," said Alissa.

"Yeah," reconfirmed Chrissy. "Why do you think it's a virginity loophole? It's so girls can bring back the guys that have gone astray."

Mindy did not want to hear anything that Chrissy was saying. She let out a loud gruff as she covered her head with her pillow.

"Go away," Mindy said.

Chrissy brushed off Mindy's demand. Her eyes rolled and then her attention was on something else. The other girls followed suit. They were done with Mindy.

The next week was worse than the beginning of the summer. Mindy was heartbroken and afraid. She was alone. Many of the girls in her cabin were getting transferred to new quarters. Soon Mindy knew she was going to be the only one there.

Then she received her first ever visitor. A brown haired girl that Mindy did not recognize quietly walked into the cabin when no one else was around. She was clearly not supposed to be there. The girl's steps were delicate. She looked out each window she passed.

At first, Mindy watched the girl sneak through the

cabin. Mindy stayed real still in her bed. Her sheets covered her from head to toe. The girl had obviously not seen Mindy yet.

Then the girl snuck over to Cora's old bed. She started opening her drawers and going through her things. That was when Mindy decided to speak up.

"What are you doing?" Mindy said as she revealed herself on her bed.

The girl nearly jumped several feet in the air. She put her hand over her heart to try and stop it from racing.

"I'm sorry," she said. "I did not think anybody was in here. Where were you?"

"In my bed," said Mindy.

"What are you doing all the way over there?"

"What are you doing going through someone else's stuff?" Mindy said, changing the subject.

The girl put up her finger to gesture for a minute of time. Quietly and slowly she closed the drawer she was looking in.

"I am a friend of Cora's. She needs help," said the girl.

"Who are you? Where is Cora? What's wrong with her? I haven't seen her for a while. She hasn't spent the night in the cabin for weeks."

"I'm Brook," she said. "Cora has been with me.

She's gotten into some trouble."

"We're all in trouble," mumbled Mindy.

Brook took the time to begin looking through the drawers again. Her face lit up when she found what she was looking for. Her hand chattered as she waved a bottle of pills in the air.

"Cora has drugs?" Mindy asked.

"Yeah, she was able to stash some away," said Brook.

"She shouldn't be taking drugs," said Mindy.

"I don't really care what she should or should not be doing," said Brook. "I'm not her doctor. I just need her to calm down. If she is in hysterics she will die here."

"How do you know she can survive this?" Mindy asked, curious.

"Because I have to try," said Brook. She kept looking out the window to see if the coast was clear even as she talked to Mindy. "Several campers have died so far. I'm not going out like them. I'm not going to give in. I'm fighting."

"God is punishing us," said Mindy.

Brook looked out the window again. She could see several campers heading in the direction of the cabin. Brook walked toward Mindy at the back of the room.

Without a thought Brook stepped over the

quarantine line. Mindy squirmed in her bed at her actions. Brook was going to be unclean because of Mindy.

"Listen," said Brook. She sat down on the edge of Mindy's bed. "I don't know what the hell is going on with you, but if you need help then I am here. I'm working on getting out of the camp. You can join me."

"I'm being watched," said Mindy. "I'm being judged."

"We all are," said Brook. "Be careful who you talk to. Do not mention me. The counselors and the campers are communicating about who is sinning. I do not want them knowing more about me. They know enough as it is."

"How are you getting out?" Mindy asked.

"I have a plan," said Brook.

Mindy was quiet for a minute. She thought about her choices. No matter what she wanted to do she could not shake the feeling that fate was watching her death approach.

"Please, help me," said Mindy. "I want to get out of here."

"Okay," said Brook. "Stay put. I'll be back for you tonight. Meet me outside."

Brook peeked over the windowsill. She could see

more campers near the cabin. Quickly she got off Mindy's bed and headed for the back door.

"Do not say a word about me," said Brook when she got to the door. "I'll get you out of this."

Mindy did not get to say thank you. Brook was gone. Seconds later the front door opened. Chrissy and the other girls returned. Mindy slipped under her covers. She just had to wait until the night.

The night was slow to approach. Mindy counted the minutes until the sun disappeared below the horizon. The counselor made her rounds. She checked in on the girls in Mindy's cabin. Chrissy and the others were quietly lying in bed pretending to sleep. They would be up for another couple of hours talking about the day. Mindy waited.

Finally, the familiar sounds of one of the girl's snoring filled the cabin. All of them had gotten used to it over the past month and could sleep through it.

Mindy slipped away her covers. She sat up and looked around. None of the girls were stirring. They were all asleep. Mindy got to her feet. She headed for the door. Before she left, Mindy looked back at her former spot in the cabin. Her stuff was still there the way she had left it. She would see her old friends soon she told herself. Then she left the cabin. Relief washed over her as she would never have to see Chrissy or the others again.

Outside, Mindy stood alone. It was too dark to see much of anything. Mindy looked all around, but she could not find Brook. Mindy waited for her by the side of the cabin. She did not want to go back inside. She had made her choice. If Brook did not show up then she would make her way out of the camp herself.

Luckily, Brook's shadowy figure came out from some bushes nearby. Mindy was relieved at the sight of her.

"What took you so long?" Mindy wanted to know. "I thought you had forgotten about me."

"Me? I've been out here for hours," said Brook. "You were taking so long I had to hold back and wait to see if you were setting me up."

"I'm not," said Mindy. "I want out of here."

"Then follow me," said Brook. "Stay close. Do not run or even walk fast. Just keep up with me. Got it?"

"Yeah, I got it," said Mindy.

Then the two girls were off. Brook led Mindy around the camp. They stayed near the perimeter for most of their journey. Mindy hated it. She hated being near the fence.

Brook never stopped. There was nothing or nobody that could get in her way. Then she directed Mindy to the edge of the fence. Bushes and leaves covered up most of the structure. They were in the area of the generators. The same spot Mindy lost Gabe at earlier in the month.

Mindy slowly came up to the metal bars that separated her from the outside world, and the Avenger of Blood.

"It's okay," said Brook. To show Mindy, she reached into the foliage. The fence opened up. It had a slight creak when it first opened. Mindy's stomach jumped to her throat.

"Don't open that," she whispered.

"I said it was okay," assured Brook. "This is still a part of the camp." Then she walked through the open gate. Mindy stayed where she was. She watched Brook walk ahead. Nothing was happening to her. Nothing was coming for her.

"Are you coming?" Brook asked.

Mindy summoned her courage and took her first step. She walked through the gates with her breath held in. Then she waited for her demise. Her body curled up in tension.

Brook looked on. She waited for Mindy to calm down. After a moment when nothing was happening, Mindy began to unwind.

"It's okay," Brook said again. "Like I said, this is

still a part of the camp. I've checked. There is more of the perimeter fence out in the distance. It looks like this part was closed off years ago."

Brook came back up to Mindy to close the gate behind her. The hidden part of the camp was dark, darker than the rest. The trees were thick. They reached high into the sky. Bushes and weeds grew wildly.

"What is this place?" Mindy asked.

Brook continued to walk forward. Mindy forced herself to keep walking or be left behind. A small trail cut into the woods. Branches blocked the path. Brook moved them aside like it was nothing new to her. Mindy ducked and tried to avoid them at all costs.

"I'm still trying to find out more about it," said Brook. "Psalm Springs doesn't exactly keep open records. All I know is it looks like something bad happened here and they wanted to wash those memories away."

The branches opened up. There was a clearing. Brook turned around to face Mindy. Behind her was a rundown cabin. The paint was weathered away. Vines climbed the sides all the way to the roof.

"It's a piece of shit," said Brook. "But I haven't seen a counselor here since day one. So to me, it's perfect."

Brook escorted Mindy to the patio. She had to avoid certain spots where the wood was giving away. The cabin was a death trap all on its own.

As Brook opened the door she knocked in a pattern of four beats. "It's okay," she said. "It's me."

A light sparked inside the cabin. The soft glow of a lantern lit up a tiny area of the room. In the light was a boy with long red hair and a splotchy beard. He did not look amused to see Brook.

"Who the fuck is that?" he asked Brook, nodding at Mindy.

"She needs our help," said Brook.

"I'm not helping her," said the red haired camper. "I don't give a shit what her problem is. I can't even deal with my own."

"I didn't ask for your help, though it would be appreciated" said Brook. "You can't keep hiding here forever."

"Watch me," he said.

Brook shook her head in frustration. She turned back to Mindy. "Mindy this is Hayden. He's been with me for a while now."

"You guys have been hiding out here this whole time?" Mindy asked. She was astonished that anybody could survive in such conditions.

"Yes," said Hayden. "There are a few of us. We get

along-"

Brook gave Hayden the dagger eyes. He shut up.

"How many of you are there?" Mindy asked.

"A few of us," said Brook. "I'm sorry, but I am not going to divulge all of that. Not yet. I still don't trust you."

"I asked for help," said Mindy.

"And that was a start," said Brook. "You only met Hayden because he doesn't want to go anywhere else."

"Fuck that," he said.

"Where's Cora? Is she here?"

"No," said Brook.

"Will I be able to see her?" Mindy asked.

"Enough with the questions," said Brook. "It's time to get some sleep. We'll need to lay low for a few days. They'll be looking for you tomorrow. You need to stay put." Brook threw a pillow and blanket at Mindy.

"I've stayed put enough," said Mindy. "You just brought me from one cabin to another."

"At least this one you won't wither away in until death finds you," said Brook. She walked over to the corner of the cabin where her own nest of a bed was.

"How do you know that?" Mindy asked.

"Because death already found this place," said Brook. "Go to sleep. We'll talk more in the morning."

Then Brook put out the lantern. The three of them were left in darkness.

When the morning came Mindy understood the final words that Brook told her. Daylight revealed the true story of the cabin. Stains of blood were soaked into the wood from the floor to the ceiling. Whatever happened at this cabin was violent.

Mindy's comfort level sunk lower than ever. She realized she had put her trust in a girl she did not know. Now, she was in a murder house with little options to leave. The best she could do was curl into a ball and hide in the corner of the room away from most of the blood stains.

Brook disappeared during most of the day. She would return periodically with food, clothes, or other supplies. Hayden did not talk much. To Mindy's amazement he had a smartphone with him, many of them. She remembered all of the campers had to give their phones up when they arrived at the camp.

"Can I see your phone?" she asked after hours of debating to herself. She did not want to bother Hayden. He was not too keen on her being there.

"No," said Hayden.

"Please," she begged.

"What for?"

"I want to call my parents, my friends, somebody," said Mindy.

"There is no reception," said Hayden.

"Then what are you doing?"

"I'm playing Magic Bird," said Hayden.   "I'm working on a perfect score, now."

"So you can't call out?" Mindy asked.

"No," said Hayden dismissively.

"Have you tried?"

Hayden looked up from his game with disbelief. "I have a phone and I haven't tried to contact somebody. I must be an idiot. There is no reception here."

"What about other places around the camp? Don't you want to talk to your family? You could call the cops."

"It's no good," said Hayden. "We're on our own."

He returned to his game. Mindy went back to her own thoughts. She thought about her family. She was sure they were missing her. She was missing them. She was missing her friends from church and school. Mindy wanted nothing more than to see them again. She wanted her old life back. She wished she had never come to Psalm Springs.

August was starting, and Brook was not ready with

her plan. There were complications for others in her group she told Mindy. They would have to wait. Hayden brushed it off. He did not care.

Mindy was upset. She was crawling the walls of the old cabin. Hayden's cell battery had died and he was whining about Brook not being around to go charge it up somewhere on the camp grounds.

Mindy could not stand it anymore. She could not hear Hayden complain for another minute. She left the camp to get some fresh air.

The area was much different seeing it in the daytime. The mystery was gone from the woods now. Mindy walked to the gate without fear. She slowly opened the door and looked around. There was nobody to see her exit.

It was a nice day out for a walk. Mindy strolled around the camp. She made sure to stay away from the groups of campers. None of them paid any attention to her as she walked through the cabins.

Without realizing it, Mindy arrived outside her cabin. It did not appear like anyone was there. She peeked her head into the window. The coast was clear.

Her stuff was still in the cabin. It had not been touched even when she had disappeared for all those weeks. Mindy just wanted a few pictures. She wanted to be reminded of home and what she was praying to survive for.

Mindy quickly went inside the cabin. She rushed over to her area. All of her pictures brought back precious memories. All of her friends were happy. She wished she was happy like that again.

Could she ever be? She knew the truth of what was out there. Were her happy friends in her pictures going to Hell? She knew they all skirted by the rules that they lived by at Psalm Springs. Their lives were acceptable outside, but here they would be one of the sinners. The world was full of sinners according to Pastor Robbins.

The cabin was nice. Air conditioning felt nice against Mindy's damp shirt. She had not been able to get a proper shower since she left and the rundown cabin was always damp and hot.

Her bed looked unbelievably comfortable. Her blankets welcomed her. The mattress called out to her. She could rest just for a little bit. Then she would have to run. She would have to run back to hiding. Hiding would delay the inevitable.

Mindy looked back down at the photos in her hands. Would she be able to save her friends and family? They were on the path to Hell. She needed to survive to return to them. If she returned home she could tell them how to protect themselves.

It suddenly all made sense to Mindy. She knew what she had to do. She knew how she could survive the summer. She was an innocent good girl. She was not sinful. She loved God, and God loved her.

Mindy put her picture back on the bedside table. She was not going to die at Psalm Springs. Her friends and family were counting on her even if they did not realize it.

She had to get out of the cabin. Brook would be wondering where she was. Hayden wouldn't care.

Mindy walked through the camp again. She did not care who saw her this time. She was on a mission of survival. Her first stop was to the counselor's office to see Pastor Robbins.

Sloth

Hayden was already bored. He did not want to be at Psalm Springs.

Hayden did not pay attention to much of Pastor Robbins' welcoming sermon. He kept thinking about the atrocity that occurred just a couple of hours ago when he first arrived at the camp. As soon as he entered his cabin the counselor grabbed the phone straight out of Hayden's hand.

"Give that back," he demanded from the counselor.

"You'll get it back at the end of the summer," the camp leader responded. "While you're at Psalm Springs you will not have any distractions from the outside world."

"It's my phone," said Hayden. "It's expensive. I'll put it away."

"Sorry," said the counselor. "Nobody is allowed to hold onto their cellphones."

The counselor turned to address the rest of the campers. He spoke up for the others to hear him.

"All cellphones, computers, videogames, mp3s, walkmans, books, please bring to me now. If I catch you with any of these during the summer you will be up for punishment. Do you all understand?"

The campers all grumbled at their counselor's announcement. One by one they delivered their cellphones and other forms of entertainment at his feet. The entire time he held tightly onto Hayden's phone.

"What are we supposed to do for fun then?" Hayden asked.

"We have a fun filled summer of activities prepared for you," answered the counselor. "Plus, you will all get a new Bible. You can even take it home with you after the summer is over."

Hayden let out a drawn out moan. The counselor was not impressed with Hayden's attitude.

"What is the problem?" he asked Hayden.

"This sounds so boring," said Hayden. "Please, give me my phone back."

"No," said the counselor.

"Fuck off then," cursed Hayden.

"Hey, watch the language," said the counselor. "We're here to have fun and make friends, not to play on our phones all day. This time tomorrow you'll forget you even had a phone."

"Whatever," said Hayden. He was tired of arguing with the counselor. He just wanted to lie down. The drive to the camp was long and boring. Unfortunately for Hayden, the sermon was coming up and all of the campers were escorted to the hall for the welcoming ceremonies.

Hayden could not pay attention during the sermon. As he sat, with his arms down on his lap, his fingers automatically held themselves in the positions as if he was playing a game on his phone. He started playing an imaginary game. He kept score of all of the moves in his head.

After what seemed like forever for Hayden the campers were dismissed from the sermon. He had not noticed when all the people around him said, "Amen."

Hayden waited for most of the others around him to get up from their seats and leave the building. He did not feel like fighting through the crowd.

The rest of the day was misery for Hayden. He was more dragged than encouraged to join in the special activities on the first day of the camp.

"I don't want to play kickball."

"I don't want to swim."

"This ice cream social is so boring."

He did not bother to make any friends the first day. He wasn't concerned with any of the people he was at the camp with. He wanted to get back on his phone. His friends were on there. If Psalm Springs wanted Hayden to have fun they would give him his phone back.

Hayden was lured to the tree line nearby the shore of the lake. It provided a lot of shade and plenty of cover for Hayden to hide in. He did not want to do any of the activities and he did not want to be bothered by any of the counselors or other campers asking him to join in. Hayden thought that was stupid and boring.

Hayden hated it at Psalm Springs. This was summer vacation, and he wanted a break. The first week he had to help build a new cabin for the camp. It was a lot of hard work. Hayden had to take a break every half hour. Really, it was just an excuse to get away from all of the hard work. He would walk slowly to the water cooler that was provided for all the working campers. Then he would drink several cups of water, usually sips at a time. Whenever one of the counselors would tell him to get back to the project Hayden would curse under his breath then begin his sluggish trek back to his post.

This routine repeated several times a day for the entire first week. As the days rolled on the counselors caught on to Hayden's stubbornness. He noticed the counselors stayed close to him. Some would try to be his buddy. They would speak words of encouragement to Hayden. Others would just order Hayden around.

Then the first sermon at the hill occurred. Hayden did not want to go. He tried to stay behind in his cabin, but the counselor kept a close eye on him. Hayden was forced to join the others to the sermon hill at the end of the week.

Pastor Robbins started his speech. Hayden was not listening. He never listened to the speeches. While Pastor Robbins spoke Hayden daydreamed about playing his favorite game. He had a lot of statuses he wanted to post to his profile page. Most of them involved the awful camp his parents had brought him to.

They thought it would be good for him to get out more. He needed to see something else other than the internet and his feet. Boy, were they wrong, thought Hayden.

But that all changed. He watched as Erika was brought out to the altar. She screamed out for help. Suddenly, Hayden's attention was completely on her. She begged for mercy, but none came. Hayden watched in fascination and terror. He thought surely somebody else would jump down and save her. He was just a spectator. He could not do anything. It was not his place.

The Avenger of Blood appeared before the campers. It brought with it a sense of dread. Hayden could feel eyes looking at him. He cowered in his seat. There was nothing he could do, so why even try.

Hayden watched Erika get taken away. Nobody had gone to save her. He looked around in disgust at his fellow campers. Why hadn't they done anything?

Before he knew it, the others around him were getting up to return to their activities. The crowd rushed to the aisles. It became a standstill. Hayden did not move. He did not want to get near any of these people. They just sat there while Erika was taken away. If they wouldn't save her then they wouldn't save him.

The tick in Hayden's hands and posture returned. He found himself hunched over on his seat looking at his hands on his lap. His thumbs punched imaginary numbers. They motioned to where the letters would be forming, *Get me out of here.*

While a majority of the campers went back to their activities after the sermon, Hayden went directly to the counselor's office. His body could not move fast enough. Every step he took was fumbled from jitters running down his spine.

The door was locked when Hayden tried to open it. He shook the knob violently. For a moment, he wanted to pick the lock, but then he realized he did not know how to actually do that.

His second instinct was to start banging on the door really hard. His fists collided with the wood paneling creating a thunderous roar.

After several minutes of the harsh knocking, Hayden finally gave up. He slumped down on the ground, braced up against the door. He would just wait for somebody to come around. Somebody would have to come down to the door. It was inevitable.

Nobody came around for several hours. Hayden considered giving up, but he did not want to go back to the others. He did not want to move. He'd rather stay and stare at the trees than hang around everybody at the camp. He never wanted to be here, and he was proven right. Instead, Hayden fell asleep. His energy waned and he wanted nothing more than to return to his bed and feel safe again.

Hayden was abruptly awoken by one of the counselors. She was only a few years older than Hayden. Her auburn hair hung in front of his face as she woke him up.

"What are you doing here?" she asked him. "Are

you okay?"

Her name tag read, Cynthia. She had a giant grin on her face. Cynthia grabbed hold of Hayden to help him up.

"No, I'm not okay," said Hayden. He shrugged off the rest of his drowsiness as he rose to his feet. "I need my phone. I want to leave."

The girl looked shocked at his words. "Why would you want to leave? This place is amazing."

Hayden returned the expression of shock. "I just watched some girl get dragged away into the woods. None of you did anything."

"You should not concern yourself with her," said Cynthia. "God judged her to be a sinner. She was not meant for this world or for Heaven."

"How can you say that?" Hayden asked stunned.

"Because God took her away. His word is law. His actions are absolute. God is infallible. Psalms 12:6, *the words of the Lord are flawless*."

"Please just give me my phone," said Hayden. "I want to call my parents. I want to leave."

"You can't leave until the end of the summer," said Cynthia.

"Like hell I can't," said Hayden. "Goddammit!"

Without hesitation Cynthia slapped Hayden across the face. Hayden crumbled in surprise and pain.

"Do not take the Lord's name in vein," said Cynthia.

Tears welled up in Hayden's eyes. He tried not to show it, but he could not help it. Cynthia tried to comfort him. She wrapped her arms around Hayden as he curled up into a ball.

"This is hard. I know," said Cynthia. "You can get through this. You just have to work at it. Accepting God is easy. Holding on is the hard part. What He does sometimes is beyond all of us. His decisions whether we like them or not are what this world needs. We are His sheep. We have to have faith and know that His actions will lead us to Heaven. Erika was filled with sin. She rejected God."

"I just want to go home," said Hayden. The tears were flowing stronger than ever. Cynthia's slap triggered his entire breakdown.

"You can't go home yet," said Cynthia. "You cannot give up now. If you leave you will be turning your back on God. His judgment is swift for those that reject His love. Please do not follow in Erika's footsteps. She was wrong to deny God."

Hayden was speechless. He could not comprehend what was going on anymore. His hands reverted to the familiar position of holding the imaginary phone.

"Listen," said Cynthia. "I know what you can do.

I'll enroll you into the gardening program."

"No," said Hayden through his tears. "I don't want to."

"Yes, you will," said Cynthia. "It will get your mind off of today, and you can start looking at all the great things the Lord does. It will be perfect for you."

"I don't want to do that," said Hayden.

"It will be good for you," said Cynthia. "I promise."

The next day, Hayden was forced out of his bed by two counselors. They were much bigger than he was. He did not even try to put up a fight. The two men practically carried Hayden to a small group of campers.

Hayden didn't say a word when he joined them. He kept his head down and frowned.

The group was taken to a far end of the camp. A field with fruits and vegetables sprawled out to the fence perimeter. Psalm Springs prepared much of their own food directly at the camp.

There was a program for some of the campers to help pick the food for the day. It got many of the teenagers more involved and active with not only each other, but with God as well.

This was the last place Hayden wanted to be. His shift lasted for six hours. They gave him a basket and told him to start picking pecans from the ground under a nearby tree.

Slowly, he picked up the pecans one by one. When he got to the end of the bunch he turned around happy that he was finally done, but all he saw was more pecans. They never seemed to clear from the ground no matter how many he picked up.

He tried to take his usual breaks, but the counselors overseeing the gardening would have none of it. They kept him working his entire shift.

Every now and then Pastor Robbins would come over to see the progress of the day. On the third day of working, Robbins came over to talk to Hayden.

"It's a wonderful day," he said to Hayden to get his attention. Hayden dropped his head. He did not want to work and he definitely did not want to talk to Pastor Robbins.

"How has your work been?" he asked Hayden. "They tell me you're struggling a bit. Can I help you?"

"You can give me my phone," said Hayden.

"Oh, I'm sure somebody has explained to you that giving you your phone would not help you," explained Pastor Robbins.

"Yes, it will," said Hayden. "This camp is awful."

"Don't say that," said Robbins. "I know you're adjusting, but harsh ideas like that will not lead to your salvation. We are here to help, Hayden. We only mean the best for you. Your phone does not. Your phone just connects you to the sinful society waiting for you. Right now, you are not strong enough to repel those influences. Once the summer is over for you, your phone will be the last thing on your mind."

"Whatever," dismissed Hayden.

Pastor Robbins patted Hayden on the back. He let out a bellowing laugh. "You'll see. I promise. This summer will be good for you. Keep up the good work. 2 Timothy 2:15, *Do your best to present yourself to God as one approved, a worker who has no need to be ashamed, rightly handling the word of truth*.

"Enjoy the rest of your day. I can't wait for dinner tonight."

Hayden was left to return to his work. As soon as Pastor Robbins walked off the counselor urged Hayden to continue picking pecans. There was no relief.

Hayden was losing his mind. Every day he worked in the field. The work never ended. He hated it. The only thing he listened to was the other campers taking turns reciting passages from the Bible.

Then one morning, Hayden slipped out early. He had not slept well that night. He dreamt about running from Psalm Springs, but no matter how far he went he was always found. The Avenger of Blood was around every corner. Eventually, Hayden was wide awake. He watched dawn approach.

Hayden left the cabin and headed down to the administrations office. First, he confirmed that the doors were locked. Then he circled around the building. There were several windows along each side of the office. He stopped at one window on the backside of the counselor's office. Nobody was around. Hayden did one last quick glance.

He picked up a rock from the ground. There was still nobody around. Then Hayden threw the rock at the window. It shattered to the ground. Hayden froze for another moment. Nobody was yelling. Nobody was coming to see what had happened.

Barely able to control himself, Hayden rushed to the window. He started to climb over the seal without even realizing he was cutting himself against the broken glass. His adrenaline was too strong to feel any pain.

He tumbled to the floor inside the building. Blood trickled across his arms and chest. His shirt was stained and ripped.

Hayden recovered quickly. The office was dark. Quietly he walked into the hallway. He did not want to turn on any of the lights. Hayden worried it would alert somebody to his presence.

His hands slid up against the wall. He guided himself through the building. He stopped at every door to examine the signs: records, office, garage, and bathrooms. It got easier with every door as the sun started to rise.

The last sign he ran into lifted his spirits. It was labeled "Storage."

Hayden dashed into the room and turned on the light. There was no window. He could move freely. The room was stuffed with all the contraband that the counselors had taken on the first day. There were mp3's, game consoles, books, and most importantly, smartphones.

He started reading all of the labels. After going through several baskets he found his cabin. His phone was right on top. He gripped it with both hands and held it close. It was like being reunited with an old friend.

Immediately, he tried to text his mother. The message would not go through. There was no reception where he was.

Hayden put his phone into his pocket and turned to leave when a new thought occurred to him. He looked back at all the phones that were still there. He did not need to debate himself for long. He grabbed several more phones from several baskets. He stuffed his pockets with them. Then he put some in his socks and shoes.

When he was completely full of phones, Hayden made his exit. He avoided the bloody window. There was a back door that would provide the cover he needed to make his escape.

He slipped out just as the sun was over the horizon. The rest of the camp would be waking up soon. Hayden chose not to return to his cabin. He started walking toward the perimeter fence of the camp. He held his phone out with his arm fully extended. The bars on his phone did not budge. There was no signal anywhere in the area.

That did not stop Hayden from trying. He reached the fence. There was still no signal. His desperation made him reach his arm out through the metal bars with his phone. It proved worthless.

Hayden started to walk along the perimeter. Every few feet he would reach out through the fence to see if there was any change in the signal.

The morning crawled on. He made a point to avoid being seen by any of the campers and especially the counselors. Hayden stuck near the fence. Most of the time there were enough bushes and trees to block his view from the rest of the camp. When a clearing came along, Hayden rushed to reach cover further up the line.

He continued along the fence. Branches and vines started to overcome the entire area. Hayden could not reach through any of the gaps to stick his phone out further. Then he saw a weak point. The branches had a small break that was big enough for Hayden to stick his arm through and look at the signal bar.

When he stuck his hand through, Hayden braced himself up against the fence. Then it gave way. Hayden slipped forward crashing on the ground as the fence opened up. He had leaned on a door.

Hayden looked up. He was on the other side of the fence. Hayden scrambled to his feet. He never let go of his phone. This was the first time he felt the pain across his chest. It made it hard to breathe.

His legs collapsed. Hayden's entire body crumbled to the ground. He laid there for several minutes. The pain was too much. He remained on the ground, silent, looking up at the tree tops and the sky beyond. He could have just laid there forever, Hayden thought.

Another hour passed before Hayden finally decided to move. His stomach was beginning to growl for food. He needed to go to the bathroom. Then it started to rain. It was just a light sprinkle, but enough to annoy Hayden to no end. He needed to move.

Hayden started to think trying to leave the camp was a mistake. He pushed the thought out of his head. He was just going to keep going.

Hayden began walking through a rough looking trail. Branches obscured the path, but Hayden could still make out the general area. It was clear this path had not been used in years.

Finally, he broke free from the tree line and emerged into a clearing. He filled with joy at his first sight.

Ahead of him was the broken down, old, cabin. With the rain coming down harder, the cabin was the most welcoming place Hayden had seen all summer. His eyes bypassed all of the neglect and damage the cabin had sustained. It was beautiful to Hayden.

He skipped through the rain to reach the porch. Immediately, he felt relief once he was under the protection of the roof. The rain ran down the gutters and hit the ground loudly. Hayden stepped inside.

The smell hit him first. Rot lingered in the air. It was dark inside the cabin. He could not make out much of what filled the room. There were several bed frames up against the wall. They were knocked over to their side. Hayden got closer to see that the bed frames were blocking another door. He shoved the beds to the side to make himself a hole.

The next room was even darker. Only one window was in that room and it was covered with gunk and dirt. Hayden tried to wipe it off with his hand, but the gunk had solidified to the window. Only little chips broke off onto Hayden's fingernails.

Exhaustion overcame Hayden. The phones in his pockets were growing heavy and uncomfortable. His hunger was getting worse. He looked around the dark room. There was nobody around. He felt secure. The pain was coming back. Hayden collapsed again. This time he let himself fall asleep. He needed to recharge. His day had already been jammed packed.

Hayden stayed in the cabin for several days. He only went outside to relieve himself. But he still had the problem of food. He did not want to go back to the camp. He did not know how to pick berries or hunt. He always thought that kind of stuff was stupid.

His stomach tightened from the lack of nourishment. Hayden started eating grass out of desperation. It tasted awful, and he felt even worse the next couple of days. It did not stop him. He believed he needed something in his stomach. He needed to eat.

His next days were spent on the floor of the cabin.

He was too weak to move. He slept through most of the day. He didn't know how long he had been out there. He didn't want to move ever again. Hayden was done.

Then he woke up one day. A girl was looking over him. Her face showed concern and worry. He could not say a word to her. She forced a bottle of water into his mouth. He took glorious sips. It was the most delicious thing Hayden ever had. Then she said something that Hayden could not comprehend. Before he knew it she was gone. Hayden could not follow her. He leaned back on to the floor and fell back asleep.

Later that day, Hayden was woken up again by the girl. He noticed he had been taken out of the back room he had fallen asleep in. The two of them were in the main room of the cabin. The girl had made a makeshift bed for him. He was placed on a pile of musty blankets and old pillows. The smell was awful, but it was better than the other room.

This time the girl had food. She cut apples for Hayden to eat. Hayden had to be fed the first time. He was too weak to move. As she fed him, Hayden listened to her speak.

"I'm Brook," she introduced herself. "How long

have you been out here?"

Hayden shrugged. He did not know the answer, and he did not want to speak.

"I'm sorry," said Brook. "I probably shouldn't ask any questions right now. I just have a lot of them. You're lucky I found this place when I did. I don't know how much longer you would have made it."

Hayden kept eating. He tried to keep his mind off of the fact that he almost died coming out here, but there was nothing else he could do.

"It's okay," said Brook. "I'll take care of you."

When Hayden was finished with his food Brook got up to leave. She stopped at the door to speak to Hayden one last time.

"Do not try to move too much," said Brook. "I'll be back with more food. I'm taking one of your phones.

"None of the counselors come to this area. We'll use this as a shelter. We're going to get through this."

Hayden watched as Brook left him alone again. He did not bother to ask her to stay. He figured she wouldn't. He went back to sleep. He was already feeling better.

Over the next several weeks, Brook would come to the cabin and bring more food for Hayden. He was getting better every day. Brook never stayed at the cabin for more than two nights at a time. As Hayden grew stronger he grew more restless.

Brook wanted him to stay put. Hayden had no problem with that, but he wanted something to do. He already killed the battery on his phone. He started playing on the other phones he had stolen, but they only lasted so long.

"You can't keep using the phones like this," said Brook once. The phones were dying left and right, and she was running out of options.

"Then go recharge them," said Hayden.

"It's not that simple," argued Brook.

"Yes, it is," said Hayden. "You're at the camp all the time. Just sneak over to an outlet and plug it in. It's not hard."

"Then you do it," said Brook.

"I can't," said Hayden. "I'm too weak to walk. Remember?"

Brook rolled her eyes. That was Hayden's excuse for everything.

June was a lonely time for Hayden. Brook came by every couple of days to stock up on their supplies of food. It was always hot in the cabin. Hayden always killed the phone battery by the afternoon and was left with only boredom to keep him company.

He came to know the cabin very well. Hayden stared at the bloodstains every now and then. Knife marks cut into the walls where much of the blood was. There was still a lot of junk and garbage that was left over from whoever lived at the cabin last. Hayden had a small laugh when he started looking through pictures that were crumbled and near destroyed. They were pictures from the 1980's. Hayden thought they all had lame hair styles.

In July, Brook started allowing more people into the cabin. Hayden always kept to his corner of the room. He hardly moved from his bed. The first two to come to the cabin were Gabe and another guy Justin.

They were a couple of some sort. Hayden did not really care. The biggest annoyance was their arguing and moody silence. It annoyed Hayden. They were like a bitter married couple.

The two of them were at the cabin for several weeks. Then Gabe went missing. Brook and Justin went out to find him. Hayden did not care. He was relieved that he once again had the cabin all to himself.

That was the last time they saw Gabe. Then Brook returned alone. She was angry. Justin had gone missing as well.

"Where's Justin?" she asked.

"He hasn't come back yet," said Hayden.

"What?" yelled Brook. "He said he was going to be back before dark. That was what we agreed on."

"Then he lied," said Hayden.

"Damn it," said Brook. "Did he say anything to you? If he got caught then we could be screwed."

"What now?" Hayden asked.

"We have to lay low," said Brook. "I can't go to the camp as much right now."

"What about the phone batteries? What about our food?" Hayden asked.

"We'll just have to conserve our stuff. We have plenty of food for a few weeks now. We'll be fine."

"And what about entertainment? I am going to be so bored after a couple of days," complained Hayden.

"You'll deal with it," said Brook.

"I want to get out of this camp, not just hide here," said Hayden.

"I am working on that," huffed Brook.

Brook got up to leave again. "I'm not staying here tonight. It'll probably be best if you stayed somewhere else as well. Just for a night or two."

"I'll be fine," said Hayden. "I don't feel like going anywhere."

"Fine," said Brook. "I'll be back to check on you.

Let me know if there is anything strange."

"Whatever," Hayden said as Brook left the cabin.

The cabin was never bothered. It was peaceful for a few more weeks. Hayden convinced Brook to start charging the phone batteries again. After that Hayden was once again comfortable. He was feeling like his old self again. He had plenty of things to occupy his time. He just needed to sit and wait until Brook figured out a way to get them out of there.

The peace would not last though. Brook brought a new girl to the cabin. Her name was Cora. Several tattoos and piercings covered her body. Hayden could see them after Brook unwrapped the blanket that was around her. Cora was in shock. She took one look at Hayden and she began to have a panic attack.

"I don't want to be here," Cora told Brook.

"It is okay," assured Brook. "You will be safe here."

"No, no, I do not want to be here. Not with him," said Cora.

"What the hell did I do?" Hayden asked.

"Fuck you," said Cora.

"Fuck you, too," said Hayden.

"Hayden, can you give us a minute?" Brook asked.

"I'm not leaving," said Hayden. "This is my spot. I found this cabin first."

"Please, Hayden," said Brook.

"No, go find someplace else if you don't want to be near me," he said.

"Damn it," said Brook. "Fine, we're going."

Brook put the blanket back around Cora. She escorted the depressed girl out of the cabin. Brook glared back at Hayden before she left. Hayden just shrugged. He did not do anything to the girl. Why was he the one getting in trouble? He was there first.

Brook eventually returned. Her time away was longer than ever before. Hayden assumed it was because she was angry at him for the other night with Cora. Later, Brook brought another new girl to the cabin. She introduced herself as Mindy.

Hayden saw Mindy as another charity case of Brook's. It was going to be another person that was going to take Brook's time away from him and getting the things he needed.

Brook left them alone for several days again. Her plan of escape was coming together and she needed to prepare a few more things.

Mindy was chatty. She wanted to know everything about Hayden, Brook, the cabin, and anything else somebody would talk about. Hayden tried to ignore her for the most part, but sometimes it was impossible. Eventually, Mindy broke Hayden down. His batteries were dead for the day. He had nothing else to do, but talk to Mindy.

"How many people do you think have died here?" Mindy asked.

"I don't care," said Hayden. "Probably a lot."

"I talked to Pastor Robbins before. He said that not everybody wants to go to Heaven. They don't want to put in the work."

"Blah blah blah," said Hayden. "Let me guess, it's a privilege not a right. You can't have everything handed to you."

"Pretty much," said Mindy.

"What people don't understand is that we do work to get to where we are," said Hayden. "I nearly died getting here with those phones. I'm not lazy. I just want to be comfortable. Is that wrong?"

"I suppose not," said Mindy.

"Maybe I don't work as hard as others, but I don't have to. There is plenty of reward to go around for everybody. Whatever these people are saying here, they are wrong."

"But if you knew you could get into Heaven, wouldn't you try?"

Hayden shrugged. "I'm sure I will. Whatever the hell is after death, I'm sure they will understand.

Psalm Springs is not right."

"I hope so," said Mindy. "I hope so."

Mindy was gone a couple weeks later. The news that Brook's plan for escape had fallen through was devastating. Brook disappeared again. Hayden was left alone. All but one phone was dead.

Hayden waited around the next day. He ate some of the food they had in reserve. There was no sign of Brook, and for the first time Hayden was tired of looking at the blood stained walls of the cabin.

Mindy's words from one of their conversations kept echoing in Hayden's head. Had he tried hard enough to find a signal? Could he still reach his family? Could he find some sign of life from the outside world?

Hayden made the decision to take the last phone and start walking around again. He had never checked the area beyond the cabin. He always assumed Brook had by that point.

His walking was slow. He had not gone for a hike in some time. The most walking he had done recently was from one end of the cabin to the other.

Every few minutes Hayden would take a break. He always rested against a tree or a rock. He'd take the time to check his phone. There was never any signal.

The perimeter fence was visible again. He started his old routine of sticking his arm through the fence to get as far out as possible.

He reached out with his phone. His arm strained against the metal bars. He watched the phone bars remain still. There was no hope, Hayden believed.

Then the phone pinged. A bar popped up on his screen for a brief moment. Hayden's heart jumped into his throat. There was a chance. He pressed himself further against the fence. It did not help. He could only hold on to the signal for less than a second. He needed to be further out.

Hayden looked over the fence. It was ten feet high. There were several places that could be used as a foothold. The decision was made. He loosened up his limbs. There was a phone signal beyond that fence. All he had to do was get to it.

He started his climb. His arms and legs cried out in pain. He was not ready for such a strenuous activity. At the top of the fence were several decorative spears. They poked at the sky with rough edges.

Hayden had to suck it up and pass the spear heads. His wounds from the broken glass were healed. He was not looking forward to getting more cuts along his chest, but he had no choice.

Hayden made the move fast. He threw himself

over the top of the fence. His move was too fast though. He could not hold himself up on the other side, and he plummeted to the ground. His body landed with a loud thud on the ground. The wind was knocked out of his lungs.

When he recovered he checked over the phone. It was still active. Hayden struggled to his feet. He dusted himself off and stuck out his hand.

The signal was still weak, but it was there. Hayden began walking further out than he had ever gone before. He was no longer in the camp. For the first time in the whole summer relief was washing over him. He was free.

Hayden watched his phone. The signal bar bounced from one to zero several times. He tried to adjust his path to find the most stable setting.

Then there it was. Two bars. Hayden found his connection to the outside world. He could call out for help. He was saved.

He was so focused on his phone he did not hear the heavy muffled breathing or see the blade coming at him.

His head burst into pain. A spearhead was thrust into his eye. Hayden cried out in agony, but the only one to listen to him was the Avenger of Blood.

Hayden fell to the ground. He rolled over to try

and see what was attacking him. His one good eye was tearing up. The pain was blinding him. He could not see the attack that was coming.

The Avenger of Blood marched over to its newest victim. It gave two cuts to Hayden's Achilles' tendons. Hayden begged for the monster to stop.

Hayden could no longer move. The Avenger of Blood loomed over him. He tried to use his phone. Before he had a chance to put any coherent numbers in, the Avenger of Blood crushed the phone and Hayden's hand with its bloody foot. The phone shattered in Hayden's grip. He could feel shards of plastic cut into his palm.

"Please," begged Hayden. "Please don't do this."

The Avenger of Blood was silent. He made His judgment.

The spearhead in the Avenger's hand swung down hard onto Hayden's face. It pierced his second eye and crushed his head.

Hayden was dead.

Envy

Neil looked at his official Psalm Springs camp shirt with disappointment.   He had asked for a size medium.   The counselor must have been too busy helping the other campers get their shirts.   Neil was given a large.

He hated large shirts.   Neil was a pleasant medium. He could pass off a snug small if he needed to. Sometimes his mother got hand-me-downs from her friends' younger children.   Neil usually avoided wearing those shirts regardless of size.   Usually they featured a TV show that Neil hadn't watched because he wasn't allowed to or the colors were too bright for his taste.

The collared shirt that he wore was striped with dark blues and browns.   It was buttoned all the way to the top.   It was nothing like the outfit the camp provided.   Neil's camp shirt was not going to give him the proper comfort around the neck.

Neil tried to put it out of his head.   Maybe later he could get a better one or trade a fellow camper for a smaller size.

He left the opening sermon with a sense of readiness. Neil was ashamed of what he had been doing. He didn't mean to click on the link to Pornbabes. But when he did he couldn't help but look. He was fixated on all the images. Naked girls were sucking, fucking, and everything in between. Then he couldn't stop. It made him feel good.

Every day he went back to the site. He throbbed and ached for those girls online. Every video he imagined he was the guy with them. The best videos were the POV. He could easily imagine it was him there. The girl wanted him and he wanted her back.

Neil started masturbating several times a day. His dad always worked late and his mother was constantly away for church meetings. After school, Neil was on his own.

He knew it was wrong, but he couldn't help it. He could not resist. None of the girls at his school would pay him any attention. He wanted a girlfriend. He wanted to be with somebody that he could love and would love him back. Kevin Blake and his girlfriend Ashley always looked so happy together. Why couldn't Neil have that as well?

The videos kept him happy. It put him in his own little world where everybody loved him and would do anything for him.

Then his mother caught him.

Neil starred at his mother from his desk with deer in the headlight eyes. His pants were at his ankles. The volume on his computer was turned down low, but you could still hear the oohs and ahs moaning from the girl as she sucked the anonymous man's penis.

That was the moment his mother made the decision that Neil was going to attend Psalm Springs for the summer. She could not imagine a world where her baby boy was looking at such horrible things. Neil was going to have to get right in the eyes of God.

Neil tried to put it all behind him. His computer was taken away which helped. Still Neil found himself looking at the girls in his school differently. During class he imagined the girl sitting in front of him was down on her knees. He could see the skin of her lower back peek out from between her shirt and jeans. Neil focused on her bare skin. He pictured her fully naked as he came up from behind and entered her. Just like in the videos.

On the van ride to Psalm Springs he sat next to a girl, Cora, sleeping against the window. She had tattoos down both arms and piercings on her face. The whole trip Neil fought off his erection. He couldn't stop looking at her cleavage. He wanted to bury his head in her breasts and have her moan in pleasure, even if she was asleep.

Neil tried to sit next to her during the sermon, but she was taken away with some of the counselors and Neil was directed a different way. Not to worry, he could try to find her later.

On the first day, Neil wandered through the camp looking at all the fun activities that were available to him. He hung around the lake for most of the day. A lot of the other campers made their way to the shore line and Neil was able to talk to many of them.

His conversations with the other groups were never very long. They were quick to jump into the water and leave Neil behind. Neil didn't want to undress to swim. He didn't like the look of his body. He was self-conscious about his size. He was skinny and pale. The last time he went swimming Jack Freeman started making fun of him. He got the rest of the class to call Neil a ghost because he was so pale. It stuck for over a month.

Neil paced on the shoreline. His yellow shirt was tucked into his blue shorts. His socks were raised as high as his calves. He thought he could play it mysterious like and wait for the other campers to grow interested in him. Then they would leave the water and have a chat with Neil.

It had yet to happen.

Neil's cabin was no better. His cabinmates talked in endless cycles about sports or whatever awesome TV show had just ended. The biggest was the fantasy show about thrones and dragons. Neil didn't know the name. He had never seen it. His mom didn't want him watching those kinds of shows. They were against God.

"You haven't watched it at all?" asked his bunkmate, George.

"No," said Neil.

"But it's so good," said George. "You have to watch them. Rent them, download them."

"My mom won't let me," said Neil.

George then frowned at Neil. He didn't know how to respond.

"God doesn't want us watching that stuff," said Neil. "It's got magic and false gods in it."

"Do you do everything your mother says?" George asked. "It's just a show."

"Most of the time," Neil said in shameful remorse.

"Most of the time? Whoa, guys, we got a rebel over here," taunted George. The other guys in the cabin chuckled.

Neil's conversations with others went just as well. At a camp for followers of God Neil was surprised when he could not talk to others about Christian entertainment or the Bible in general.

He overheard a group talking about their friends back home. One of the campers said they missed their friends, some of whom were gay.

Neil decided to interject. He was curious as to why they would have friends that were against God's will. It said so in the Bible.

The entire group stared at him blankly. Some nodded their heads and quickly changed the subject. Once they were gone Neil did not see them again.

Later in the week, Neil's cabin was scheduled to go through confession. It was a great way to heal the troubled soul. Many of the problems that teenagers had could easily be solved by letting go of their embarrassment and irrational anger.

When Neil and the others arrived they saw several more campers already in line. Many of his bunkmates said hello to people they recognized. Neil stayed quiet. He did not know any of them.

They all gathered into a single file line. Up ahead there was the confessional booth. Pastor Robbins was on one side of the booth behind the closed doors. He made the time to listen to every single camper.

Each confession only took a couple of minutes, but it was still a long wait in the chapel. The campers were growing bored. Naturally, conversations started to pick up volume. Neil stayed quiet as he listened to the others talk about their homes and their schools. Neil loved listening to other people's stories. They always seemed better than his life. Neil imagined he was in the same scenarios and pictured himself doing all the cool stuff that others did.

Then they started talking to him.

"Neil, Neil," said his bunkmate, Michael. "Who was your last girlfriend?"

"Her name was Kara," lied Neil. He usually lied in this situation. It made things easier. Kara was one of his favorite searches.

"Did you have sex with her?" Michael asked.

"No," said Neil. "I'm waiting until I get married."

Michael shrugged. "That's good. But how far did you go with her?"

"We kissed," said Neil. He tried to keep things vague.

"Just kissed," said Michael. "She didn't get you off or anything? Come on, man. That's lame."

Neil didn't respond.

"Alright, lay off of him," said one of the friends in the group. He had natural blonde hair that looked like it belonged to a movie star. Neil wished he had hair like that. Then maybe the girls would like him more.

"We're just messing with him, Morgan," said Michael.

"And it's over now," defended Morgan.

"What are you going to confess?" Michael turned back to Neil.

Neil stayed quiet. He did not want to talk about his problems.

"Do you have anything to confess?"

"Yeah," mumbled Neil.

"Let me guess. You stole some gum from the store. No wait. You had a cookie before dinner," Michael joked.

The group around them laughed at Michael's jab toward Neil. Neil kept his head down. His face was turning red. He was getting embarrassed.

"Lay off of him," defended Morgan.

"I'm just saying I don't think Neil needs to be here," said Michael. "He's a goody two shoes."

"So stop messing with him," said Morgan.

"Fine. Whatever," said Michael.

While the conversation was going on Neil did not notice that the line was growing shorter. It was his turn up to the confessional booth.

The booth was dimly lit. Neil sat down on the small chair provided. He could not see Pastor Robbins on the other side of the booth. The mesh screen was too dark for visibility.

"Hi," said Neil. He was nervous. He was so nervous Neil did not realize he didn't fully close the door. The streak of light coming from the outside of the booth went unnoticed.

"Good afternoon," said Pastor Robbins. "Thank you for joining me."

Neil sat in silence. He waited for his instructions. He did not know what to do.

"You can take your time," said Robbins. "Tell me and God whatever is bothering you. This is your chance to set yourself straight."

"Okay," said Neil. He did not want to come right out and say he watched porn. Suddenly, Neil got the idea from Michael. He wanted to start off small.

"I told my Mom I had never watched a rated R movie. She doesn't approve of it. I went over to my friend's house. It was on TV. I just wanted to know what it was about. Everybody else talks about it. It was good.

"And I cheated on a test once. I looked over Lindsay's shoulder. She's really smart."

"Anything else?"

"I sometimes sneak extra food when I'm at school," confessed Neil. "It's nothing big. Just some extra chips or another dessert."

"Do you realize you are breaking one of the Ten Commandments? When you sneak food or watch shows without your parents knowing you are dishonoring them. Even if it is just a little bit."

"I know," said Neil. "But it does no harm. Everybody else seems fine."

"Do not be deceived, Neil," said Pastor Robbins. "They may appear good and well, but they are rotting on the inside. You should listen to your parents."

"Okay," said Neil.

"How has everything been since you've arrived at Psalm Springs?" asked Pastor Robbins. "Have you had any problems?"

"No," said Neil. "It's been fine."

"Neil, what is said in here is private," said Robbins. "If you are having any problems please let them out. If you keep things bottled up then God cannot help you."

"I saw this girl," said Neil, and just like that all of his problems started to unravel. "She was so hot. I can't stop thinking about her."

"You're going down a slippery path, Neil," said Pastor Robbins. "Do not covet her."

"I can't help it," said Neil. "I've been watching these videos online. I imagine her and me doing those things. I know it's wrong, but they just pop up in my head. I see her naked lying in front of me. I just want to kiss her all over.

"I actually think about a lot of girls like that. I see Jerry and Dawn holding hands in the hallway all the time. He told me that he did a fish eye to her once. I looked it up. I can't see Dawn without thinking about that now.

"What if I'm not good enough? What is wrong with me? I can't get these ideas out of my head. When I go to church I start to daydream. Cathy is a friend of mine. She has been for years. I like sitting next to her. She always smells nice. Sometimes I lose focus on what is going on and just think about her. She doesn't have a boyfriend."

"Okay, Neil," Pastor Robbins interjected. "I understand. You need to learn more self discipline. Focus more on God. He will clear your mind. This summer you will have to learn to handle your urges. Stop thinking of women as a prize. When you begin to drift in your mind say a prayer. God will listen. God will know you are fighting off the offerings of the devil.

"You need to keep these words in mind. Galatians

4:9, but now that you know God- or rather are known by God- how is it that you are turning back to those weak and miserable principles?   Do you wish to be enslaved by them all over again?

"God will give you freedom from physical desire. You just have to put your faith in him fully."

"Okay," said Neil. "I understand."

"Good," said Pastor Robbins. "You are stronger than you think, Neil. I know you can do this. You may go."

Despite his talk with Pastor Robbins, Neil still felt ashamed of his desires. He got up from his seat and pushed the door to the confessional booth open.

He put on a straight face to hide the fact that he just went through a lot with Pastor Robbins. As he walked out he saw the campers in the waiting line all looking at him.

They were all smiling and chuckling quietly to themselves. Several people pointed in Neil's direction.

It was then Neil realized how easy it was to open the door. He never closed it. Many of them had heard what Neil was saying.

Michael's grin was as wide as his face. He was nodding his head and giving Neil a thumbs up. Some of the girls in the line could not look at Neil directly. They turned away as he walked past them. The story of his confession was already being spread.

As Neil passed Morgan he got a pat on the back. It was a simple gesture, but Neil felt the support of at least one person.

The rest of the day Neil could see more people talking about him around his bunk. They were all hearing about what Neil confessed. He couldn't look anybody in the eye after that.

The next day Neil's confession was all but forgotten. Everybody moved on, but Neil could not let it go. He kept quiet around his bunkmates. They were all chatting about other things. None of them were paying any attention to Neil.

Then a group of their friends appeared. Morgan was among them. They all had baseball gloves.

"I thought we were going to the softball game?" Morgan asked through the screen door of the cabin.

"We're coming," said Michael. He grabbed his baseball glove from his chest at the foot of his bed. "What's the hurry?"

"I like playing baseball," said Morgan. "Let's go."

The cabin began to empty out. Neil remained in his bed reading a book that he checked out from the camp library.

Morgan looked over at Neil. "Do you want to join

us?" he asked.

Neil looked up. He couldn't hide his smile even though he wanted to. He didn't want the others to know how excited he was that he was invited to something.

"Sure," said Neil. His voice cracked and stuttered a bit. His one word came off as two.

While the others in the cabin did not say anything they all gave Morgan a stern look. None of them were happy with his invitation.

As they walked down to the field Neil tried to start up several conversations or join in others. Whenever he asked a question the reply was usually just a one word answer.

"Have you guys heard of the band, Praise He?" Neil asked. It was his favorite band that his mom would let him listen to. Confidence was coming back to Neil. Morgan's invite was a step in the right direction.

"Yup," responded one of the guys next to him.

"Do you like them?"

"Okay," he said.

"They have a great message about following God and listening to the scripture."

"Yeah…"

When it looked like someone's attention had gone another way Neil tried his approach on somebody else.

"I was thinking about getting my ears gauged," said a camper to Neil's left. The guy already had several piercing in his ear and eyebrows.

"Why would you do that?" Neil asked.

The guy looked over at Neil with a dumbfounded look on his face. At first he didn't respond back.

"We should be keeping our bodies pure," Neil said to drive his point home. "It says in Leviticus, you should not make cuts on your body or get any tattoos."

"It's just some piercings. Besides, I can take them out if I wanted," he said.

"I'm just saying it's wrong according to the Bible," said Neil.

"That's no longer relevant," he said. "It's cool now."

"Oh," said Neil. He didn't believe the pierced camper, but he didn't have a further argument.

"You know your stuff," said Morgan. He started walking next to Neil. "I was wondering if I could borrow your Bible later. I misplaced mine yesterday, and I need to read up on some things. I'm having a couple of problems."

"What's wrong?" Neil asked.

"I don't want to get into it, but I just need a little guidance," whispered Morgan.

"Can't you ask one of the counselors for a book? I only have the one," said Neil.

"I know," said Morgan. "I just didn't want to get them involved yet. I don't think it's anything, but I don't want to worry them. I thought since you know the Bible so well that I could borrow yours. You don't really need it."

"Yeah," said Neil. His mom went through the Bible every night. She picked out scriptures for him to read. When he was finished she would explain them to him and help him understand the context of the world.

"That should be okay," said Neil.

"Great, thanks," said Morgan. "I'll give it back tomorrow. Thanks. You're a life saver."

A game was already going by the time the group got to the field. It didn't matter. They just rotated in and picked up where the game left off. The innings were reaching into the double digits and the score even higher. There was no need to start over. The campers just wanted to play. It didn't matter who was winning. Much of the time people were changing teams whenever they felt like it.

Neil was never able to make it to first base. He struck out every time. When he was in the outfield he was told to go to right field. The ball rarely made it his way.

For a few minutes Neil stopped paying attention to the game. He looked out to the tree line of the camp not too far away from the field. He couldn't help but think somebody was watching him from out there. When he finally turned back to the game he noticed that his team had gone to the bench and his opponents were on the field. The game was continuing. Nobody bothered to alert him.

The game could have continued until dusk. The day was perfect to be outside and the rotating list of campers that came and went kept the game going with fresh faces and energy.

But it all came to a halt when a young girl came running across the field.

"THEY ARE LYING TO YOU!" she yelled out. All of the players stopped what they were doing to listen to the girl. The ball landed off in the distance with no one watching.

"GOD IS NOT OUR SAVIOR!" she yelled out again. "IT IS ALL A LIE!"

Counselors followed the girl out onto the field. They shouted at her and told her to stop.

"Erika!" yelled one of the women in green. "Stop disturbing the others. Please come with us so we can talk about this."

Erika turned to the counselors approaching her. She was winded. Clearly she had been running and screaming for a while.

"This is all bullshit!" Erika yelled. "God isn't watching over us and protecting us. We're suffering all on our own. He's just laughing at us while we crawl around at His feet."

"That's not true," said the counselor. "God has a plan for us all."

"Then His plan sucks!" screamed Erika.

"Do not say that," said the counselor.

"I want to go home," Erika demanded. "I do not want to be here. I hate this. I hate you. I. HATE. GOD!"

Then Erika fell to the ground from exhaustion. She was out of breath and out of energy. The counselors took the opportunity to surround her.

Neil could hear her begging to be let go. He stood motionless at the dugout. He was shocked at Erika's words. How could anybody hate God?

Erika was brought to her feet. The counselors all had a hold of her. She struggled to fight them off, but eventually she walked off with them.

She continued to scream "God does not care about us!" before her tears finally covered up her words of hatred.

Neil never thought he would see Erika again. Then it was the first Sunday of the summer. He was eager to get to the sermon on the hill with Mindy. On Monday, He was going to be starting class taught by Pastor Robbins. Neil couldn't wait to hear what he had to say.

He sat in stone cold silence as they dragged Erika out onto the chancel. She yelled at the audience and screamed at the counselors.

Neil listened to Pastor Robbins give his explanation. Erika had turned her back on God. She had not only lost faith in Him, but publicly renounced Him.

He couldn't help but feel a little pleased when they started to carry her out past the gates. She did not belong at Psalm Springs.

Then Neil saw it. The Avenger of Blood appeared from the trees. He stood regal with the camp. He was the king and the campers were his subjects.

The Avenger of Blood grabbed hold of Erika and lifted her from the ground with ease. She fell back to the ground hard. Then the Avenger of Blood began to drag her away into the woods by her hair.

Neil was stunned. He couldn't believe what he was seeing, but in the back of his mind it all made sense. Erika had turned her back on God, so God damned her to Hell. It's what He had done for ages in the Bible.

Suddenly, Neil's heart sunk to the floor. The reality

of the situation sunk in. Neil was a sinner. He couldn't help it. Neil had been sinning and despite everything he did that was good he was still a sinner.

The Avenger of Blood waited for him as well. Neil would be damned to Hell if he couldn't change his ways.

He had to breathe. He had to relax he told himself. His parents would not send him here if they did not think he could get through it. Neil could change. He could change for God. Neil would be accepted into Heaven.

That's what Psalm Spring was all about. It was here to help people like Neil. His sinning had to stop, even if he didn't want to.

Class began early Monday morning.

Thirty students filled the small classroom. Not a word was spoken. Solemn from the other night still hung in the air.

The desks were aligned four in a row and five in a column. Neil found a seat in the middle of the right side. The front row was already taken by five campers who arrived even earlier than Neil.

Neil's seat was next to a poster of Jesus with his arms wrapped around a young boy and girl. They basked in his heavenly aura as the surrounding other children held their fists up to them. The poster's caption read: Cast out in sin? Jesus will be your lifesaver.

Neil wanted to put himself in the young boy's shoes. He wanted to hug Jesus and never let go. That would protect him from the Avenger of Blood.

Looking around, Neil only saw one other camper that he recognized. He was happy that it was Morgan. After the first week, Morgan was the only one that was genuinely nice to Neil.

"You got a new Bible," Neil said to Morgan from two desks over.

"Oh, yeah," said Morgan. He looked down at his blue covered Psalm Springs issued Bible as if he just realized it.

"I guess I can get mine back then," said Neil.

"Yeah, I'll get it to you later," said Morgan. "I don't have it on me."

"You owe me one," joked Neil. Morgan nodded his head. The joke fell flat. So Neil tried it again.

"You owe me one," said Neil. Morgan looked back over. He nodded again. This time Neil just smiled back, satisfied Morgan had gotten the gist.

More campers began to pile into the room. Desks were starting to fill up. Neil was glad he got there early. He liked his seat. Then he turned to talk to

Morgan again. Neil was surprised to see a different face in the seat that he was just looking at a moment ago. Morgan was gone.

Pastor Robbins entered the classroom a few minutes before seven o'clock. He greeted everybody with a warm hello then stood in front of the class completely ignoring his desk behind him.

"I know you all have a lot on your mind," said Robbins. "There are a lot of questions. That's okay. That is perfectly normal. That is why we are all here. I'm here to guide you to a path of understanding. The sight of God's work is far more awe inspiring than just hearing about it. He truly is an awesome god.

"On our first day, I usually just leave the floor open to questions. You are all young adults. You are all smart and should not only hear the truth, but be given the chance to come to terms with it. You have bear witness to God and God as bear witness to you. Every one of you is now under judgment. Over the next few months your choices will decide if God allows you to continue your path toward Heaven or end your sinning now and banish you to Hell.

"Please, don't be shy. Ask whatever is on your mind."

Hands started to stretch into the air. Pastor Robbins smiled. He pointed at a girl sitting in the front row. When she started talking all the other hands went down, forced to wait their turn.

"What happened yesterday?" she asked. "With the girl?"

"Yes, Erika," began Robbins. "She was troubled. We spoke to her on several occasions last week. She arrived here thanks to her parents. They believed that she needed to be shown that what God does is actually for the good of the world. Erika did not believe that. She turned her back on God a couple of years ago. I was told there was an incident with her friend. Since then, Erika hated God. She believed him to be evil. No God could allow cruelty and pain in this world, she said.

"That's a wonderful thing to believe in, but unfortunately it is a lie. God does not allow cruelty, pain, suffering, or evil into Heaven. The world is a different story.

"The world is a filter. Imagine a strainer resting over a bowl. Then you place noodles into the strainer. All the boiling water and little debris fall through the holes into the bowl. That leaves you with clean noodles perfect for dining. The strainer is the world. It is here to separate the good from the bad.

"Erika could not accept that. She refused to accept that. Instead she chose to continue to spread the lies that the devil wants you to believe. Her actions earlier in the week did this camp no good. She spread sin to several of you, and it will now be even more difficult to fight off the demons that lurk in the shadows just waiting to influence you.

"She had to be stopped before her sin had the chance to reach any more of you. The Avenger of Blood judged her like he will judge every one of you by the time this camp is over."

More hands shot into the air. Robbins picked a boy in the back.

"What are we being judged on?"

Pastor Robbins let out a little laugh. "This isn't multiple choice or anything. You can't necessarily cram for it. Rarely does this happen overnight, but once you have heard the word of God then you must begin to make your choice.

"Accept God and Jesus Christ as your lord and savior. Follow in His footsteps and obey His law. I will tell you it is more than simply following the rules to the letter. You have to want to follow the rules. I have seen too many false followers ended by the Avenger of Blood because they thought they could beat the system. At the same time I have seen those who have faltered along the path and gone on to continue spreading the word of our Lord because they kept Jesus close to their heart, repented their sins, and wanted to do what was right. It is simple instructions, but a difficult task."

Pastor Robbins picked out another camper near the window of the classroom. She was caught gazing outside toward the trees. She gave a slight jerk when Robbins called her out. Neil thought it was funny.

"You had a question earlier," said Robbins.

"Nevermind," said the girl.

"You can ask me anything, Brook" he said. "It is crucial that you get your answers. It is the only way to find spiritual salvation. With your experience you should know that."

"Why are you doing this? That girl is dead because of you? So many are dead because of you," Brook asked.

All of the campers slowly turned back to look at Pastor Robbins. They wanted to hear the answer.

Pastor Robbins' shoulders dropped. It was as if he put a fifty pound book bag across his shoulders.

"I want to make something perfectly clear. I have done nothing to harm any of you. Every summer when the camp opens I pray that we lose none of you. I pray that every night. I do not pray to God. Of course he is listening. I pray to your souls. I pray that they listen to my pleas and expel the sin that consumes them.

"I live here under the grace of God and under the eye of judgment brought down by the Avenger of Blood. There is no difference between you or me. We are all children of God and we are all here to have judgment passed over us.

"My duty is to prepare you for that moment. But I cannot force you to accept God. That has to come from within. I can only tell you and explain to you the situation. The rest is up to you."

"Then why even open the camp?" Brook asked. "If people are going to die then why bring us here?"

"Because I believe the truth is far more important," said Robbins. "Mark 16:15-16, *and he said to them, 'Go into all the world and proclaim the gospel to the whole creation. Whoever believes and is baptized will be saved, but whoever does not believe will be condemned.'*

"We are all going to die. It doesn't matter if it is tomorrow or fifty years. If this camp was not open then you could very well live until you are old. You could have a family. They would love you, but then when you passed away your soul would go to Hell. And so will your children's souls, and so on and so on. It isn't because you did something wrong. It is because you didn't know the whole truth.

"There are people out there telling you to follow

God. You ignore them. They are just strangers. What do they know? You believe that your life is good enough. But that is a lie you tell yourself because you just want to delay the inevitable.

"Now or later does not matter for Hell, but it does matter for you and for all the people that you know. Sin spreads from soul to soul. It corrupts one then interacts with another like a sickness.

"It is God's wish that everybody achieves entrance into Heaven, and some day that may be possible, but first He must stop the spread of sin.

"Psalm Springs allows God to reach out and save you or strike down the sinful soul. Only the pure of heart will remain.

"Coming face to face with the truth allows that. Denying the inevitable is the sure path to Hell, fast or slow. Do not live in ignorance or half truths.

"God is real. God is powerful."

Neil spent the next few weeks going to class and trying to make new friends. Mindy stopped coming around as much. Her failed Bible study group really got to her. It did not matter much to Neil. She was friends with a homosexual. Neil knew God didn't approve of that.

He began volunteering at the medical ward of

Psalm Springs. The camp saw it as an opportunity for many of the teens to help out their fellow campers. Many of the patients there were going through various levels of withdrawal. The transition to Psalm Springs was a rapid one. Some people could not adjust to it so easily. They were taken away from their dependents. Their addictions went unanswered.

Neil's job was to help make them comfortable until they were ready to take part in the camp and embrace God like they should.

The job ended up being very boring. Neil hardly interacted with the campers that were staying at the medical ward. They usually kept quiet around him.

The head nurse, Virginia, was a sweet lady. She reminded Neil of his grandmother. They had a similar smell. She let Neil eat lunch with her. Morgan volunteered at the medical ward as well, but not the same days as Neil. It left Neil alone often. Virginia was always there to be good company.

At the end of his day Neil was on his way out, but Virginia grabbed his attention and asked him for one more thing. Neil was told to grab the lunch tray from one of the patients. Neil was exhausted. He wanted to go lie down and read, but he did as he was told. Now was not the time to be disobeying orders. The Lord was watching.

To Neil's surprise he recognized the girl that was lying in bed. He would never forget the tattoos that graced both of her arms. Her nose piercing was gone and she looked deathly ill, but he would never forget her.

A quick look at the door revealed her name as Cora. He loved that name. Neil entered the room. His steps were now awkward. He tried to correct it and make himself look casual and loose, but it only resulted in an even more unbalanced stride.

No words were coming out of his mouth. He looked at the beautiful girl in front of him. Just like in the van ride he could not take his eyes off of her or her magnificent breasts.

Neil got out of there as quickly as he could. He lucked out he thought. He didn't think Cora noticed him. He would have another chance to play it cool and become her boyfriend.

"Don't over think this," Morgan advised Neil. After Neil told him about Cora being in the medical ward Neil needed to know what to do next. He was nervous and never had an opportunity like this before. Usually the girls he liked stopped going near him.

"You don't want to come on too strong," said Morgan. "You have to play a little. If she sees that you want her too much she will use you up and throw you away."

"But what do I do?" Neil asked.

"Okay, you drop off her lunch. Throw in an extra dessert or something. Something small just to let her know that she is special, better than the other girls."

"That's easy," said Neil.

"It is easy," said Morgan. "You just make it too complicated. Be yourself. Relax."

"Maybe I should pray for God to help me?" Neil suggested.

"Couldn't hurt," said Morgan.

Neil began his campaign to get Cora to fall in love with him. It started out with an extra piece of fruit. Then it rolled into dessert and milk. Cora took notice. She said hello to Neil whenever he came by.

Some days were better than others. Neil would pop his head in to her room to see if she needed something. She'd beam a smile back at him and ask for a small snack or a new blanket. Other days she would have no time for him. Cora would roll away from him. Audible groans were her way of telling Neil to go away.

After weeks of pining for Cora and presenting her little gifts Neil's chance finally arose.

And he blew it.

Cora was unusually disconcerted that day. Her entire bed was covered in sweat. Usually she threw Neil out of her room, but this time she called for him.

She was desperate. Neil had gotten so much for her already, but she needed just one more thing. The camp had taken away her pills. It was her medicine, Xanax, and she needed it. It would put her right. Cora said she would do anything to get them back.

Neil wasn't sure how to respond. There was a medicine closet that Virginia and some of the campers had access to. Neil was one of them. The closet contained lots of medicine that was confiscated from the campers on their arrival. Virginia saw to it that it was properly distributed back to the owner.

Neil could get in there and get Cora's medicine. But that would be breaking the rules. How would God react?

Then Cora propositioned him. She offered him a blow job for her pills. Neil's mind raced. This was what he wanted. This was what he had wanted for years.

Then the Avenger of Blood entered his mind. The stalking behemoth was waiting for him. The monster was waiting for Neil to slip up and fall back into sin. He had been doing so well since arriving at Psalm

Springs.

Neil froze. He ached to have her look up at him while he was in her mouth, but that wasn't love. This wasn't what God wanted. This wasn't allowed.

He shook his head at Cora and walked out. He couldn't do it. He couldn't be with Cora like that.

After the awkward incident, Neil avoided Cora's room. He couldn't face her. He was embarrassed for walking out on her like that. He wanted to help her, but he knew it was the wrong thing to do. The best he could do was not mention it to Virginia.

The only person Neil did tell was Morgan. Morgan laughed at the situation, but when Neil got defensive Morgan told him that he did the right thing. God would approve.

"You never see the devil in action," said Pastor Robbins. "He's a puppet master. He pulls on the heart strings of every individual in the world. Some of them are too weak to resist. They follow the devil's will because he can give them immediate gratification.

"Do not give in. Heaven is the ultimate gratification. You just have to earn it. Be patient. Your reward will come."

"How does the devil influence us?" Neil asked. Neil needed to know how he could avoid any poor choices.

"By example," said Robbins. "The devil does not sit back and wait for your souls to sin. He is impatient just as his sinners are. So what does he do? He gets in the minds of greedy, sleazy people that prepare a package to the world. They make TV shows and movies about how you should be living your life. You should do drugs because they make you cool and make you feel awesome. Go have sex with as many people as you can because it turns you into more of a man. Ladies, you are not strong and independent for having sex. You are selling out your body and soul for gratification. Men do not respect you for it and neither does God.

"You see stories about men and women who murder people because they feel they have the right for revenge and justice. That is not for you to decide. God is our final judge. Not man.

"You have to remind yourself that this is not how life is. What you see in the world of fiction is life through Hell tinted glasses.

"God will not go easy on you because you lived the life you saw on TV or read in a book. There is only one way to live life accordingly and that is through God's law."

Every night Neil prayed for Cora. He wanted her

to find peace. She was starting to get better. Though Neil avoided her he couldn't help but check up on her status every now and then.

It wasn't before long that Cora was released from the medical ward. Neil was ecstatic. This was his second chance. God was giving him and Cora a new beginning.

As soon as she left the building Neil was making his apology. He didn't know why he did it, he had done nothing wrong, but it felt like the right thing to do.

Cora shrugged it off and acted like nothing had happened. They spent the rest of the day together and Neil couldn't have been happier.

But Neil's paradise was rotten. Morgan joined them the next day. He took them to a secret spot tucked away from the rest of the camp. It was a small clearing just a little ways into the trees. It was the perfect place to get away.

Neil thought it was a really cool hideaway. He wished he had known about it earlier. Several days over the past month Neil could have used it to get away from some of his cabinmates. They still gave him a hard time any chance they could get.

Once Cora and Morgan were settled by a tree Morgan pulled out a joint from his sock. Neil was surprised to see it. What was Morgan doing with it?

Neil took a step back. He did not want to be associated with drug use. Cora and Morgan laughed as they each took a hit.

Cora wasn't better. She was still doing drugs. And she had gotten Morgan involved. Neil was devastated. His heart sunk down to his stomach.

Then they offered him the joint. They were so casual about it. Neil couldn't understand how they were so relaxed. Didn't they know they were being watched? Judged? They just didn't care.

Neil left. He was not going to go down the path of sin. That was the path to Hell. Neil had to remain clean and pure. It was the only way to get to Heaven.

Once again, Neil tried to stay away from Cora. He also steered clear of Morgan. It hurt him because Morgan was his only friend at Psalm Springs.

Every day Neil woke up with pieces of paper scattered all over his bed. His bunkmates made a game out of how many they could get on him without him waking up.

Neil's days were lonely. He was left alone in the cabin whenever he didn't have class. He'd go out and try the activities that were going on, but they were hard to do when you were alone and nobody asked to join you.

Every so often Neil would go to the secret hiding

spot. Cora and Morgan met there often. Others started to pop up. They would pass around weed or other pills that Morgan had access to. Another camper bragged that he was given access to a lot of the buildings. He had a ring of keys that jingled when he talked. He was able to get their group alcohol.

Neil felt terrible for his friend. Morgan had fallen under the spell of sin. The devil's influence was gripping them tighter and tighter.

But they were happy. Neil watched them laugh and make jokes. Nobody was being bullied. Neil wished he had a group of friends like that. Morgan's arm was around Cora. She snuggled into his embrace. It was everything Neil wanted.

Often Neil just sat in the trees watching the group acting like he was there. He'd laugh when a funny joke was said. Sometimes he'd even pretend to smoke a joint or take a drink.

There were times when it was just Cora and Morgan in the spot. Morgan would start to kiss her neck. Cora would lean back and take another hit.

Neil watched Morgan as he moved his hand down into Cora's blue shorts. She began to moan from the pleasure of Morgan's fingers.

Neil listened to his crush's ecstasy. He'd close his eyes and imagine it was him fingering Cora. Neil could only do it for a short time. He'd become erect and run off in shame.

Night was a harder time. His thoughts would go back to Cora and Morgan in the woods. He imagined making out with Cora. Then she would graciously move down to give him a blow job just like in the movies.

Neil would grow in his shorts. His body would begin to rub up against the mattress as he lay on his stomach. It felt good against his erection.

He tried to stay as quiet as possible. He didn't want to draw the attention of his bunkmates. Every time he masturbated it felt wonderful, but he always ended with tears in his eyes.

This was not what God wanted. This was the actions of a sinner, but Neil could not help it. He wanted to feel desired.

In July rumors started to spread. Cora was caught naked in the bed of one of the boys' cabins. Neil heard the others talking. She had been escorted through the camp, wrapped in a blanket, to the counselor's office. The campers were calling Cora a whore.

Nobody knew who she was having sex with. Neil had a suspicion, but he didn't want to say. The only thing on his mind was wishing it had been him.

"Do you know what I was doing before I took over the duties at Psalm Springs?" Pastor Robbins asked the class.

The class was silent in their response. This was the first time that Pastor Robbins ever spoke about his past with them.

"It's nothing dramatic. They wouldn't tell my story if I had died. I worked at an office. It was the same thing every day. I used to dream of the weekend, but before long even that became boring and monotonous. I was hollow inside.

"That was the moment I realized what had happened. Sin had gotten inside of me. It burrowed into my soul and was slowly eating it away. If I really had died back then my soul would have gone to Hell. I was a vessel for sin."

Neil sat up in his chair as he listened to Pastor Robbins. He hung on every word. There was still hope for him.

"I'm not going to deny that. It's the truth. I wasn't doing anything bad, but I wasn't doing anything good. And that is where the problem lies. Proverbs 18:9, *whoever is slack in his work is a brother to him who destroys.*

"Sin spreads through the indifferent minds of

individuals and the idleness of their actions. If you want to shake off the sin that is in your soul then you must move.

"I'm not talking about running from yours sins. That will never work. Run as fast and as far as you like, but when you turn around it will always be right behind you.

"The only way to get rid of your sin is to fight back. Stand toe to toe against your sins and say, 'No more.' Show God that you are not going to stand for this corruption. You want to live. You want to live under the grace of God.

"He will envelop you in His love and His protection. Then when sin comes to tackle you back to the ground you will find that God is standing behind you. He is bracing you up.

"God will have your back as long as you have His. That is the covenant that you make with Him. He will stand you up and dust you off. All you have to do is move forward. Tell everybody you know that God has your back.

"Will they scoff at you? Will they turn their heads? Sure. But that is their choice. Their decision is to turn from God. Your decision was to spread the word.

"It is not your place to judge. It is God's."

There was no more time to waste, Neil decided. Pastor Robbins was right. Neil was a good boy, even if he was fighting off his own sins. He did nothing to help Cora. Now, she was the devil's sex toy. But there was still time to save Morgan. Whatever he was going through, Neil wanted to help.

He confronted Morgan the next day. Once Morgan's cabin was empty, Neil went inside. He did not want to do it in front of a crowd. When Neil made his presence known, Morgan nearly jumped out of his shoes.

"Whoah," Morgan yelled. "Don't do that. Knock."

"Sorry," mumbled Neil. "I just wanted to talk to you."

"That's fine," said Morgan. "It's just weird to sneak up on people. I could have been naked or something."

"I looked inside before I came in. I made sure you were decent."

Morgan stared at Neil for a moment. "That's not any better."

"Can we just talk?" Neil asked, getting the subject back on track.

"What do you need?"

"I know about you and Cora," said Neil. "I saw you guys out in the woods."

"We were just hanging out," said Morgan.

"No, you had your hand down her pants," said Neil. "You were fingering her."

"So what if I was?" said Morgan. He gave up on defending himself.

"She started to have sex. Everybody is calling her a whore, now. You knew I liked her. You knew I wanted to be with her. Why would you do that? Why did you open the road for her to become a whore? Everything is ruined."

"I did not ruin anything," said Morgan. "You don't understand what happened. Cora was helping me. I have my own problems that you don't know about. She would let me do things to her to get me to focus.

"Come on, Neil. You remember. She offered to give you a blow job for drugs. She was a whore. I didn't turn her into anything. She wanted to have sex with me. I said no."

"I… I just thought if she had been with me I could have saved her," said Neil. "We could have found pleasure in each other."

"Then why did you say no to her earlier," asked Morgan. "Your chance was there."

"I don't know," said Neil. "I couldn't do it. It didn't seem right."

"That's because you're not ready," said Morgan.

"But how do I get ready?" Neil asked.

"Practice," said Morgan. "That does not mean watching porn. No, that's not the way to do it. You have to actually be with a girl. That's the only way you can learn what you need to do, and when the time comes to truly pleasure your future wife you will be ready."

"I can't have sex with random strangers. That's a sin."

"You can't have vaginal sex," said Morgan. "That is an act that requires a real bond between not only the two partners, but also God. With those three parts in place you can create a life."

"So what do I do?" Neil asked.

"Butt sex is the way to go," said Morgan.

"Really?"

"It's close to the real thing, and is not as sinful," said Morgan.

"I don't know," hesitated Neil.

"You have to trust me on this," said Morgan. "It's used as therapy for a lot of sinners. Women help bring homosexuals back to the grace of God with anal sex. Sometimes people make the wrong choices and they have to be steered back."

"How do you know this?" Neil asked.

"Because I've been having problems with homosexuality. I tried to change before, but it didn't work. It wasn't until I learned about these methods that I've been making progress."

Unconsciously, Neil took a step back. He didn't want to be near a homosexual. Had they been dating all this time?

"Don't worry," said Morgan. "I'm getting better. Cora was helping me. She just wanted to take it too far."

"So what are you doing now?"

"There are some others that are helping me," revealed Morgan. "I can talk to them. Maybe they can help you, too. If you want."

Neil thought about it for a minute. He wanted nothing more than to be like everybody else. He wanted to be like people he saw everywhere. This was his chance.

"Okay," said Neil.

It took several days before Morgan got back to Neil. As a favor for Morgan, Neil returned a shovel and rope to the supply shed of Psalm Springs. Morgan said he was too busy to do it himself. Neil was happy to help. After all, Morgan was doing so much for him.

Finally, the girls were ready. They would meet them out in the woods. Morgan found several new hiding spots around the perimeter of Psalm Springs. No one would disturb them.

Neil waited anxiously next to one of the trees. He was already hard. He couldn't help but readjust his shorts periodically. Morgan was getting the area ready. He had a couple of blankets from the cabin laid out on the ground. Morgan told Neil to calm down several times, but his advice did no good.

Footsteps were heard approaching their area. Twigs and grass were crushed and brushed aside. Then the two girls, Chrissy and Alissa, appeared.

"Hey," said Morgan as he walked up to the girls to greet them. He put his arm around Chrissy. She snuggled up inside his hold.

"Neil, this is Chrissy and Alissa," introduced Morgan. "Chrissy has been wonderful at helping me out. I feel so much better since meeting her."

"He had a problem, so I helped him out," said Chrissy. "It's what God wants."

"Say 'Hi' to Alissa," urged Morgan.

Suddenly, Neil realized he had forgotten to speak. He was so nervous. "Hi," said Neil.

Alissa smiled back and waved her hand. Then she started walked toward Neil. Morgan and Chrissy went to a blanket on one side of the clearing they were huddled in.

"Neil, right," said Alissa on approach.

"Yes," croaked Neil. His leg wouldn't stop shaking.

"It's okay," said Alissa. "This will be fun."

She took Neil by the hand. Together they walked to the other blanket. Neil looked over at Morgan. Morgan was already making out with Chrissy. His hand was wandering down her body. Then Neil looked back at Alissa. Without thinking he reached out and grabbed her breast with his free hand. She jumped a bit from surprise.

"Excited?" she quipped.

When they got to the blanket Alissa sat down and leaned back. She looked up at Neil.

"Come on," she said, waving her hand across the blanket.

Neil looked down at her. She was incredibly hot. There were few girls back at school that matched her looks. He couldn't wait to join her, but he could not move. Once again he looked back at Morgan. Chrissy was now on her hands and knees. Her shorts were at her feet on the ground and Morgan was behind her.

"Look at me," said Alissa, drawing back Neil's attention. "We can do that, too."

She adjusted to her knees and knelt right in front of Neil. The imagery was so familiar. This was what

Neil had wanted. He could feel her warmth so close to him. He looked down at Alissa kneeling in front of him. He could not move as she reached for his shorts. Slowly, she pulled them down. A cool breeze sent a shiver down Neil's spine.

Then he lost it.

Alissa never touched him. Neil could feel his underpants getting wet from his ejaculation. His stomach dropped and embarrassment filled his heart.

Alissa stepped away when she saw the stain forming in front of her. She looked up at Neil with disappointed eyes.

"That's okay," she said while holding back a smile.

Neil could barely hear her. The sound of Morgan and Chrissy going at it filled the woods.

"Neil," said Alissa. She was now on her back. Her legs were slightly spread. She was inviting him in. "Eat me out. Then we can go back to you."

Neil remained frozen. All of his excitement had vanished. It had washed away into his pants. Now, he just felt hollow and alone. He could feel eyes watching him. They all waited for his next decision.

"Come on," said Alissa. "Do something."

Then Neil did do something. He turned around and began to leave. He could not be with Alissa. Not like this.

"Are you serious?" Alissa called out as Neil left the woods. "Asshole."

Neil did not care what she called him. Relief flooded his body. He was at peace again. Nobody was watching him.

It wasn't until the next day that Morgan found Neil. Neil was alone reading through one of the camp's Bibles.

"What happened to you yesterday?" asked Morgan.

"I couldn't do it," said Neil. "It wasn't right."

"I'm sorry," said Morgan. "I thought you were ready for that."

"I guess I wasn't," said Neil.

"That's okay," said Morgan. "You just have to start smaller."

"I don't want to do anything else."

"You want to be alone forever?" asked Morgan.

"No," admitted Neil.

"Then you need to take the steps to being with someone."

"I don't know how," said Neil.

"No problem," said Morgan. "First, we need to get your mind off of Cora. Is there anybody else you like?"

"I don't know," said Neil.

"Come on, there are plenty of cute girls here.

There has to be somebody that you're attracted to."

"They are all hot," said Neil.

"I see that now," joked Morgan. "What about that girl, Brook? She's cute. She seems nice. I've never seen her with a core group of friends. Maybe she's looking for one. You should talk to her. I bet she would like you."

"Do you really think so?" Neil asked.

"You guys would be great together," said Morgan.

The idea of Brook and him together started to sink into Neil's thoughts. He pictured her long brown hair and her matching eyes. Maybe Morgan was right. Neil just needed to find somebody that was nicer, more his style. The more Neil thought about it the more he started to like Brook. She was smart. She was good looking.

Now, Neil just had to find her.

Brook was not an easy person to track down. She rarely stayed in one place twice after class. Neil became infatuated with her and the mystery of where she went in her free time only made her more desirable.

He sat next to her during class. Every now and then he would say hello. She would respond, but it would end there. Neil could never get more than a one word answer out of her.

After class he would try to invite Brook for lunch. She always said she was busy.

After every failure to get close to Brook, Neil sought advice from Morgan. He told Neil to not give up. This was good for him. Neil just needed to try harder.

Then Neil started to follow Brook. He kept his distance because he was scared and did not know what to say. Neil thought if he figured out what she liked then he would know what to talk to her about. Later he could "randomly" bump into her at one of those spots and they would hit it off.

Neil followed her from the cafeteria to the bathroom to several of the cabins, and then along the perimeter of the fence. She circled around the administration office and the chapel.

Neil had no idea what she was doing. As her walk continued Neil put himself further and further from her. He could feel he was getting in too deep and if she caught him then he would be in trouble with no way to explain it. He couldn't help it though. He liked her now, and he wanted to know everything about her.

The routine continued. Brook would always go to the cafeteria and grab extra food. Then she would wander through the camp, every now and then picking up items. Later she would disappear. Neil would lose track of her somewhere along the back of the camp near the generators.

"Have you talked to her yet?" Morgan asked Neil after two weeks of encouraging Neil to get out more. It was approaching August. Neil was running out of time.

"No," said Neil. "She doesn't give me a chance. I try to after class, but she doesn't sit still. She just wanders around. Then I lose her. Every time. I think she knows about me."

"Maybe she does," said Morgan. "But that's a good thing. Then there is no reason not to talk to her. She's probably waiting for you to make the first move."

"You think so?"

"Totally," said Morgan. "Just go talk to her for once."

Neil did not need to make the first move. Brook did it for him. Later in the week, Brook came right up to Neil to confront him.

She wanted to know about the campers that had access to keys. Brook needed help. She said Cora needed help.

Neil was hesitant, but he could not refuse somebody in need. That was what he was here for. He wanted to be the one people relied on. That was what God wanted. If he helped Brook and Cora then he could get closer with them. He could show them how great God was and they would be grateful, so grateful they would want to be with him.

Neil was finally going to be as happy as everybody else was.

That night Neil could barely contain himself. The day kept repeating in his head. He told Brook about Carl. He was the one with the keys. He wanted to do right by Cora and Brook. That was the path of the righteous.

He told Morgan about his conversation with Brook. He tried to keep some details out of it. Brook didn't want people to know what she was doing. Neil did say that she was looking for Carl. Morgan knew Carl better and Neil wanted to know if he had told Brook about him accurately.

Neil told Brook that Carl volunteered at the administration office and the chapel. That was why he had so many keys. Morgan said that was right, and Brook would be happy that Neil was able to help her out.

Neil was beaming with confidence. Everything was coming into place for him. He stood with God and now God was granting him the blessings of friends and family. Morgan had his back. Then perhaps Brook or Cora would be so thankful that Neil helped them out they would give him a chance and be with him.

He was going to have everything that everybody wanted. Neil was happy, and he had God to thank for that.

Neil was finally ready for the Night of the Tenth.

Lust

Gabe desired a better summer than this.

He left the opening sermon with the same loathing and annoyance that he arrived with at Psalm Springs. Every minute he put up with at the camp was another minute he was going to yell at his parents.

They had forced him to come to Psalm Springs, but they didn't have the courage to drop him off. Gabe was brought to the camp in one of the white vans. He wasn't even able to prepare for his trip. One day he returned home from work and men were waiting for him outside in the driveway. They practically shoved him into the van. Gabe had enough time to see his parents watching the entire incident from the front living room window. His mom stood there crying while his dad just shook his head in disappointment.

The van had a protective cage for the drivers. Gabe

could only yell obscenities and pointless demands as the van drove him away.

Gabe came out to his parents a year ago. It broke his mother's heart. His father did not speak to him for several days. Even Gabe's older brother moved out of their joint room.

It was the following Sunday after Gabe's announcement that his family got together to discuss the matter. His parents told Gabe that they supported him, and they would pray for him to get through this.

What they said only infuriated Gabe. They didn't understand, even if they said they did. He didn't want them to pray it away. This was who he was. He was gay. Instead, Gabe just sat there and nodded his head. He realized that it took him years to come to terms with who he was. He had to give his family some time too.

The following months were filled with his dad offering advice on how to pick up women. His brother rarely came around to hang out with him anymore. He wasn't allowed to hang out with his friends anymore, at least not his guy friends. Every Sunday, his parents would drag him to church. During prayers his mother would squeeze his hand tightly. She was trying to transfer her spiritual strength to Gabe.

Gabe thought the troubles were over. Things were starting to get back to normal at home. The next thing he knew he was on a van to Psalm Springs. He just decided he would put up with the whole thing.

The timing was actually convenient in one aspect. Gabe just broke up with his somewhat boyfriend a few days ago. They had been dating under the radar for a couple of months. Gabe hated the secrets. He wanted to be official, but Trevor did not want to do it. They were rarely intimate. Trevor was not ready. It eventually broke them apart. Now, Gabe was glad he was away. It gave him a chance to heal his broken heart.

The first day of activities was not exciting. Ice breakers always bothered Gabe. While they involved mostly new people there was usually one or two people that knew Gabe or knew of him. They always expected Gabe to make a point of saying he was gay like that was the one thing that defined who he was.

The only thing he was glad about this time was that nobody knew him there. He kept to himself through the beginning of the day. Gabe could tell a lot of the other campers were not going to be too keen on him being homosexual.

Then Mindy came along. She caught him ogling one of the counselors in an arts and crafts corner.

Gabe was embarrassed that he was caught. He tried to get out of the conversation with Mindy, but she was persistent. As much as he hated to do it, Gabe finally gave in to being Mindy's gay best friend for the day.

The next day Mindy found Gabe walking with his cabin group to prayer service. She pulled him away so he could join her and her activities. They spent the rest of the afternoon together. Mindy dragged him with her to meet new people. Gabe just wanted to keep to himself at the moment, but she never gave him that chance. Then they met a camper that Gabe could not resist.

"I'm Morgan," said the camper. His blonde hair was slicked back. He worked out enough to show his frame. He wore a shirt that was one size too small. Gabe was instantly attracted to him.

"Gabe," he replied. Gabe gave Morgan a small smile when he spoke his name. Morgan smiled back. It was a moment that Mindy or the other campers around them did not share.

"Isn't this place great," said Mindy. "Everybody is so cool here. I met Gabe yesterday. He is awesome. We can talk about anything. We just clicked."

Gabe just nodded his head in silence. He rolled his eyes several times as Mindy kept going on about him. He was embarrassed. She didn't go right out and say he was gay, but she might as well have. As Mindy talked the other campers started to eye Gabe more and more. They were realizing what Mindy was saying. None of them wanted to acknowledge it.

"It sounds like you should be everybody's friend," laughed Morgan. "We were going to go swimming later if you guys want to join us." Morgan looked directly at Gabe when he offered the invitation.

"Yeah," said Gabe. He was excited to see more of Morgan.

"Great," said Morgan. "We just have to go to Bible study first. We'll be at the lake in a couple of hours."

After their introduction to Morgan and the others, Gabe and Mindy continued on to meet other people at the camp. Gabe could not concentrate whenever somebody was talking to him. He could only think of Morgan.

They met for swimming later that day. There was a policy at Psalm Springs that all the girls had to wear one piece suits. There was nothing said about what the boys had to wear. Gabe was secretly relieved at that.

Mindy hung around the shallow end of the lake. Most of the girls stayed on the shoreline getting tans while the boys were out in deeper water. Mindy tried to stay in the middle of it all.

Morgan was swimming out further than any of the

others. Gabe decided to follow. It gave him a chance to be alone with Morgan for a change. Mindy was usually right by his side.

The lake had several docks floating all across it. They were cool hangouts for the campers if they wanted to make the swim out to them.

Morgan was on the ledge of the closest dock. He hung his feet in the water. Gabe caught up to him. His first impulse was to jump up to the deck and grab hold of Morgan, but Gabe had to play it cool. He did not want to look overeager.

"Mind if I join you?" Gabe asked casually.

"Sure," said Morgan.

Gabe pulled himself out of the water and sat near Morgan.

"I'm surprised Mindy isn't joining you," joked Morgan. "She's attached to your hip."

"I know," said Gabe. "She's alright, I guess. She just tries too hard."

"So are you two together?" Morgan asked.

"No," answered Gabe. "She's not my type."

"Fat," said Morgan.

"What the fuck," said Gabe.

"I mean she's got a cute face," said Morgan. "She's just a little big. It's fine if you like that. Go for what makes you happy, bro. I don't judge. Declare this a judge free deck."

"It's not that she's a little big," said Gabe.

"So she is fat, you agree," interrupted Morgan.

"Moving on," said Gabe. "It's not that she's fat. It's that she's a girl." Gabe paused to let Morgan make the connection.

"Oooooh," said Morgan. "You're homophobic."

"No," said Gabe. "Wait, what?"

"Clearly, you don't want to say the word 'gay'. You must really hate yourself."

"I don't mind saying the word. Shut up," said Gabe. "I'm gay. I'm gay. Are you happy now?"

"A little," said Morgan. "Gay."

"So what the hell is Mindy doing?" Morgan then asked.

"I don't know," said Gabe. "She wants to be cool with a gay friend."

"Then she's at the wrong place," said Morgan. "I don't know how kindly they take to that."

"That's why you can't tell anybody," said Gabe. "Please. I'm trying not to make a big thing out of it."

"Your secret is safe with me," said Morgan. He put his arm around Gabe's shoulders. "After all, I always wanted a gay friend."

"Fuck you," said Gabe.

The two of them hung out on the deck for another

hour. They talked about what brought them to the camp. Morgan attended a Christian school. He got in trouble with many of the teachers for challenging them on their history and science books. His parents decided Morgan needed a better disciplinary track and they sent him to Psalm Springs.

Before Gabe left the lake he had already made plans with Morgan to meet again the next day. All Gabe had to do was ditch Mindy.

Early the next morning, Gabe was the first to get ready in his cabin. He didn't wait around for the others to leave. Gabe made his exit as fast as he could. The coast was clear as he made his way through the camp. He knew if he waited any longer Mindy would have found him.

Gabe waited outside the recreational hall for an hour. It was still cool in the morning so it did not bother him. Morgan appeared in the distance. Gabe stood to his feet while he tried to hide his excitement.

"You got rid of Mindy," said Morgan. "Good job. I'm glad we could hang out without her. She was kind of annoying."

"Yeah, I'm glad we could get together again," said Gabe. "What do you want to do?"

"Doesn't really matter," said Morgan. "I'm skipping

prayer service. Let's go find a game to play. You can drool over the boys while we kick their asses."

Gabe and Morgan went down to the volleyball courts. They played several rounds against different teams. Nobody was particularly good. It usually ended up in a no contest. The scores were always wrong between the teams and Morgan would start to argue in their favor every time.

They grew tired of that and went to wander the camp. As the afternoon hit the sun was bearing down for one of the hottest days of the summer so far. Gabe found a shady spot in the tree line. He and Morgan went to relax there for a while.

They were leaning up against the trunk of a tree. Even in the shade the heat was near unbearable. Gabe and Morgan were drenched in sweat.

"I could have taken him," said Morgan. He was referring to their last game of volleyball. Morgan got into a fight against his opponents. He was arguing with the other camper over a ball that landed on the line. Eventually the argument broke down into name calling and if Gabe hadn't broken it up, fists would have been involved.

"I believe you," said Gabe. "You're big and strong."

"Nope," said Morgan. "I just fight dirty."

Morgan laughed at his own joke. Then he shifted

his hand. It overlapped with Gabe's.

"Seriously, though, thanks for pulling me aside. I appreciate it. If I got into a fight here the discipline would be worse than detention," Morgan said.

Gabe kept his hand where it was. He liked the attention. "I just didn't want to see the guy punch your face in. That would have been a travesty."

Morgan gave Gabe a curious look. "Are you hitting on me?"

Gabe tried to laugh it off, but this was his chance. "A little," he said. "I'm not going to lie. I kind of like you."

Morgan was quiet for a second. Then he slowly began to smile. His hand took hold of Gabe's. Gabe's heart skipped a beat. He could no longer contain his happiness.

"I like you, too," said Morgan.

Then Gabe leaned in. Their first kiss was gentle. They were feeling each other out. Then the kiss progressed. Gabe could feel Morgan's tongue embrace his.

Gabe was feeling wanted and desired for the first time in months. His ex-boyfriend never touched him like this.

Morgan rolled Gabe over onto his back. He climbed on top of Gabe. They breathed in unison.

Morgan did not say a word. He kissed Gabe again. As they made out Gabe could feel Morgan's hands drifting down to his waist. Gabe's shirt was slowly rising up to his chest.

Then Morgan began to crawl down Gabe's body. He kissed Gabe's uncovered chest and stomach. Gabe did not resist. He grew bigger each second that Morgan got closer to his groin.

Gabe closed his eyes as Morgan began to pull his blue shorts down to his knees revealing his underwear. He felt Morgan wrap his hands around him. Then he was pulled out. Morgan's hands were warm, even warmer then the summer air.

Gabe forgot all about his problems at home. He put aside all of his issues with his ex-boyfriend. He no longer cared about what the people at Psalm Springs thought about him. The only thing he wanted to concentrate on was Morgan and his mouth wrapping around him.

Gabe spent every day of the rest of the first week with Morgan. They would get together early in the morning and spend much of the day together. No matter what they were doing that day Gabe and Morgan would always find themselves hidden in the woods by the afternoon. In the privacy of the trees they would hook up. They had a special spot hidden in the tree line near the fence.

It was Gabe's release from his own problems. He just wanted to have some fun. Every time together they got more adventurous with each other. Gabe started to let Morgan take him from behind. There was nothing more that Gabe wanted now.

It was Sunday. The first week at Psalm Springs was over. All of the campers were ordered to attend the service at the sermon hill. Gabe and Morgan tried to ditch it, but before they could escape out to the woods they were caught by one of the counselors. The counselor made sure they were in attendance at the service.

Gabe was ready to sneak out of the massive group of campers. He wanted to get to the woods to be with Morgan. It had been on his mind all day. He wanted to taste Morgan again.

Morgan discreetly grabbed hold of Gabe's hand and gave him a little squeeze. It was his sign that they would get away later. They had all evening still.

Before the service began Gabe could hear his name getting called out across the hill. He immediately knew who it was. He hadn't spoken to Mindy since the beginning of the week. He had hoped she had moved on, but not to his surprise she was still looking for him.

"Your girlfriend is calling you," Morgan teased.

"Shut up," said Gabe. "Don't look at her."

"We should call her over here," said Morgan.

"Don't do it," said Gabe. "She'll befriend you too."

"I could go for a little cushion on the pushing. It's no big deal to me," said Morgan.

"Fuck you," said Gabe.

He continued to ignore the many times Mindy called out his name. She finally stopped to the relief of Gabe. It hurt him to just ignore her that way, but she did not have what he wanted. She was only going to get in the way, no matter how much she understood.

The sermon began. Gabe did not pay too much attention until Erika came out. He watched in surprise and horror as she was dropped outside the gates. When the Avenger of Blood appeared a chill went down Gabe's side.

He realized he was not at any regular camp. This place was much more serious. Erika screamed for help. As her cries pierced the sky, Gabe found himself slowly separating from Morgan. Now, more than ever, he did not want anybody to know about him.

The sermon was over once Erika was carried away

into the woods. Gabe did not wait around. He shuffled away with the crowd. He did not wait for Morgan either. He did not want to escape to the woods anymore. He didn't even want to be near Morgan at the moment.

Gabe's whole body felt filthy. There was now a target on his back. He ran straight for the bathroom. Before he even got to the stall he could feel vomit rising in his throat. It spilled out to the stalls around him, but he reached the toilet before the majority of it came out.

He threw up his lunch until he was dry heaving. His parents had warned him. They said he needed to change or he would go to Hell. Were they right?

Pastor Robbins said Erika was taken away because she turned her back on God. Is that what Gabe was doing? That monster was out in the woods near the fence. Had it seen Morgan and him?

His stomach tried to vomit even more out of its empty system. Only bile and stomach lining drooled out of Gabe's mouth.

The next stop Gabe made was to the church at Psalm Springs. The doors were always opened for the campers to come in as they pleased and speak directly with God. Gabe picked an open pew in the back and sat down.

He prayed for acceptance. It was the first time he prayed in years. All those times going to church with his family, he always just sat quietly while the others said their prayers. Gabe never had anything to say to God. This time he did.

"God," Gabe began, "I don't know where I am, or how long I am going to be here, but you have to get me through this. I just saw a girl get taken away. They said it was because she turned her back on You. But You would never do this. You love and accept everybody. Please accept me.

"My family does not. My church does not. But Mindy does. She understood who I was. She says You still love me. Please give me a sign that she is right. I need to know that You are watching over me. I need to know that I am going to be alright."

Gabe was silent after that. He listened to the sporadic sounds from inside the church. The other people inside sniffed their nose, or adjusted in their seats. Gabe listened for anything that he could take as a sign. But nothing came. Gabe was not going to get an answer.

His breathing grew rapid. Gabe was starting to hyperventilate. He kept telling himself to calm down. There was nothing to worry about. He would just keep his head down, and he would be fine. Then

Morgan popped into his head. He remembered how good it felt to be with him. He wanted nothing more than to be in his embrace. Morgan could give him comfort.

Just thinking of Morgan made Gabe hard. He tried to separate his thoughts from Morgan, but it was even harder than his previous break up. Morgan had accepted all of Gabe. This was the first time anybody had done that. Gabe could not just give up on Morgan so easily.

The next couple of days, Gabe tried to lay low. He did not see Mindy the entire time. She had disappeared. Gabe avoided Morgan as best he could. He never got up to meet him in the morning. Gabe always stayed with the other guys in his cabin. They went to prayer service and Bible study.

Then Morgan finally caught up with Gabe. Gabe was not paying attention and Morgan snuck up on him from behind while Gabe's group was on their way to the activity center for carpentry lessons.

"Where have you been?" Morgan whispered into Gabe's ear.

"I've been busy," said Gabe.

"Too busy to see me?" asked Morgan. "Come on, let's get out of here."

"No," said Gabe.

"What's wrong with you?" said Morgan. His voice was slowly rising.

"We can't be seen together," said Gabe.

"Then we won't be seen," said Morgan. "I'll meet you out there."

"We can't risk it," said Gabe.

Morgan reached out for Gabe's hand. Gabe let him take hold of it for a moment before he pulled it away. They were starting to draw the attention of the other campers around them.

"Oh, come on," said Morgan. "Fuck these people. I thought we had something special. We were having fun."

Gabe came in closer to keep his voice low. "Quiet down. I enjoyed it too, but you saw what happened. These people are not fucking around."

"We don't know shit," said Morgan. "That was for show. That girl is probably a part of the whole bullshit camp. They want us to be afraid. They want us to not go near each other because they know they have nothing to stop us."

Morgan once again grabbed Gabe's hands. He slipped in a small kiss. Then Gabe pulled away again.

"No," said Gabe.

"What! You weren't saying no when I was fucking you in the ass, you fucking faggot!" Morgan screamed.

At this point everybody in the area was watching and listening to Gabe and Morgan's fight.

"Fuck you," said Gabe.

"Yeah, I fucked you. You were begging for it," said Morgan. "I bet you didn't care then if anybody caught us."

The crowd of spectators was growing larger with every word spoken. Gabe just stood in silence. He had nothing further to say to Gabe. His secret was out. Already he could feel the judgmental eyes on top of him.

"Oops," said Morgan. He turned around and shoved his way through the crowd. He nearly knocked over Chrissy and her friends. They eyed him down as he walked away from the spectacle.

Gabe could not move. He was in shock. Claustrophobia was starting to kick in. The campers around him started to close in on him. He was going to pass out. His knees grew weak. Black spots appeared in his view. But before he could fall two counselors grabbed him.

They propped him up. All of Gabe's strength was gone.

"Come on," said one of the counselors. "We'll get you out of here. You'll be taken care of."

Gabe could not say thank you. He finally let

himself go.

Gabe woke up later in a small room with a cot and a tiny window. He sat up. His throat was dry and begged for water. There was a sink in the corner of the room. Gabe unsteadily walked over to it and got himself a drink by cupping water into his hands. He finished at the sink by splashing water onto his face. It helped relieve the rest of the drowsiness that was hovering over him.

He did not have to wait long for the door to his room to open. Pastor Robbins was the one to greet him. He brought in his own chair to sit on. He gestured for Gabe to have a seat on the cot.

"How are you feeling?" Pastor Robbins asked. "I heard you passed out earlier. I'm glad to see you are on your feet already. I wanted to be notified as soon as you were up. Nobody should have to wake up to a strange room alone."

"Thank you," said Gabe. "I don't know what came over me."

"You're in a fight, my son," said Robbins. "A fight for your soul. Of course it will wear you down."

"So you heard," said Gabe.

"Do not blame yourself," said Pastor Robbins. "Society is to blame. It influenced you to start looking at men as you would look at a woman. It said that it was okay to lay with a man like it is with a woman. Well, society is wrong."

"What can I do?" Gabe asked.

"You've already started," said Pastor Robbins. "You have to fight your urges. You have to stay away from the temptations of the body. A man's body cannot offer you anything. It is a sin that will drag you to Hell. Romans 1:27, *in the same way the men also abandoned natural relations with woman and were inflamed with lust for one another. Men committed indecent acts with other men, and received in themselves the due penalty for their perversion.*

"I want to pull you from your cabin. You'll stay here. You'll have classes that will help you fight your temptations. I want to see you succeed by the end of the summer."

"Okay," said Gabe.

"You see, this will be easy for you. You are already trying to become the man you are supposed to be. God is proud of you for making the right choice."

Gabe was starting to feel better about himself already. He knew he could change if he tried. He had to.

"I'm going to warn you though," said Pastor Robbins. "This is not going to be easy. It does not happen overnight. You will have to repel every advance made by society and the devil lurking out there."

"I can do that," said Gabe. He was still dizzy from his fainting. Pastor Robbins words were comforting to him.

"Do you trust me?" the pastor asked.

Gabe nodded his head.

"Good," said Pastor Robbins. Then he got up from his seat. "I want you to rest now. Tonight you will start your realignment. We'll get you straightened out."

Pastor Robbins reached the door. He signaled to people outside in the hallway. Two counselors appeared at the doorway. Robbins stepped out of their way.

Gabe watched as the two counselors approached him. Gabe was too slow to react. They grabbed his arms and shoved him down to the bed. In flawless motion his arms were strapped to the bed posts. Gabe was too stunned to fight back. Before he knew it his feet were strapped to the posts at the other end.

"This is for your own good," said Pastor Robbins. "We don't want you to give in to any kind of desire right now. Your mind is your worst enemy."

Gabe tried to fight from the restraints. He grew

tired quickly. The restraints would not give. The door closed behind Pastor Robbins and his counselors. They left Gabe alone in his tiny room.

Hours passed for Gabe. He was stuck with only his thoughts. He spent a lot of the afternoon and evening in and out of sleep. The sun had gone down. It was night time and Gabe was growing even more tired.

The door to his room opened. Relieved, Gabe looked over. He wanted to get out of the restraints. The silhouette at the door was that of a girl. Gabe did not recognize her, but she wore the familiar yellow and blue camp outfit.

"Please let me out?" Gabe pleaded.

"I was told I was to sleep here tonight," said the girl.

"What? Why?" said Gabe. He tried once again to get out of his restraints with no use.

"Pastor Robbins said you need to get accustomed to sleeping in bed with a woman."

"No," said Gabe. "That's okay."

The girl did not listen to Gabe's plea. She closed the door behind her as she entered his small room. Gabe tried to tell her no again, but she crawled into bed with him.

He couldn't move as she cuddled up with him. "Stop complaining," she said. "I'm not going to have sex with you. We're not married."

Gabe was stuck. The girl wrapped her arms around him. He could feel her breath on his neck. Her breasts pressed up against his side.

"Just try to get some sleep," she said. "I'm really tired. We can talk in the morning if you like."

Gabe did not answer. He couldn't put up a fight so there was no further use in arguing. He closed his eyes and forced himself to go back to sleep with the warm embrace of the girl lying next to him.

The days that followed left Gabe in a state of distress. He was being held in one of the buildings on the camp. The perimeter was fenced off. During the day Gabe and his class were allowed time outside. The rest of the camp continued on with their day while Gabe watched on from his confines. They all looked happy on the other side of the fence. Gabe just wanted to be free.

Instead, he spent his days in class learning about the proper roles of men and women. His group was lead by two counselors, Richard and Michelle. The two counselors were always beaming with joy. Their smiles rarely left their faces. Each day they encouraged their campers to follow the path of the Lord as they taught them about the true sanctity of marriage.

"There is no real connection in a relationship

between man and man or woman and woman," said Michelle. "What you are experiencing is friendship mixing with the desires of sin."

"I have a friend named Eric," said Richard. "I hang out with him all the time. I text him every day. I give him advice. He gives me advice. We are pretty much inseparable. That does not mean that I am going to have sex with him."

"Sex should only occur once you are married," said Michelle.

"Exactly," said Richard. "Sex is the accumulation of the love you share with not only your husband or wife, but with the connection you have made with God. Sex is the beginning of your family, and you should not start a family until you have a structured base. You can only have that base with a mother and a father. They both play crucial roles to raising children under the path of God. It says in Proverbs 1:8, *Listen, my son, to your father's instruction and do not forsake your mother's teaching.*"

"Being a father means having the responsibility of the family on your shoulders," said Michelle. "You are the leader. Your decisions should be for the best of the family, not just one or two of the members."

"And there would be no leader without the full support of your wife," said Richard. "Being a wife and a mother means being the glue that keeps the family working. Without one or the other the family falls apart."

"Sure it seems like plenty of families get by with only one parent or homosexual parents, but that is not the case," said Michelle. "That is a façade for the rest of the world to see. In their hearts they are struggling, and their souls are crying out for help. God is there to help them, but they have to be the ones to admit their faults and reach out to Him. In this world they might be fine, but eventually Heaven's gates will be closed to them because they faltered from the path. Living in denial about your fate will only bring it upon you faster."

Gabe hardly listened to the counselors. This was all stuff he had heard before. His parents told him his lifestyle was wrong. The pastor at his church told him that God may have loved him, but He did not love his choices. Gabe did not care. All he wanted back then was to be with his boyfriend.

His eyes began to wander around the room. He didn't recognize any of the faces in his class. Each one looked miserable. It was clear they were all captives to this seminar.

Gabe's attention stuck on one guy in particular. He had dreamy black hair and blue eyes that Gabe got lost in. He kept his head down frowning at the floor. His unpleasant look only made Gabe want to hold the guy more. The counselors continued talking, but Gabe stopped listening. The only thing Gabe wanted to learn was the guy's name.

It took two days to find that out. Gabe's new infatuation was named Justin. He was able to learn that through the group of girls that were in his class. Each guy was partnered with a girl. The girls were a part of the rehabilitation treatment. Gabe's partner was Cindy. She stuck to him like a little puppy. It was through her he learned the names of the rest of the residents and his new crush. After Cindy grew comfortable with Gabe she would constantly talk to him. At night when they shared Gabe's bed she would talk endlessly in the dark before finally falling asleep.

During class the campers were encouraged to share stories about when they had feelings for somebody else. If their feelings were expressions for somebody of the same sex then the counselors would explain how their feelings were misdirected.

Friendship is a part of every healthy relationship. It's common for youth and the inexperienced to confuse a friendship for love, especially when a physical embrace is desired. The counselors explained the key was to keep your desires directed in God's path. Sex was supposed to feel good. If the devil had his way then you would fornicate with anything available. It was the devil's favorite trick; use God's generosity against the weakness of man's desires.

Gabe listened as Justin told his story about when he realized he was gay. Justin had a girlfriend, but he never felt comfortable. He always felt stiff when they cuddled on the couch. He was always uncomfortable with her in his arms. She would text him and Justin would ignore the message for hours. She was never his priority. Instead, Justin just wanted to spend his time with his friend, Mike.

The counselors told Justin that what he was feeling was completely normal. He just needed to realize that he wasn't gay he just wasn't with the right girl. He wanted so desperately to be with somebody that he forced it onto this girl that showed him a little affection. When that did not work instead of looking for another girl he took the easy way out and redirected his desires to a more comfortable choice in his best friend, Mike.

During one of the sessions the campers were given the task to write down who they were attracted to. After they had done that they were instructed to drop the paper into the bucket in the middle of the room. From there the counselors would set the pieces of paper on fire. It was a way to visually cleanse the soul. They could start to let go of the sinful things that they wanted and start anew.

Gabe instinctively wrote down Justin's name on his piece of paper. After reading it to himself Gabe had second thoughts. He would have to hand that paper over to the counselors. What if they read it? Gabe crumbled up the paper and put it to the side. Quickly, he wrote a new name. The name meant nothing to him. It was the name of his neighbor back home. The guy was fifty years old and had a goiter. Gabe was not attracted to him.

Gabe watched the bucket of names go up in flames. The other campers looked at the display in a calm solace. Ashes fluttered into the air and then settled back down into the flames. The fires of Hell were burning away at their sins.

The crumbled piece of paper was still at Gabe's feet. He nudged it with his shoe several times. The fire was warming up the room, but the piece of paper with Justin's name on it was burning a hole in Gabe's thoughts.

Gabe scooped up the piece of paper and held it in his hand for the rest of the class. He had to get rid of it before any of the counselors could find him with it.

Finally the session was over. Gabe was one of the

first to get up. As he headed for the door he passed Justin still in his seat. Panic and opportunity filled Gabe's heart. Without a second thought Gabe dropped the crumbled piece of paper onto Justin's lap. He didn't stop to wait for a response. Gabe kept walking out of the room with the rush of other campers more than eager to leave.

Every day the campers were offered time outside. The area was fenced off from the rest of the camp. Beyond the fence they could see the rest of the camp go on without any notice to those that were stuck in the sexuality rehabilitation clinic.

Gabe and the others were free to roam around the yard under the supervision of the counselors. It was still early in their classes and their movements were monitored heavily. If a guy got too close to another guy the counselors would call them out on it and bring in one of the girls to restore the balance.

While Gabe kept his distance he constantly glanced over at Justin across the yard. There were several times he caught Justin looking back at him. He had gotten Gabe's note.

The summer rolled into June. The classes were filled with awkward moments for every camper in attendance of the classes. Each day was filled with scenarios that were built to help the campers return to a life of normalcy and blessings.

The counselors artificially created moments that men should share with a woman in order to get Gabe and the others to have better experience for what God expected of them.

Cindy was asked to lie down on the floor. Then Gabe was placed on top of her, and in between her legs. They remained fully clothed in the missionary position for several minutes while the counselors explained the roles of a husband and wife.

Gabe couldn't look Cindy in the eyes during their training. He was too embarrassed. He kept looking up and toward the other campers surrounding them. It did not help the situation. He focused on Justin. They shared a quick glance before Gabe looked away again. Gabe could have sworn he saw a little smile on Justin's face. That only made the situation more awkward. Gabe started thinking about him and Justin. He could feel him getting hard and starting to press up against Cindy. It was uncomfortable. He wanted to adjust but could not do so discreetly. Gabe looked down at Cindy. She was looking back up at him with an encouraging smile.

As the classes progressed the mood of the campers was beginning to change. There was less grumbling from them. Many of the boys started to get excited to go start the day. The counselors began introducing more intimate topics. They wanted the boys to hold the girls, even share a kiss. Changes were happening. A few of the boys were caught making out with their sleep partners. The counselors always put a stop to it when they found them, but the punishments were never harsh. The counselors were almost proud that they found their campers in such situations.

One night while Gabe was trying to sleep he could feel Cindy's hand moving down to his groin. While still in a daze from sleep he imagined Justin holding him tightly. When he opened his eyes he saw the truth. Cindy was riding up against him.

"What are you doing?" Gabe asked groggily.

"Shhh… It's okay," she said. "It's okay." She kissed him several times on the lips. It wasn't the first time they had shared a kiss. Gabe even made out with her a few times in the past weeks. It had never gone farther until this night. He could feel her getting wet as she rubbed up against his hip.

"Please stop," said Gabe. "I can't move." He was still restrained at night. His straps were too tough to break.

"I'll take care of you too," said Cindy. She grabbed hold of Gabe. He hardened in her grip.

Suddenly, Gabe wanted nothing more than to give in. This whole summer had been a nightmare. Was it too much to ask for one night of pleasure?

"Please…" said Gabe. "I want to do this."

Cindy stopped for a moment. She looked at Gabe with that encouraging smile that he had seen before. She reached down off the bed where her pants were discarded on the floor. She fumbled for a second through the pockets then gleefully presented a key.

Gabe's eyes grew wide. She had the key to his freedom this whole time. First she undid his feet. Then she undid his hands.

Gabe sat up nearly tossing Cindy off of him. She rolled over on the bed against the wall. Gabe turned back and leaned over Cindy. He held her wrists down across the mattress. Their heavy breathing grew in sync.

He tried to position himself between her legs, but Cindy refused. "No, we can't do that. We're not married," she said. Gabe was growing frustrated. He was throbbing and needed to find relief. Cindy started to twist in his arms. She turned on to her stomach.

"We can do other stuff," she said looking back at him.

Gabe did not protest. He readjusted then began to guide himself into her asshole. Cindy whimpered from the pain, but she did not cry out or tell him to stop.

He moved back and forth. Cindy started to move with him. Gabe could hear her mumbling. As he listened he could here Cindy saying a prayer. She was praying for Gabe.

As Gabe continued he started to think about Justin again. This made him press harder against Cindy. Tears welled up in her eyes, but she did not tell him to stop. She only kept praying.

Then Gabe finally finished inside of her. He moaned in pleasure before releasing Cindy. When she was free she curled up into a ball and turned her back to Gabe. She lied there staring at the wall. The sound of her sniffing her noise echoed in the quiet room.

Gabe collapsed onto the bed. He did not say a word to Cindy. They slept for the rest of the night with their backs to each other.

That was not the last night Gabe and Cindy were together. July arrived. Cindy let Gabe take her several nights during that time. Gabe never argued against it. Cindy was there to help bring Gabe back into the light of God. She would do anything that was needed.

The classes were going well for all of the campers. Everybody was actively participating and playing their proper roles of manhood. They were going so well that the counselors believed they were ready to finally be reintegrated with the others in Psalm Springs.

Gabe was thrilled to hear the news. He wanted nothing more than to be free again. Cindy was a nice distraction, but it wasn't what he wanted.

The final night before they were to be released from the center the camp held a dance between Gabe's group and another group that was located in another building. The other group was a number of girls that had been detained for rehabilitation.

The dance was held in the hall where the campers first met Pastor Robbins. The hall was filled with both rehabilitation campers and their sleep partners.

Music played and the campers mingled amongst themselves. At the beginning of the night the campers kept to their groups. Then the counselors started to encourage the groups to mix. The sleep partners helped the counselors in this regard. They expanded the groups and eventually were able to break the ice and get the groups talking.

The dancing started soon afterward. The guys asked the girls to dance. The songs jumped from letting the campers go free style to slow dancing where the couples kept themselves at arm's length in front of the counselors.

Gabe danced with several different girls. He tried to get into the night. He should have been excited. They were going to be free to return to the rest of the camp tomorrow. He had a cute girl in his arms. He couldn't deny that.

But he still wasn't feeling it. He rarely made eye contact with her as they danced. He was just going through the motions. Gabe felt very little had changed in him. Every few seconds he would turn his attention to Justin. He watched as Justin danced with one girl after another. They all wanted a chance with him.

The night started to wind down. Gabe was getting tired of dancing and was almost ready to call it a night. Then he watched as Justin left the hall. Nobody was paying him any attention so Gabe did the same. He walked through the exit just a moment after Justin. There were bathrooms and drinking fountains beyond that door. Nobody would give his exit a second thought.

Gabe let the door close behind him before he called out Justin's name. Justin stopped and turned around. The hallway was much quieter than the music filled room beyond the door. The silence left the moment between Gabe and Justin almost deafening.

"Hi, I'm Gabe," he said.

"I know," said Justin. "You left me that note a while back."

"Yeah," said Gabe. He couldn't help but feel a little embarrassed about that moment of hopeless romance.

They stood in awkward silence. Gabe had no idea what to say next. He hadn't thought this through enough.

"Did you mean it?" Justin asked. He took a step closer to Gabe.

"The note?" Gabe asked. "Yeah, I had a pretty big crush on you when I first saw you."

"Oh," said Justin.

"But that's gone now," Gabe said hesitantly. "I'm over it. This class, you know."

"Yeah," said Justin.

Unbeknownst to each other, Gabe and Justin were still taking steps forward.

"I just wanted to say hello," said Gabe. "I thought maybe we could be friends."

"Sure," said Justin. "I'd like that."

"Cool," said Gabe.

They were closer than ever. Whatever they were saying was going over their heads. They did not want to be friends.

Gabe leaned in and kissed Justin.

Justin kissed him back.

This was what Gabe wanted. Every time he was with Cindy he was thinking of this moment. There was no amount of training or prayer that was going to turn Gabe away from what he really wanted.

They got lost in each other's embrace.

They were so distracted that they did not hear the door opening or the music roaring to life for that brief moment.

"What are you doing?"

Gabe and Justin stopped. Their faces were frozen in terror. Gabe knew that voice. It was Cindy.

"No, Cindy, no. This isn't anything," said Gabe, stumbling over his words.

Justin remained quiet. He was too afraid to speak.

"You were making out with him," accused Cindy. "Haven't you learned anything? I thought we had something. I thought I was helping you."

"Cindy, it's just… I'm sorry," said Gabe.

"Sinner."

"No."

"You are a sinner. You are going to Hell! SINNER!"

Every time Cindy spoke her words grew louder. She was screaming at the top of her lungs by the end of it.

"SINNER!"

Gabe tried to keep her quiet, but she fought him off. Justin could not handle it. He ran off down the hall away from the scene.

Cindy ran back into the dance hall. She continued to scream as loud as she could. Her voice was so loud it could be heard over the music.

"SINNER! GABE IS A SINNER!"

The music cut off. All of the attention was on to her. Gabe froze at the doorway. He did not know what to do.

"Gabe has turned is back on God once again. He has given into his own desires. He is a sinner," Cindy told her audience of counselors and campers.

They all turned to look at Gabe. There was nothing further to say. Gabe made a run for it.

He ran as fast and as hard as he could. The door crashed open behind him as the mob of God-fearers started to chase him down.

Gabe had enough distance between him and the others that when he ran through the exit door to the outside he could change his path without them noticing. As soon as he hit the fresh night air Gabe made a run for the nearby bathroom outhouse.

He didn't run inside to the first door. Instead he ran around the small building to the entrance on the other side. It was the side for the women's rooms.

The bathroom stalls were all empty. It was late enough that the lights were all out in the bathhouse. Gabe walked on the balls of his feet. He tried to be as quiet as he could, but he was scared.

He knew he couldn't hide in there for long. He had to run, but to where? They were in the middle of nowhere. He had no idea where he was. How could he escape?

It was deathly quiet. Gabe could hear his hunters looking for him and Justin. They shouted orders to start spreading around and begin the search.

The voices got louder. They went into the bathrooms, but on the men's side. The walls were thin. Gabe could hear everything. They started checking every stall. Gabe kept his legs lifted up above the toilet even though they had not entered the women's restroom yet.

Suddenly, the voices grew louder and more excited. Then Gabe could hear sobbing in the midst of the celebration. The counselors had found Justin.

"No! No, please, don't!" shouted Justin through the wall. He continued to beg as the others ignored him with their laughter.

Justin's cries changed as Gabe could hear them taking him out of the bathroom. He told them he was sorry. He said he would never do it again. He said it over and over, but his words were only falling onto death's ears.

"Take him to the gates."

Gabe heard the orders. It was quieter; calmer than the others. Pastor Robbins had joined the search.

Gabe could no longer look away. He quietly snuck to the door of the women's restroom. Gently, he cracked open the door. The counselors were holding Justin to his knees. Pastor Robbins stood over the young man. His head was down. He looked ashamed at the camper.

"There is nothing left we can do for him," said Robbins. "He has heard the message. It is now time for his judgment."

"No! No! No! Please, don't do this. Please!" Justin yelled out.

The crowd started to move. They walked away from the bathrooms. Gabe did not have much room to see. With only a few steps the group was gone from his sight.

It grew quiet again as Justin's pleas for mercy drifted away. Gabe took the chance to open the door further.

He peeked his head outside. The coast was clear. Everybody had gone with Pastor Robbins and Justin.

This was the moment that Gabe needed. Now, he

was in control of the situation. They weren't looking for him at the moment. It gave him the advantage.

Gabe kept his pace slow. He did not want to draw any undue attention. He needed to stay oblivious. There were people walking in the distance. They did not look like they were looking for anybody.

The sun was touching the horizon. The campers would be heading inside soon. It would give Gabe near freedom then. He just had to wait.

He kept walking. He made his trek in a roundabout way. There was only one place he knew he could go and be sure he was safe. He had to go to the gates where the others were taking Justin.

That way Gabe would know where the group of searchers was and where they were looking.

There was no way out that Gabe knew of. If he ran blindly through the camp he would be found. He needed a plan.

By the time Gabe arrived at the hill the gates were open. Justin had been placed just at the edge of the camp. None of the campers dared go near the exit to the woods on the other side.

Gabe circled around. He stayed in the shadows near the fence line. None of the counselors or other campers were going near the area.

"You have been returned to your Father's doorstep.

It is time you enter through to the Kingdom of Heaven," said Pastor Robbins. "My heart goes out to you. May the good Lord judge you with right."

Justin took a shaky step forward. He could barely stand on his feet. "I just want to go home. Please, let me go."

"You are free," said Pastor Robbins. "You have chosen the path of sin. There is nothing left for you here at Psalm Springs. Through those gates is your home."

"No," said Justin. "No, not there."

Justin took another step forward. He was brought to a halt by a rock striking his chest. The blow knocked the wind out of Justin. He groaned in anguish.

When Justin did not move back farther more stones began to get thrown. All of the counselors and campers partook in the activity.

Strike after strike of rocks hit Justin. Finally he started to back away from his firing squad. The rocks kept coming so he took more steps. Then his steps turned into a flea. He ran from his pursuers through the fenced gates of Psalm Springs.

As soon as he was off the property two counselors shut the gates behind him. They were quick to put the lock in place.

The rocks stopped. Justin ran back to the fence. He pressed his body as far as it could go to the metal bars. He tried to squeeze through the little space between them, but he was too big.

His arms reached out into the camp. He grabbed for anything. Anything that could help him get to safety.

"Open the gate. Open the gate," Justin begged. "Please, open the gate. I don't want to die."

"It is not death you should fear, young man," said Pastor Robbins. "It is Hell."

Justin started to break down. "I don't… I don't want to go to Hell…"

"Then you should have heeded our warning. We were only trying to help you. Psalm 9:17, *the wicked return to the grave, all the nations that forgot God*," said Pastor Robbins. Then he turned away from Justin. He began to walk away while talking to his counselors. "Find the other one. His judgment is still at hand."

The group dispersed at his orders. They left Justin to his fate with the Avenger of Blood.

Gabe ducked down into the bushes near the fence. He did not breathe as the group of campers passed him by. Once the sound of footsteps was gone the only thing that could be heard was Justin's crying sobs.

The search party disappeared. They did not want to

be around to see the Avenger of Blood claim his next sinner.

Gabe retreated from the shadows. He hesitantly walked closer to the gates and Justin. The night sky was getting darker. It was hard to see, but Justin had not moved. He was still by the fence. His attempts to force himself in were over. He limply leaned against the fence on the ground. Justin looked out to the woods for his killer.

As Gabe walked closer the leaves and grass shuffled under his feet. Justin heard the sound and looked around.

"Gabe!" he exclaimed. "Gabe, please help me!"

Gabe looked at his crush in silence. He began to shake his head.

"Please help me. Help me open the doors. I need to get back inside," Justin begged.

"I can't," said Gabe. "I can't open the gate."

"What? Please."

"I can't," said Gabe. "I'm sorry. It wasn't supposed to be like this."

"What the fuck are you talking about? Help me," demanded Justin. "I thought you liked me. Help me!"

"No," said Gabe. "I just… I just wanted to be with somebody. I'm sorry."

"Fuck you! Fuck you, fuck you, fuck you," said

Justin.

Gabe could not say another word. There was nothing left to say. Justin was not worth it to try to open the door and risk the attack from the Avenger of Blood.

The leaves in the woods nearby started to rustle. Justin stopped his cursing of Gabe to turn and look behind him. There was movement in the shadows coming toward him.

Justin's breathing grew shallow and rapid. He looked back at Gabe with wide eyes. Gabe turned away. He could not watch.

"It's okay," said a girl's voice. "I'm here to help you."

Gabe turned back around. Standing outside of the perimeter was another camper he had not seen before. She was not a part of the search party looking for him.

"I'm Brook," she said. "I can get you back inside. You have to follow me."

Gabe and Justin stared at her in stunned silence.

"We have to move now or you are dead. I am not waiting out here for long," said Brook.

Justin started to nod his head. He stepped toward his savior, Brook. She took his hand and led him into the shadows along the fence line.

"Wait," said Gabe. "What about me?"

"Fuck you," said Justin.

"Follow the fence," said Brook, ignoring the broken camper in her arms. "When you reach the section with the generators, wait for me there. I will come and get you."

"I can't be out here for long. They are looking for me," said Gabe.

"I will be as quick as I can. I have to get him to safety first. He can barely walk."

"Fine," said Gabe. He did not wait around for any more of the conversation. He started to make his way along the fence to the generators. Brook and Justin disappeared into the woods. Gabe's only chance now was Brook's word.

And her word was true. Gabe waited for twenty minutes hidden behind the generators. He only passed a few of the campers on his journey there. When they were in sight he pretended like he was looking for somebody along the fence. It was enough to be ignored by the true search party.

Once Brook showed up she showed him the way to the hidden cabin. Gabe was hesitant at first, but with no real options he followed her.

The first night at the cabin was awkward. Another resident in hiding, Hayden, started complaining about the extra people.

"Now, who the hell is here?" he said when Brook and Gabe arrived.

"They needed my help," said Brook. "They would have died had I not brought them here."

"This is my cabin," said Hayden. "I say who can stay."

Brook groaned and shrugged off Hayden's decree.

Justin was in the corner of the room. Bruises started to appear all over his body. Blood was staining his yellow camp shirt. His eyes were bloodshot and filled with rage. He stared at Gabe without a word.

"You two need some rest," said Brook. "There is another room. One of you can have that. The other can stay in here. I don't care which. It's not perfect. Hell, it's disgusting, but we're not being hunted here."

Justin stood up and hobbled over to the extra room. He slammed the door behind him. Brook grunted and frowned.

"And please keep it down," she said. "We're alone out here, but that doesn't mean we need to take too many chances."

"He's just going through shock," Gabe said as an excuse. "He'll be fine."

Brook turned to Gabe. "I know what you did. I was watching the whole thing. I should have left you there."

"Then why didn't you?" Gabe asked.

"Because I'm trying to save people's lives here," she said. "And I need help."

The next few days Gabe and Justin laid low. They did not speak to each other. Gabe usually sat outside the cabin during the days. Justin remained inside with Hayden. Hayden was usually too busy playing on his cell phone to care about either two.

Eventually, Brook came to Gabe for help. She had a plan to get away from the camp but she was going to need supplies. She couldn't do it all alone. Gabe volunteered to head back to the camp. He said he wanted to help, but really he wanted to get away from Justin. His one moment of weakness with Justin turned into a debt he would have to repay.

Before Gabe returned to the camp Brook cut his hair. It was as short as she could get it. While not a perfect disguise it would help Gabe not get noticed right away. As long as he stayed unnoticed he would be fine.

Every time Gabe went to the camp he was asked to sneak food and water from the cafeteria or simply watch counselor rotations around the administrative building. Hayden had told them about the broken window and the layout of the building from what he had seen. He remembered where the office was and the location of the garage.

Gabe discovered the window had not yet been fixed. There was only a piece of plastic covering up the opening. Everything he saw he reported back to Brook. They could sneak in if they needed to.

It looked like the search for him had died down. When he walked around the camp he did not notice anybody actively looking for him, at least nobody that was trying to judge him.

He spotted Mindy several times during his missions. Gabe tried to avoid her as much as he could. He still felt bad for ditching her in the first week, but she was getting clingy. Now, she could ruin the whole thing if she found him. Gabe didn't know if she would turn him in or not.

One day she saw him. Gabe was watching the schedule of the counselors when he had to retreat. He did not want to full out run. It would draw the attention of the other campers, but he could not let Mindy approach him. He hurried as fast as he could. Surprisingly, she kept up with him. When Gabe rounded the corner of a cabin he made a run for the generators. Mindy had started to slow down, and Gabe was able to hide behind the noisy machines.

He looked back and saw Mindy looking all around

for him. She wasn't giving up so easily. She started to walk toward him. Staying low Gabe was able to get to the entrance of the hidden part of the camp. The gate was still slightly ajar from when he had entered the camp.

As quickly and quietly as he could he hid behind the bushes that clung to the fence line. Mindy approached the generators and looked behind them. She found nothing. Gabe remained still. He waited for Mindy to look all around. Her faced was confused. She could not understand where Gabe had gone. Then she walked off. Gabe was relieved. He was still safe.

Hayden was growing more frustrating. Now, whenever Gabe returned to the camp he had to take the extra phones with him because Hayden just had to play his games. Brook said they were going to need whatever phones they could get once they escaped the camp. They needed them fully powered.

Brook and Gabe started to hide them from Hayden, but he noticed. He complained and yelled until he got a new one to play with.

Finally, Gabe had had enough of Hayden. When Hayden started on one of his tantrums Gabe took the dead phone from Hayden's hand and threw it across the room. The phone shattered against the blood stained wall.

"What the hell, man?" Hayden yelled.

"Stop dicking around with the phones. We need them," said Gabe. "If you want to get out of here then you need to help out."

"Hey, I'm sick," said Hayden. He cuddled his stomach when he said this.

Brook stood up to try to get between Gabe and Hayden.

"Leave him alone," defended Justin. His right leg was bandaged. He could barely walk on it. They did not have the knowledge to properly fix it.

"Hayden is not sick. He's lazy," said Gabe. "He needs to start pulling his weight around here."

"I found this cabin," said Hayden. "I saw the layout of the office. I found the phones."

Brook rolled her eyes. "I also found the cabin."

"I found it first."

"You say you've been in the office. Then you need to go back. We need the keys. I don't know where they are. I'm sure they are in the building. You'll have a better chance," Brook told Hayden.

"Fat chance. I'm not going back there," said Hayden. "If they catch me they'll put me back to work."

"If they catch me they will kill me," said Gabe.

"Because you're a fucking faggot," said Hayden. "You and your boyfriend."

"He's not my boyfriend," said Gabe.

"Yeah," confirmed Justin. "He was going to leave me to die. You shouldn't even be here. I don't know why Brook is helping you."

"Fuck off," said Gabe. "I was just looking for a hook up, okay. Fuck. I didn't owe you shit. I don't love you. You were a cute guy. That's it. Get over it."

Justin charged toward Gabe, but Brook intercepted. It was not hard since Justin could not move very fast.

"Gabe, please head to the camp," said Brook. "Get us some food. We all need to chill for a little bit."

"You go," said Gabe.

"I'm not leaving you three together," said Brook. "If we don't start working together then we are all dead. We die in this cabin, get killed by the Avenger of Blood, or die trying to walk our asses out of here if we do not get keys to a van. So, we all need to bring it down a notch, and move on."

"Fine," said Gabe. "I'll get us some food." He turned and left in a huff.

Hayden flipped Gabe off as he left. "Take a phone!"

Gabe did not go directly to the cafeteria. He

walked around the camp for a little while trying to clear his head. He had gotten used to being able to walk around the camp without being noticed. The search for him must have died down if not gone away entirely.

He was so consumed in his own thoughts that he did not see Mindy come up from the side. She was dolled up like never before. The blush and eye shadow was applied very liberally. The excess use was a sign of somebody who did not use makeup very often.

She proposed the idea of them being together. She knew how to save Gabe. If they were together she could cure his gayness.

Mindy's smile irradiated from her dark red lips. She was confident that she had convinced him to be with her.

Gabe only got angrier. There was nothing to save in him. He did not believe he was doing anything wrong. He liked who he liked and that was it.

Then Gabe exploded on her. All of his rage from the past weeks at the camp and hiding in the cabin came exploding out on her.

She took his wrath. Her smile quickly faded. Tears welled up in her eyes. Her makeup began to run. Gabe could not stop. He scolded her for the idea. He berated her for trying to change him. She could not have him.

When it was all over Mindy ran off. Gabe had just broken her heart.

Adrenaline was coursing through Gabe's body. He needed a fix. He needed to get his energy out. Then he remembered Morgan. He hadn't seen Morgan in the rehabilitation center. He could still be out in the camp.

Gabe knew Morgan would listen to him. Morgan would understand and help him. Morgan was always up to help him.

Quickly, Gabe went to Morgan's cabin where they used to always meet in the morning. Just thinking about Morgan and the first week of the summer made Gabe hard. He was growing more excited by the second.

Gabe knew Morgan did not play by the rules of the camp. It was why he tried the cabin first. Morgan was more than likely still there doing whatever he wanted.

One peek through the window confirmed it. Morgan was inside. He was shirtless and sweaty. Gabe grew even tighter in his shorts. He moaned over Morgan's damp hair as he swished it out of his eyes.

Gabe hurried over to the backdoor of the cabin. He opened it and as soon as he saw the room was empty except for Morgan, Gabe pounced.

Morgan turned around to the sudden surprise of Gabe shoving his tongue down his throat. Gabe was relieved to get some of this energy out, but he wanted more.   He grabbed hold of Morgan, but Morgan reached down and took Gabe by the hands.

"What happened to you?" Morgan asked, pulling him away. "You went and disappeared off the entire camp. I thought you were gone."

"No," said Gabe, nearly out of breath. "I was taken to a rehabilitation class. They had me locked up."

"I guess it didn't work," said Morgan.

"Am I glad to see you," said Gabe. His elevator eyes reached every tip of Morgan.

"That's a change from when you last saw me," said Morgan.

"I've been going through a lot of stuff," said Gabe. "This camp is insane."

"I know," said Morgan.   He reached over and grabbed a bottle of pills from his nightstand.   He passed the bottle over to Gabe. "Here take this. It'll help. You look like a mess. This will calm you down."

"I don't want to calm down," said Gabe. "I want you."

"Okay," said Morgan. "First take these. You'll feel better. Then you'll have to tell me what the hell you have been doing since the first week. We can get to the other stuff later."

Gabe looked down at the bottle. It was a prescription of Xanax for a girl named Cora.

"Where did you get this?" Gabe asked. Then he started to look around. When he first came into the cabin he was so focused on Morgan that he did not see in a nearby bed there was a girl.

Her tattoos reached all the way down both arms and to her back. She slept under the covers completely oblivious to the situation going on right at her side.

"Holy shit, is she okay?" Gabe asked. Cora did not look well, even in sleep.

"She's fine," said Morgan. "I'm helping her out. She just took a little bit too much medicine. She's sleeping it off now."

Gabe sat down on another camper's bed. He needed a moment to process the new information. He had nearly confessed everything to Morgan while somebody else was in the room. If she had not been asleep then he could have been ruined.

Morgan sat next to him. He put his arm around Gabe. "It's going to be okay," he said. Then he kissed Gabe's forehead.

"God, you look exhausted," said Morgan. "Lay down. Get some rest. I'll join you."

Gabe could feel Morgan gently laying him down on

the bed they were in. Suddenly, all of Gabe's energy was waning. He wanted nothing more than to sleep. He was crashing and Morgan was there to catch him.

Morgan put his hand under Gabe's head and rested him down on the pillow. "Nobody will be back for a while," said Morgan. "We'll be fine."

"Thanks," said Gabe. He reached out for Morgan to get his former lover to join him.

Morgan grabbed the second pillow on the bed. He fluffed it up several times as Gabe smiled back at him.

Then Gabe's vision went dark. Morgan had placed the pillow over Gabe's face.

It pressed down tightly across Gabe's nose and mouth. He fought to break free, but he was too weak. All of his energy was gone. His screams were muffled by the pillow.

All of Morgan's weight was on top of him. His legs pinned down Gabe's arms. It was a familiar touch that Gabe knew all too well.

"You fucking come here after all this shit started going down?" Morgan said through the pillow. His voice was muffled. Gabe could barely hear it.

"Do you want me to get caught? I'm not dying here," said Gabe's former lover.

Those were the last words that Gabe ever heard.

Gluttony

All Cora wanted to do was relax.

She hardly remembered the first week of camp at Psalm Springs. Her last full memory was being at a party hosted by a friend of a friend. After only a couple of hours her friend, Trish, disappeared. It wasn't the first time Cora had been ditched by Trish. She didn't think it would be the last either. It didn't really matter. Cora was able to snag a few drinks and many of the guys there kept offering her shots. Once she found a group she liked that was passing around a joint Cora stopped caring where Trish had gone. Cora was settled.

Then a fight sparked later in the night. Cora remembered driving home in a fit of rage. Some douchebag, she had forgotten his name (if she had ever learned it), wanted to take Cora home with him. He said he had some better stuff there. Cora thought about it, but she wasn't in the mood. Then the guy got angry. Core ended up storming out, not even bothering to find out if Trish was still at the party or not.

That was when her memories started to fade. Cora remembered seeing her house. Her neighbor's lights were on. It was unusual for that time of night.

Then there was a struggle. Cora's vision was gone. Muscular arms wrapped around her waist. She was taken off her feet. Like a ragdoll she was tossed inside a vehicle. That was the last thing she could remember of that night. Everything else was a blank.

The next morning Cora was being forcibly woken up by a group of upper twenty adults in green shirts and blue shorts. She was sitting in the window seat of a van.

Her head was pounding, and her stomach felt like it was swimming in acid. She needed a drink, anything to ease off the pain.

Out the window she could see a sea of teenagers and young adults all walking to the entrance of the camp.

The group of counselors had to drag Cora out of the van. She stumbled several times once she reached her feet outside. They braced her up. One of the counselors, John, looked Cora over.

"She's fine," he said. "You look pretty bad though,"

John said directly to Cora. "We'll provide some new clothes for you, and some toiletries. You'll need those for your stay."

John bent down and began patting Cora's boots and pant legs. He knocked her right boot and it rattled back. He hit it again to the beat of acknowledgment. Without asking, John dug into Cora's boot. His hand shuffled around for a second. Cora did not fight it. Then John released her with a bottle of Xanax left in his hand. Cora typically hid her pills there. It was uncomfortable, but Cora had gotten used to it. Most people didn't find them.

"I'll be taking these," John told her. Then he continued talking, but Cora started to drift out again. She could not concentrate. The sun was bearing down on her. The light hurt her eyes. She blinked repeatedly to try to adjust to the change.

"…to the welcoming hall," John was telling her. "Do you understand me?"

Cora nodded. Her body shifted. Her knees wanted to give way. The rocky gravel looked like the most comfortable bed in the world.

Then Cora threw up.

The counselors bounced back to avoid any backsplash. They all groaned and moaned in disapproval. Several of the counselors walked off.

They had other campers to handle.

Cora was bent down. She stared at her vomit that was splattered all over the ground. For one brief second she felt better. Then the nausea returned.

Another round was coming. She felt John put his hand on her back to comfort her. He gently lifted her hair out of the way. When Cora started throwing up again she was in the clear.

"Let it out," said John. "There will be food and water provided before and after the sermon today. I suggest you take it easy. You'll get through this. We are praying for you. God will help."

The sermon was a blur. Cora could not listen to Pastor Robbins talk for very long before her mind started to wander off. She was starting to shake. The camp was only providing fruits and water for their morning snacks. It would not be enough.

The only thing Cora could do was sit quietly and concentrate on not throwing up any more or even dry heaving.

The rest of the day was spent lying in her bed. Her cabin counselor, Lisa, told Cora that she could not have any medicine for her hangover. Psalm Springs was designed to keep the youth of the world pure in mind and body. After Lisa left to attend to other business Rose was responsible for the cabin. Rose saw to it to look after Cora.

"I've seen your information," said Rose. "Drinking, drugs, your tattoos. You've gone down a sinful road, Cora. We're here to help you. It's not going to be easy to bring you back to the grace of God, but it is possible. He's waiting for you to make the first step. That is getting cleaned up. When you are feeling better please join us outside. We've got a lot of fun activities planned for the next week."

Cora's only response was a barely audible groan. The light was still too much for her. She pulled the covers over her head. It blocked out the nagging sun and Rose's nagging voice.

Cora was in such distress that she never thought to ask where she was. She just wanted the pain to go away.

Throughout the day several girls came in and out of the cabin. Two girls, Chrissy and Alissa, snickered at Cora as they walked past her bed. Cora watched, from a small break in her covers, Mindy for an hour as she put together her living space in the cabin. Mindy had a couple of bags worth of stuff she had brought with her.

Eventually everybody left the cabin, and Cora was given the chance to relax. It did not help. Her heart was racing. She needed something to help mellow out. Wherever she was she was kidnapped. They were being nice to her, but for how long? Whenever she thought about her situation panic ran through her body.

Before she knew it Cora's bed was soaked from sweat. Her body shivered from chills, and she could now smell the moist sheets covering her.

She wanted to feel better. She needed to feel better. But her pills were gone. She needed a drink. She needed a smoke. She needed something.

She could feel her spine start to spasm backward.

Then she blacked out.

When Cora regained consciousness she was in a new room. It was air conditioned. Gospel music hummed in the background. Her bed rustled under every little move she made. She was lying down on a long sheet of paper. A light blanket was placed over her.

A few moments later, Cora noticed a bell on the nightstand next to her. It took all of her strength to reach for it. Her entire body hurt. Her head felt as if she had been struck hard. The top of her skull throbbed.

The bell felt so far away. Her fingertips could

brush against the handle, but Cora did not have the energy to make the final reach. Her coordination was off. When she pushed forward her hand went too far. The bell fell to the ground. It ringed for a brief second before it settled down on the hardwood floor.

The noise did the trick. Just a minute later the door to Cora's room opened. An old woman entered. She wore an oversized sweater and dress that matched. Her hair was a faded blonde. She smiled when she saw Cora was awake.

"Hello," said Virginia. "You gave us a scare."

Cora looked at the old woman with curiosity. She could not put together what was going on. Her thoughts were a mess.

"Everything is okay," said the old woman. "My name is Virginia. You were brought to the medical ward by your bunkmate, Rose. You were having a seizure."

"Yeah…" said Cora. It was the only word she could come up with.

"You are lucky," continued Virginia. "You knocked your head against the bed rail. There was blood all over."

Cora reached for the back of her head. She winced at the slightest touch to her wound.

"You need to get some rest," said Virginia. "Drink

some water and go back to sleep. You have a difficult time ahead of you. Your body needs to adjust to the sudden lack of alcohol and whatever else you have been doing."

"My medicine…" said Cora.

"I don't think so," said Virginia. "We don't want you abusing any more drugs. That's the devil's path. You need to get off of it as soon as possible. Health and pleasure must come from God, not from man's sinful creations."

Virginia left Cora soon after. Cora was not the only patient in the medical ward.

There was nothing left to do. Cora laid her head back down on her pillow. Her wound gave off a sudden surge of pain then settled. Before she knew it Cora was asleep.

The rest of the week Cora spent in the medical ward. She had two more seizures in the next couple of days. Virginia was there to comfort her when she came back to.

The nights when Cora was awake she cried. She wanted to be home. Cora still did not understand fully what was going on. She was at a camp, but she did not know why. She was not a bad girl. She did not do anything terrible. She did not deserve this.

On Sunday, Cora was starting to feel a little better. Her strength was coming back. She was able to eat without throwing it up. She had not had a seizure for several days. Virginia was excited to see Cora more alert. It was just in time.

Sunday, Cora was escorted with several other residents of the medical ward to the sermon hill. It was exhausting for Cora. She had very little energy to make the walk.

The hill was crowded with the rest of the campers of Psalm Springs. It amazed her that there were so many of them. None of them were trying to run away or even looked scared. Cora had been kidnapped to be there. She couldn't fathom that the others had come there willingly. There had to be somebody that could help her.

Cora listened to Pastor Robbins give his speech. His words dug deep into Cora's thoughts. They were bringing in kids that did anything out of line. Cora tried to shrug down and become invisible. Her stomach was turning upside down.

Then they brought out Erika. The girl was screaming obscenities at the counselors and campers. Cora freaked. That could easily have been her up there.

Cora was quiet as she watched what followed.

Erika was thrown out of the camp gates. Then the Avenger of Blood appeared. Cora's heart sunk further. She turned away as Erika was dragged out into the woods.

Then Cora threw up her dinner. This time it wasn't because she was physically sick. She was sick from fear.

Virginia patted Cora on the back. She let Cora compose herself. The rest of the campers were starting to return back to their cabins. The day was over.

"It's okay," said Virginia. "You needed to see that. Now you know what you are fighting for. This camp is to help you save your soul. If you don't clean up your act then God will banish you to Hell."

The next week wasn't great for Cora. She spent every day bed ridden in the medical ward. Some nights she woke up with sweats and cravings for a drink. Her anxiety came back with a vengeance once she knew what was going on at the camp.

Every night she dreamed of the Avenger of Blood. The behemoth stalked her around every corner. She could keep out of reach, but every night the monster was getting closer. Then she would wake up screaming or she would wake up by someone else screaming. That was every night.

As the summer continued into June more campers started to appear at the medical ward. They were there to work with Virginia and help out with the patients.

There was a constant rotation of campers at first, but eventually Cora began to notice one camper returning to her room periodically. He eventually introduced himself as Neil.

It was to Cora's amusement to watch Neil walk around her room. It was like he was constantly walking up hill.

She first noticed Neil when he brought her an extra glass of water. Then there started to be extra portions of food on her tray. Whenever Neil walked by her doorway he stole a quick glance inside and smiled.

Cora could tell Neil was smitten with her. It was like middle school all over again. Cora was one of the first to develop breasts. It brought a lot of attention to her from the boys.

She started to test how far she could take Neil. She asked for a third or fourth cup of water. He happily obliged. Then she started asking for food that wasn't available at the medical ward. The next day Neil would appear with what Cora had asked for. Usually it was just extra fruit or a granola bar. Cora didn't really know what was all available at the camp. When she asked for a soda Neil lowered his head in shame. He did not know how to get that.

What Neil was getting for Cora was good, but she needed more. Her cravings had not disappeared. Many of the days came to a crawl. She wasn't allowed out into the camp yet. Virginia was worried that Cora was not ready yet to fend off sinful temptation.

The day finally came that Cora needed something stronger. Neil could get her all the water and snacks in the world, but it would do her no good.

Finally, one day when Neil came around Cora offered a proposition.

"Neil, I need a favor," she said.

Neil's eyes perked up. He walked over to her bed so they could talk more privately. "What's up?"

"I am desperate. I need a drink," said Cora.

"I can get you some water," said Neil.

"No," corrected Cora. "I mean a real drink. You know, vodka or something."

"Oh," said Neil. "We're not supposed to be drinking. It's against the rules."

"I know that, but I am dying here. I need a drink. This place is awful. I can't get through it. Please."

"I don't know…" said Neil. He took a slight step back. He couldn't look Cora in the eyes anymore.

"What about my medicine? I had some Xanax

when I arrived. I don't know what they did with it. That will help," suggested Cora.

Neil turned to the doorway like he was looking for something. "There is a storage closet where they put medicine that campers brought in. It might be in there," he revealed.

"Can you please look?" asked Cora. Her eyes grew wider in desperation. She could feel her mouth salivate. Her heart raced in anticipation.

"I'm not supposed to," argued Neil.

"Please, I will do anything. I will give you a blow job if you can get me my medicine," Cora offered.

Neil took another step back. His face gave off the expression like she had offered to kill his family. Cora was surprised at his reaction. Usually she could pay for her drugs, but every now and then she would have to offer something else. It typically went over well.

"Um… um… I should be going. I… I can't," stumbled Neil. Then he rushed out of the room. Cora was left on her own with nothing gained.

Later that day a new camper appeared in Cora's room. She immediately thought about how cute he was. His devilish smile was something she could get used to.

"Who are you?" she asked.

"I'm Morgan," he answered. "I'm a friend of Neil's."

"Oh," said Cora. She tried to look innocent for Morgan. She did not know what he knew.

"I heard about the offer you gave Neil," said Morgan.

"I don't know what you're talking about," denied Cora.

"I can get you your pills," said Morgan. "That is, of course, if the offer is still on the table."

Cora smiled. Not at the thought of just getting her pills, she wouldn't say no to Morgan.

"Whatever," she answered.

Morgan smiled back. As he left the room he adjusted his shorts. Cora lied back down thankful that she was going to be able to relax again.

The next day Morgan was good to his word. He came into Cora's room during a quiet part of the day. Virginia was gone from the medical ward. Many of the other campers were off to lunch.

He rattled the bottle of pills to bring them to Cora's attention. Cora waved her hands in the air like a baby bird getting food from her mother. Waves of anxiety and excitement surged through her.

Morgan threw the pills on to her bed. Cora scooped them up in haste. She did not wait for anything. The lid was flipped off and three pills went down her throat. She did not even need water.

A rush of relief came over her. Finally, she was going to be able to relax. With her head on straight she could figure out what to do next about this camp.

The edge started to come off of her feelings even before the medicine kicked in. Cora was basking in the knowledge alone that she had her pills.

Then Morgan cleared his throat. It brought Cora back to the room. She looked over at him. He was standing at her bedside by her head. His grin went from ear to ear.

Cora rolled her eyes. Boys were easy to manipulate.

"We had a deal," said Morgan.

"I remember," said Cora.

She reached over and pulled down Morgan's blue shorts. He was ready to go. She put him in her mouth and began to pleasure him. He earned it.

Morgan was louder than Cora wanted. He kept moaning his satisfaction as she flicked her tongue around him. She didn't want to alert anybody to what she was doing. If they found out she had gotten her pills back then she knew she would be in trouble.

Then he suddenly pulled away. Cora was surprised at that. Then Morgan started to come. He released himself all over Cora and her bed.

"What the hell?" she said.

"Sorry," said Morgan. He pulled up his shorts when he was finished. Then he headed for the door. He didn't bother to get Cora anything to help clean up.

Cora was left with the mess that Morgan made. She used her blanket to wipe off her face and neck then rubbed it across the bed to cover up the rest of it.

As soon as Morgan was gone he was out of Cora's mind. Her hand wrapped around her pills. They were her new security blanket. After a quick glance she slipped the bottle under her mattress. They would be safe there.

Then for the first time since arriving at Psalm Springs, Cora began to relax.

From that day on Cora was able to keep her composure. Virginia was thrilled to see Cora's progress. She believed Cora was getting through her withdrawals better than expected. What she didn't know was that Cora was back on her pills.

Cora went through her remaining pills in the first week. She regrettably had overdone it, but she did not want to fight it. She just had to get past this hump then she could start cutting back. That's what she told herself.

When Cora was empty she got Morgan to steal

more pills. It came with the same price as last time.

Her healthy improvement allowed Cora more freedom. Virginia did not need to check on her as much. Eventually, Virginia decided that it was time to allow Cora to return to the main camp.

"This is going to be a lot of responsibility, Cora," Virginia told her. "When you are out there every decision is your decision. If you fall back onto the sinful path then God's judgment may fall down upon you. We cannot always protect you."

Cora nodded her head. She was always quiet around the old lady. A smile crept across Cora's face. She was happy to be released, but she was even happier that she was putting one over on Virginia. Her bottle of pills was tucked safely in her shoe like usual. It was stuffed with pieces of her blanket to ensure the pills would not rattle around and alert Virginia to their presence.

"Please use the rest of the summer to regain God's embrace. He will surely be disappointed if you fall."

Cora said thank you and headed out. At first she walked through the camp. It was the first time that she was able to see it. Cora had no idea where her cabin was. She still wasn't sure if she wanted to even go there. There were still a lot of unanswered questions.

Out of the corner of her eye Cora saw her opportunity to get some of those answers. Neil was off in the distance. He had been following Cora since she left the medical ward.

Cora walked toward him. She let out a little wave to indicate that she was coming to him. Neil froze. He looked as if he wanted to run, but he was too afraid. Cora had not seen him since she propositioned him for her pills. She figured she had freaked him out.

"Hi, Neil," said Cora.

Neil's stance turned into a shy curl. "Hi," he whispered. "I'm sorry I stopped coming around."

"That's okay, I need some help," said Cora.

"I don't know if I can help you."

"I just need to know where I am," smiled Cora. "Nothing else."

"You're at Psalm Springs," he answered.

"Which is what? Why is everybody here?"

"We're here to be shown the true power of God. We're all sinners and this is the way to get us straight."

"You're a sinner?" Cora said. She looked Neil up and down curious to what he had done.

"In the eyes of God, yes," said Neil.

"How were you brought here?"

"My parents had me picked up. They explained to me that if I didn't take care of my problem now then I would be destined for Hell. They could not live with me knowing that I would go to Hell."

"You came here on your own?" stunned Cora. "Is that how everybody else is?"

"Most of them," said Neil. "It's the right thing to do. We need to get out of the sinful world if we're going to make it into Heaven."

"And this is okay with everybody? We saw somebody killed."

"People die all the time," said Neil. "The world is terrible. Heaven is meant to be peaceful and a sanctuary for the innocent. God cannot allow the sins of the world to infiltrate His home."

"So He kills sinners. That is not peaceful," said Cora.

"We are not in Heaven yet," said Neil.

Cora didn't like where the conversation was going. Her stomach dropped. She leaned in and used Neil as a brace to stay standing.

"Are you okay?" Neil asked.

"I'll be fine," said Cora. "I just need a little pick me up."

Neil held onto Cora for a couple of minutes. His hands stayed at her waist and shoulders. He looked stiff while he held her.

"Can you find Morgan for me?" Cora asked Neil.

"You guys are friends, right?"

"Yeah," said Neil. "I'll let him know that you are looking for him."

"Thanks," said Cora. "I appreciate it."

It took only a day for Morgan to find Cora. Neil had also stuck around. He spent much of his free time hanging out with Cora. She did not mind. Neil was able to tell her more about the camp, and introduce a lot of the people in the area.

Cora returned to her cabin briefly, but she did not want to stay. The girls there eyed her down when she arrived. She recognized the two girls that insulted her on her first day, Chrissy and Alissa.

Cora decided that she would only return to the cabin when only necessary. That meant just nightfall. The counselors were strict about having campers in their cabins for curfew.

Morgan found Cora and Neil walking around the camp.   Cora found the constant movement comforting. If she stayed put then she would start her cravings. She always needed something to do.

"I've been looking for you guys all over the place," said Morgan. "I'm glad to see you got out, Cora."

"Yeah, thank you for that," she said.

"What are you guys up to?" Morgan asked.

"Nothing," said Neil. "We're just walking around."

"If you want we can head over to this spot I know. It's pretty secluded. We won't be disturbed," said Morgan.

"For what?" Neil asked.

"I've got some stuff," said Morgan.

"Like what?" Cora asked.

"About an ounce," said Morgan. "I don't know if it's any good. I found it in the contraband room at the medical ward."

"You stole something?" Neil accused.

"It is fine, Neil," said Morgan. "They stole it first."

"I'm in," said Cora. "Lead the way."

"Great," said Morgan. "Neil, you coming?"

Neil looked flustered. His head darted from Cora to Morgan then back again.

"…Okay," said Neil, finally.

Morgan was thrilled to hear that Neil was in. He led them to a spot hidden in a cluster of trees. They were out of view from the rest of the camp.

Cora got as comfy as she could next to a tree. Morgan sat next to her. Neil stayed on his feet. He shifted his weight from one foot to the other.

Cora took the weed and paper from Morgan. He was more than happy to oblige. Cora liked to roll her own. She enjoyed the practice.

"Are you guys going to smoke that?" Neil asked.

"Yes," said Morgan. "Sit down. You need to chill out."

Neil did not move.

"Isn't it bad for you?"

"You'll be fine," said Cora. "It'll help you relax."

"And that's something that we really need a lot of around here," said Morgan.

"What if they catch us?"

"What are they going to make us do? Say a Hail Mary," said Morgan.

"We could die," said Neil.

Cora stopped rolling and looked up at Neil. Morgan did the same. The three of them shared a quiet moment.

"They won't catch us if they don't know about us," said Cora. "I've been back on my pills for weeks now. Nothing has happened."

"This whole place is an illusion," said Morgan. "That whole thing the first week was just for show. There is no way they killed that girl. She's just one of the counselors that sets an example and then disappears for the rest of the summer. God is not trying to kill us."

"It looked real," said Neil.

"Yeah, that's what makes it effective," said Morgan.

Cora returned to her duty. She licked the last edge of the paper and secured it all together. It was a work of art she thought.

"Can we please stop talking about this?" said Cora.

"Of course," said Morgan. He handed her a lighter.

"Thank you," said Cora. She took the first hit from the joint. It warmed her lungs with a familiar touch.

"Is it good?" asked Morgan. He was leaning over to whisper in Cora's ear. His hand was on her upper thigh.

"Not bad," she said. Then Cora reached and offered a hit to Neil.

"No, no, thank you," he said.

"Come on," said Cora.

"No," said Neil. Then he backed away from the two of them.

"Neil, Neil, don't run away," said Morgan.

But it was too late. Neil was gone from their hiding place.

"His loss," said Morgan.

Cora leaned back against the tree. She was enjoying her smoke.

"Good find," said Cora. She handed the joint over to Morgan. He took a hit and passed it back.

"What do I get for getting you this?" he asked.

"There was no deal for this," said Cora. "You don't

get anything. This was just a friendly gesture."

"Are you sure?" Morgan asked. His hand started to move up her thigh. It snuck underneath her shorts.

Cora took another hit. It was a long deep breath. She felt Morgan's hand brush against her crotch. Then he started to pull back.

"Don't stop there," said Cora. She took another drag.

Morgan's hand returned. He rubbed her up and down.

Cora closed her eyes. She was feeling good.

All through July, Cora and Morgan met for parties nearly every day. Sometimes others would join them. They were all campers that were scared of being there and needed a break. They were usually invites from Morgan.

The campers were at Psalm Springs for several reasons. Some were delinquents and their parents were running out of options to straighten them out. Some were gay. One girl was caught leaving an abortion clinic. A lot of them were there because they were caught drinking and doing drugs. They were following the influence of Satan and needed to see the light of God.

Neil stopped coming around. It was a small relief

to Cora. He was getting annoying. Every now and then Cora would catch a glimpse of Neil watching them from the distance. It was creepy. She hoped he would found another girl to pine over eventually.

One day a friend of Morgan's, Carl, brought with him a couple bottles of wine. He worked at the church with several of the counselors. He was able to get a hold of some of the wine used for communion.

Carl passed around the bottles to the group of five that were together at the hidden spot in the trees. It was one of the biggest groups they had had so far.

Cora had taken some Xanax earlier that day before Morgan came around for another party. The atmosphere was lively and upbeat. Cora paid no attention to how much wine she started to drink.

It tasted bitter. Cora squirmed as it went down her throat. Then she took another drink.

The party lasted for some time. Cora did not give it any thought. Her thoughts danced as the wine kept making its rounds through the group.

Morgan had his arm draped around her. She brushed him off several times. He was keeping her too warm. The shade was only doing so much against the summer heat.

The ground swirled back and forth underneath Cora. It felt like a ride at the carnival. Usually she enjoyed the sensation, but this time it was becoming too much. She wanted to settle down.

The party was still going. The others were laughing and having a good time. Cora liked that. She did not want to miss it, but she had to lie down. Her usual spot on the tree felt like sandpaper. She could not lean against Morgan. He kept moving around.

Finally, Cora had enough. She got up and started to leave the party. As soon as she got to her feet she fell back down. Her vision went black for a moment and all feeling in her body was gone.

"Whoah, where are you going?" Morgan asked.

"I need to lie down," Cora said or at least she thought she said. The actual sound that came out of her voice was more of gibberish.

Morgan chuckled at her. "Okay, it looks like she's done."

He braced Cora back to her feet. "We'll see you guys later," he said. Then he grabbed Cora's hand and made it wave good-bye at them. The group laughed at his joke.

Cora mumbled some more as Morgan led her through the camp. She tried to tell Morgan that she wanted to go to her cabin, and he could return to the party, but none of those words came out.

Instead of taking Cora to her cabin, Morgan

brought her to his. The cabin was empty. His bunkmates were elsewhere in the camp doing whatever that day's activities were.

Morgan laid Cora down on a bed. Immediately, she wrapped herself up in the covers.

"Thank you," she garbled.

"You know, I was hoping we would have some time to ourselves," said Morgan. He sat on the bed next to Cora. He placed his hand on her waist. Then he brushed hair out of Cora's face with the other.

Cora shrugged him off. She just wanted to sleep. She wasn't feeling well.

Then she felt Morgan cupping her breast with his hand. She again brushed him off.

"Stop it," Cora tried to say.

"Come on," said Morgan. "I've been getting you stuff for over a month now. I should get some appreciation for that."

Cora said something incoherent. Even she did not know what she meant to say.

She turned to look up at Morgan. Before she could say another word she felt his tongue breaking into her mouth. Then Morgan pulled back and looked Cora in the eyes. She stared back at him, the two of him that she saw.

"That was nice, wasn't it?" Morgan said. "Just go

with it."

Morgan shifted on the bed. He put his full weight on top of Cora. She could not push him off.

He started kissing her down her neck. She struggled harder, but it only helped Morgan. The blanket was shoved up and out of his way. He forced himself in between Cora's legs.

She could feel him getting harder.

"No, no, please don't," she begged. The entire bed was spinning. Cora could not tell which way was up anymore.

"Just relax," said Morgan. "I'm here for you."

He kissed her several more times. Cora's shorts were pulled down to her knees. Morgan rubbed up against her.

"Stop," said Cora. "Go away."

"You've wanted to do this. I know," said Morgan.

Then he entered her.

Cora winced in pain as Morgan started to thrust back and forth.

He held her arms down as he continued.

All Cora could do was close her eyes and cry. The room never stopped spinning. Mercifully, she blacked out.

Cora woke up later that afternoon. Her head hurt.

She wanted to throw up, and she was sore down below. Her eyes began to focus on the room and the cabin she was in. It was unfamiliar to her, and a group of guys were surrounding her.

She was lying in bed naked. She could feel the sheets touching her bare skin. All of the guys in the cabin had the look of accusation on their faces. Cora couldn't look them in the eyes. She covered herself up as best as she could.

The cabin counselor, Brad, approached her. He looked stern. There was no remorse for what had just happened.

"What are you doing here?" Brad asked.

"I don't know," said Cora. "I don't remember. Please, help me."

"What are you doing in my bed?" asked one of the campers. Cora looked over at him. He was a short, pudgy kid with freckles. She had never seen him before.

"I don't know," answered Cora again. Tears welled up in her eyes.

"Were you having sex?" the counselor asked.

Cora looked at him. Her mouth twitched holding back her emotions.

"No, yes, no. No. I… I was raped," said Cora.

"Okay, okay," said Brad. "Let's get you out of

here."

The counselor got up from the bed. He tried to comfort Cora, but she shook him off.

Cora did not want to be touched by anyone right then. Even the blanket she wrapped herself in was rough. It reminded her of what had happened.

"Let's go," said Brad. "We need to have you checked out."

Cora did not move. She stayed standing by the bedside. All of the boys continued to stare at her. Some of them had smirks on their face. Others could not look at her.

Brad grabbed hold of her. This time he did not let go when Cora tried to break his hold.

"We need to go," he said. He led Cora out of the cabin.

Once outside, Cora kept her head hidden by the blanket. She peaked through a hole to see where she was going. As she walked she could see the campers all around them. They looked in her direction. They all looked at the shameful naked girl. Heads turned and Cora tried to make herself invisible. It did no good. Every camper along the way saw her.

Brad took Cora to the familiar sight of the medical ward. Virginia rushed to them as soon as they entered the building.

"You poor thing," said the old woman. "What happened?"

Virginia took Cora from Brad's hold. She gently put her arm around Cora to try and comfort her.

Cora began to cry. Everything she was holding in on her walk to the medical ward was finally coming out.

"It's going to be okay," said Virginia. "God will make this right. He always does."

Virginia waved Brad away. She would take care of Cora from there. They walked together to a new room. It was similar to the one Cora spent the start of the summer in.

"Lie down," said Virginia. "We will get this all sorted out soon."

Cora did as she was told. The sterile paper and clean sheets were enough to welcome Cora home. Virginia rushed over to a closet to get Cora some clothes to cover up with.

"Now, get some rest," said Virginia. "Try to remember what happened. It's going to be difficult, but it's the only way we can fix the situation."

Cora nodded. She then stopped listening to Virginia. Her head hurt, and she just wanted to be alone.

Cora was woken up by a gentle hand on the shoulder. It gave her a chill down her spine. Virginia smiled back at her. Cora's drowsiness started to wear off. Then she looked over and Pastor Robbins was sitting across the room. He was far enough away that Cora was not too afraid of him.

"Good morning, Cora," said Robbins. "I understand you have been through an ordeal."

Cora nodded her head. She didn't want to actually say what happened to her.

"My counselor, Brad, he said that you told him you were raped," said Robbins.

Cora nodded her head again. She looked down, no longer able to look back at Pastor Robbins or Virginia.

"Is that true?" Pastor Robbins asked.

Again, Cora nodded her head.

"I'm asking because Brad also found some pills beside you. We know your history with drug abuse. Were you high when this happened?"

Virginia looked shocked at Pastor Robbins' reveal. She shook her head in disappointment at Cora.

"Yes," said Cora. "But they were helping me."

"Drug use does not help," said Robbins. "God does not approve of your actions. I've met several girls like you over the years. You learn early on that you can get whatever you want by offering your body to boys.

How can it be bad if it feels good? It feels good because that's what the devil wants you to believe.

"The devil will make things easy for you. It's not a challenge to go to Hell. That is simply a participation award. And the more people that just participate then the less will go to Heaven.

"The devil does not offer his pleasures because he wants you in Hell. He does it because he does not want you in Heaven. If he can't go then no one should go. He wants God to be lonely.

"The more sin spreads the more people go to Hell. That is why God will strike down the sinner. One less sinner in the world means one less sinner to spread corruption to another innocent soul.

"Do you understand, Cora? You have been spreading sin. Your body is a temple that you have destroyed, and in order to keep it destroyed you have roped in the lives of innocent men to enable you. You pervert them for your own gains. Because it feels good."

"No," said Cora. She was curled up in a ball. Every word of Pastor Robbins made her tighten up.

"Yes," said Robbins. "The boy you had sex with was corrupted because you wanted to feel good. Mark 7:20-23, *and he said, 'What comes out of a person is what defiles him. For from within, out of the heart of man, comes evil thoughts, sexual immorality, theft, murder, adultery, coveting, wickedness, deceit, sensuality, envy, slander pride, foolishness. All these evil things come from within, and they defile a person."*

"I thought you were over that, Cora," said Virginia. She looked away from the young girl when she said it.

"They make their own choices, Virginia. It is the only way they will get to Heaven," assured Pastor Robbins.

"I didn't want this to happen," said Cora.

"Your choices were made by you," said Robbins. "This can still be fixed though. There is a chance to turn sin into redemption. The two of you must forgive each other's sins. Sex is between a man and a wife. It is a sacred vow to God.

"Who was with you? He must pay reparations and then we will see to it that you two find happiness together under the guidance of our Lord."

Cora shook her head. For the first time she stared directly at Pastor Robbins. Sorrow, confusion, pain, absurdity all went through her mind.

"No," said Cora. "I don't remember who it was," she lied. She was never going to say who had raped her. She never wanted to see Morgan again.

"Very well," said Pastor Robbins. "Then you will stay here for treatment again. I hope that in your time at this camp you will remember what happened to you and realize that you can still have a fulfilling life ahead of you. The Day of the Tenth is approaching. I pray that you will be ready."

Pastor Robbins got up from his chair and left with the final word. Virginia followed him. She held her head down in shame for Cora.

Cora did not have many visitors. Virginia was the only one that came to her room. The old woman would drop off Cora's food then leave without saying a word. Her usual friendly mood had dropped off.

One day Cora heard voices outside of her door. It sounded like girls, but Cora would never know. They never came in. Later, when Virginia came to drop off her dinner, Cora saw that whoever had stopped by had written the words WHORE under her name on the door.

Cora's first and only true visitor finally arrived. Neil shuffled into her room early one morning. He kept his distance unlike before.

"Please, go," said Cora. She knew Neil was friends with Morgan, and she wanted nothing to do with him or anybody associated with him.

Neil stood silent for a minute. Then he got up the courage to speak.

"Why not me?" he asked.

"What?"

"Why didn't you want to be with me? I liked you. I did things for you. That's what boyfriends are supposed to do. Why didn't you get with me?"

"I didn't get with anybody," said Cora.

"Everybody is calling you a whore," said Neil. "They said you were having sex with the other campers. I just thought that we could have been together, instead."

"They are lying, Neil," said Cora. "I didn't have sex with anybody. I was raped. Somebody took advantage of me. Is that what you wanted? Do you want to use me, too?"

"I just wanted us to be together," said Neil. "But you never gave me a chance. We could have been good together. I could have helped you."

"You have no idea what you are talking about," said Cora.

"Yes, I do," said Neil. "I liked you, and I would have treated you well."

"It wouldn't have worked, Neil," said Cora.

"Oh," said Neil, defeated. He dropped his head in embarrassment then walked out the door. All of his courage to say those words was for nothing. He left Cora alone.

It was her only visitor so far, but Cora knew it was for the best. Whatever Neil's problem was she did not want to be a part of it. She believed he still had a chance.

The next several days brought the return of Cora's withdrawal symptoms. Her body needed her drugs and it craved more alcohol. Virginia would give her nothing. She was only offered water and crackers to help ride through the pain.

Cora was up every night with cold sweats. She never remembered the seizures. Virginia would appear every now and then to offer words of encouragement.

"It's never easy to get into Heaven, my dear," she would tell Cora. "You have to endure."

One night Cora was dreaming again that the Avenger of Blood was creeping towards her. She had not dreamed of the monster in the woods for weeks. This time it was the most terrifying. She slipped in and out of consciousness. Every time she opened her eyes she saw something move in the shadows of her room.

The Avenger of Blood was getting closer. The blade of the spearhead dangled over Cora's bed. It glistened in the moonlight.

Then Cora had a hand cover her mouth. It was

real. It wasn't a dream. She squirmed to try and break free. The hand immediately came off.

The room filled with the sound of someone trying to shush Cora. There was no longer anything attacking her. Cora lied still in her bed. She didn't dare move afraid it would alert whoever else was in there with her.

"It's okay," came a girl's voice from the shadows. "It's okay. I'm here to help."

Then she revealed herself. It was not the Avenger of Blood or even Morgan as Cora had feared.

"My name is Brook," she said. "I want to get you out of here."

It took little convincing for Brook to get Cora out of the medical ward. There was no help there anymore. They were letting Cora remain in her room to rot.

Brook told her that she could take Cora some place safe. The counselors did not know of her hiding spot.

On their walk through the camp Cora had to make sure she was not still dreaming. Brook led her through a hidden gate along the fence. The new part of the camp was darker, and chaotic.

Cora did not like the look of the place, but she did not want to be alone. She kept up with Brook, a complete stranger that she trusted.

"There is a cabin up ahead," said Brook. "It's not pretty, but it's been safe. There is already somebody there. His name is Hayden. He's not great company, but he was there first."

Suddenly, Cora froze. She stood outside of the cabin. It hid in partial shadows. Foreboding filled the air around them.

"No," said Cora. "No, I can't do it."

"What? You've come this far. Please, just come inside," said Brook. "You'll be safe here."

"No, not with him in there," said Cora.

"Hayden is harmless. He's an asshole, but he's harmless."

"I don't care. I'm not hiding out in a cabin with a guy," argued Cora.

Brook paused to think. She looked at the cabin then out off in the distance. Then she turned back to Cora. "Let me talk to Hayden. Maybe he will relocate for a little bit. There aren't many places we can go, Cora. We're all in hiding. We're all making sacrifices."

"I know," said Cora. "I just can't."

Brook took Cora by the hand and brought her inside the cabin. She wanted Hayden to see Cora for a bit of sympathy.

It did not work.

Hayden did not care about Cora's situation. He was not leaving his cabin. He found the cabin first, and he believed it was his. Cora would have to find someplace else to hide.

Brook and Cora returned outside. Cora was in tears. She did not want to go back to the camp. They were not going to help her.

Brook looked off in the distance again. She was mulling something over in her head. Cora stood and waited. She did not want to disturb Brook while she was thinking.

"Come with me," said Brook. "What you see stays with just us. Hayden does not know about this. I prefer to keep it that way. Understand?"

"Yes," said Cora. She could keep a secret. She knew that.

"I've got a plan to get us out of here. If you ruin it I will drop you from the group. We all have to play a part. You're in this now. Don't screw up."

"Got it," said Cora. She was starting to get cold. Her entire body jittered.

Brook led her deeper into the woods. The moonlight was getting lost. Then they approached a clearing. Cora looked out and saw another building. It was slightly smaller than the cabin. The walls were made of stone unlike the wood cabins. She recognized the building as she got closer. She had seen them before.

It was a communal bathroom. The cabin in the cut off zone had one too.

"You don't want me to talk about a bathroom," Cora said as they walked to the entrance.

"It's not just the bathroom," said Brook. "It's who's here."

Brook knocked on the door several times. It was a password.

"Who is that with you?" said a girl on the other side of the door.

"This is Cora," said Brook. "She needs our help."

"What's wrong with the cabin?"

"Hayden is wrong with it."

There was silence for a minute then the door opened. Brook gestured for Cora to step inside.

The inside of the bathroom reeked. It smelled of sewage and burnt food. A fire was going in the corner of the room. Part of the roof had caved in giving proper ventilation for the smoke.

By the campfire was a girl in the familiar yellow and blue camp outfit. Her shirt was torn and bloody. Cora looked the girl up and down. She recognized her, but she could not place from where.

"Cora, I would like you to meet Erika," said Brook.

Then Cora remembered where she had seen her. Erika was the girl the counselors had thrown past the gates the first week. The Avenger of Blood had taken her. She was supposed to be dead.

"It was fake?" said Cora. "You're alive. This whole place is a lie. Morgan was right."

"Nope," said Erika. "This place is as real as it gets."

"Then how are you here?"

"I got away," said Erika. "I've been hiding ever since."

"Oh my God," said Cora.

"Tell me about it," said Erika.

"Will you be okay here?" Brook asked Cora.

"Yes," said Cora.

Brook looked over to Erika. She did not have to say a word.

"It'll be fine," said Erika. "It's been getting boring out here anyway."

"Thank you," said Brook. "It won't be much longer now. Cora, we're going to need to talk about some of the people you've met. It's why I came looking for you. There were parties. I heard you had contraband. How did you get them? They must have had access to parts of the camp that I can't get to. I need to know who they are. They may be able to help."

"I'll do what I can," said Cora.

"Good. Then we'll talk tomorrow. Get some rest tonight. I can figure out a plan after that. Shit is falling apart. We need to figure out something new."

Brook left Cora with Erika after that. She said she was going to return to the camp. Despite her attempt at escape she still spent most of her nights there. Nobody was looking for her yet.

Brook started to solidify her plan over the next few days. Cora told her about some of the people they met. She mentioned one guy who said he had keys to several of the buildings. It was how they ended up with alcohol, but Cora couldn't remember everybody that was at her parties. She did not remember the guy's name, but Neil would know a lot of them. Neil was spying on her during the parties. If Brook could find Neil then they had a chance of finding the guy with the keys.

Brook hoped that meant he had the keys that lead to the garage. The only way they were going to really escape from Psalm Springs was with proper transportation.

While Brook was getting excited as time went on Cora was getting sicker. She was not recovering well from her withdrawals. She constantly found herself shaking. Several times Erika had to tend to her.

The stress of being on the run at the camp was too much for Cora. She wanted nothing more than to feel free again. She asked Brook several times to find Carl and get her some wine. She knew it would help. Brook refused the suggestion. Wine was not something Brook wanted to risk getting.

"Please, please, I need something," Cora begged. "I can't do this. I just need a little bit. Just a little bit to take the edge off. Then I will be fine. I can handle this."

"I can't risk it," said Brook. "I'm already putting my neck out when I have to recharge batteries. Carl is already risking a lot for the van keys. I can't have him get more wine."

"What about her medicine?" Erika asked. Cora told her about her Xanax. It had been taken away by Brad when they found her in Morgan's cabin.

"I have some in my room!" Cora exclaimed. "You can get it. It's under my bed. I had so much. I collected them from the parties. They took what was on me, but I kept some. I kept some on the side. Please. Please get it for me. I need it."

Brook contemplated her decision. Erika was nodding her head. She knew Cora needed something.

"She can't quit cold turkey," said Erika. "If you can

get her something then we can try and wean her off. It's that or she freaks out when we need her."

"Fine," said Brook. "But that's it. We need to concentrate on getting out of here, not just surviving."

Cora was ecstatic the next day when Brook arrived with her pills. She clutched them in her hand like a lost child. She took several of her pills without a second thought. Cora was once again feeling on top of the world.

A new girl popped up, Mindy. Erika and Cora never met her, but Brook mentioned that she was staying at the cabin. She had been exiled back at the camp.

"Chrissy and Alissa," said Cora. "I'm sure they were behind it. They are trying to stay innocent by shaming anybody that does anything wrong."

"That makes six of us," said Brook, staying on task. Cora usually didn't pay attention whenever Brook came around talking about the plan. Cora did not want to worry herself with it. She just wanted to sit in the corner and relax.

"Carl says he can get us the keys to a van. After he does that, then when we are all ready we make a run for it."

"Still no word from Gabe?" asked Erika.

"No," said Brook. "He's probably dead, too."

"Could he have turned?"

"I don't think so," said Brook. "Somebody would have come by here by now if we were told on."

"I hope you're right," said Erika.

But soon everything changed.

Brook returned to the bathroom. She did not leave for several days. Her plan had gone wrong.

Cora sat in her usual corner. She listened to Brook tell Erika that everything was falling apart.

"After Mindy left all of the locks in the camp started getting changed," explained Brook. "Carl lost access to a lot of things. It'll take some time to get new keys."

"No more wine?" Cora mused.

"Now, Hayden is gone," said Brook. "I can't go back to the cabin. It's not safe."

"Do they know about this place?" asked Erika.

"I never told Hayden or Mindy about it," she said. "But we have to keep a look out. Just because they don't know we're using it doesn't mean they won't check it out. They could still know it exists."

Brook's words dug deep into Cora's head. She took another pill. She wanted to forget about the feeling of dread that was overcoming her. Every day it was getting worse. The Night of the Tenth was approaching.

Brook never came up with another plan. Cora stayed in the bathroom with Erika the rest of the summer. She had run out of pills the previous week.

Cora was anxious every moment of every day. She wanted to run out of her own skin. Erika and Brook were talking about new plans, but they rarely involved Cora in them. Or Cora never tried to get involved. She could not remember nor did she care.

It was the final night of the camp. The Night of the Tenth was upon them. Brook saw it as their last chance to make an escape. Tomorrow the vans would be gone and they would be stuck there.

Whatever the Tenth was Brook hoped they could take advantage of the change of schedule and simply break into the garage and steal one of the vans. It was their only hope.

Brook and Erika were gathering their things. Cora could not move. She was gripped with fear. She had nothing to comfort her. She had nothing to gather up. She was alone.

"Let's go," said Brook. She looked over at Cora. She and Erika were at the door of the bathroom waiting for her.

"I can't," said Cora.

"There is no more time," said Brook. "We have to go now. It's our last chance."

Cora shook her head violently. "I can't do it! I don't want to do it! I just want to stay here and not fucking deal with it. I can't. I already have too much to handle."

Brook came up to Cora. She knelt down to meet face to face. "I told you when you first arrived that if you messed up I would have to drop you. Do you remember?"

"Yes," said Cora.

"This is it," said Brook. "I'm trying to help you, but if you don't want to be helped then I can't do it. We are all scared, but we do not want to die here. Erika and I want to get out. We're not dying because somebody else believes something different."

Cora looked at Brook with tearful eyes. "Just take me with you. I can't do this. Just take me."

Erika shook her head across the room. "We can't drag you along."

"Please, I don't want to be alone. I just want to be okay."

"Sit here," said Brook. She looked back at Erika's disapproving glance. "If we can we'll come back for you."

"No, no, please, don't leave me alone," begged Cora.

"Let's go," said Erika.

Cora reached out for the two girls. She tried to grab invisible lines that would pull them back, but the girls kept going forward. Then they were gone from the bathroom and she was left alone.

Cora crawled on her hands and knees to the door. Tears and snot flowed down her face. The bathroom door was left open. Cora crawled outside.

It was dusk. She moved slowly across the ground. Brook and Erika were gone. Cora eventually stopped moving. Tremors returned to her body. Every inch of her body itched. It demanded relief, but Cora could not offer it anything. She was empty. She had overindulged and now there was nothing left.

The night started to grow cold. Cora wanted to make a fire, but she did not know how and she did not have the strength to move.

She could only stare up at the stars. The heavens were clear. As she laid there Cora could have sworn that she felt the Earth move. It swayed her gently through the stars.

The sounds of the woods amplified. Animals croaked and chirped out in the distance. Every few seconds a thud echoed through the trees.

Cora was mesmerized by the sounds. The thud was growing louder. It was the warning of the approaching storm.

Cora opened her eyes when the sound of the thud finished. In its place was heavy breathing. She looked up. The stars were gone. Instead there was the leathery face of an old bearded man.

The Avenger of Blood eclipsed the sky. He stared down at Cora with hollow eyes. His spearhead glistened in the moonlight.

Cora tried to scream. She tried to run, but there was no more fight in her.

The Avenger of Blood stepped down on Cora's hand. His boot crushed her fingers. She finally let out a deathly scream.

The pain paralyzed Cora in fear. She could not move. She could not fight back.

The blade came charging down. It pierced into Cora's arm. The Avenger of Blood's strength held Cora down. Then he began to saw the blade through her skin.

The Avenger of Blood peeled away at Cora's arms. She felt every slice of the blade. The pain made her alert. She was alive for the first time in years.

When the Avenger of Blood finished with her first arm he moved to her other. Drapes of tattooed skin were thrown across the ground. Blood soaked into the grass underneath Cora's mangled body.

Cora screamed and screamed, but nobody heard her. The pain was becoming too much. Cora started to black out. Her memories were growing jumbled.

She snapped back into consciousness. Cora was being dragged across the woods. Her arms were bloody. They tingled and burned.

Then she woke back up to see she was at the apse at the bottom of the sermon hill. The camp gates were wide open.

The Avenger of Blood stood over her. He gripped her wrists and dragged her to her feet. Then she dangled in the air. The Avenger of Blood held her with ease.

He lifted her farther. She dangled by the wrist. Her hand was placed up against the cross that decorated the sermon hill. Then a sharp pain went through her arm just below the wrists.

There was no more voice for Cora. Her face screamed silently into the night.

The Avenger of Blood let her go. She hung in the air stuck to the cross by her arm and a nail. Then the monster grabbed her other arm. He lifted her to the other side. Cora started to black out again.

She woke up one last time. Her arms were

stretched out. They were in even more pain than before. Blood dripped to the ground. Torches were lit all around her. She could hardly breathe. Every breath was a struggle.

She looked down and out. Campers were surrounding her. They all stared at her in terror. She hung crucified for display.

Behind her the gates were open. The Avenger of Blood had disappeared.

She was the first sacrifice. The Night of the Tenth had begun.

Pride

Brook could not believe it.

Her father had left her there. The summer was supposed to be the chance to spend time with him. After her parents' divorce four years ago her father moved to Colorado. It was states away from Brook and her mother in Virginia.

The plan for months had been that her dad would pick her up and they would road trip it back to Colorado. Just the two of them. But when they hit Kansas things changed. They were soon off of the interstate and driving along the highways and backroads of the Midwest.

Brook's mother was calling non-stop. First her father's phone. Then hers. The reception was spotty. Brook could never hold a conversation with her mother longer than two seconds.

When her mother finally got a hold of her father

the only thing he kept repeating was, "This is for her own good. She needs to be shown the light. You can't keep raising her like this."

It made Brook tense, but her father brushed it away with a beaming smile. He reassured Brook they were going to have fun this summer.

Then they pulled into Psalm Springs. Brook eyed the beaten and weathered sign that greeted them at the entrance. She had never heard of the place.

She knew her father found religion shortly after he moved. He constantly name dropped the Bible during their conversations over the phone. She never realized it was enough dedication to stop by a camp on their father/daughter road trip.

When he parked the car Brook's father turned to look at her. She was confused. Hundreds of other new campers walked past the car through the front gates of Psalm Springs. This was not part of the plan.

"I need you to listen to me, Brook," he said. "Your soul has been corrupted. I'm sorry. There was nothing I could do before. Your mother, God bless her soul, does not know what she has done. She led you astray."

"What? Dad, I'm fine," said Brook. "What is going on?"

"You're staying here for the summer," said her dad.

"No," said Brook. "We were going to spend the

summer together. I didn't agree to go to some camp."

"There is no arguing this, Brook. You are going."

"No," she said. "Take me home. I am not staying here."

"Yes, you are," he said. Then her dad took the keys out of the ignition. "This is as far as you go. You can get out of the car and go to the camp or we'll just sit here."

"This is crazy," said Brook.

Her dad remained silent. His stare went straight ahead. Brook found no argument that would turn him around.

"I want to go home," she said.

"You will go home when the summer is over. I believe in you," said her father. "You can do it."

"I'm not religious, Dad," she said. It was the first time she ever said those words to her father.

"I know," he answered back. "That is why you are coming here. I don't want you going to Hell. I am your father and I need to protect you."

It took another half hour of back and forth between the two in the car, but finally Brook gave in. She could no longer spend another second near her father. Brook got out of the car and slammed the door shut. Campers and parents around her gave her plenty of distance as they walked past her.

Before he left Brook's father said to her, "You'll do well here. I know you will. You're my daughter. You'll understand, and come to love Him. I expect to see you at the end. I'll pray for you."

Then he was gone. He was a dust trail in the horizon.

It was all Brook could think about during Pastor Robbins' welcoming sermon.

Every word he said, Brook laughed at. Pastor Robbins sounded as delusional as her dad. They spoke as if God was real. Brook knew better. She refused to believe that even if there was a God then somehow only one group of people got it right about Him.

Nothing was going to change her thinking. She could listen to every sermon Pastor Robbins wanted to give. She could read every page of the Bible. It wasn't going to change her mind. She thought religion was a crutch for people who couldn't handle their lives. She didn't need it or even want it.

Brook had to get out of there. She knew there was no way her dad was going to come back to get her early. He was adamant about Brook staying for the summer. She was going to have to rely on her next plan of action.

The health and safety of the campers was always a

huge concern. Brook had to rely on overcautious counselors and directors if she was going to be able to leave.

Brook decided to wait another day. It was only the first week. If she went to the nurse's office too early it would clearly look like she was trying to scam them. Another day would offer cushion and believability.

She could say it was the food. She wasn't used to it and now it was making her sick. They'd have to let her go home. Maybe it was the traveling? They were at different sea levels. It could be affecting her sinuses. Perhaps she was prone to migraines? They would have no way of knowing that. Did her dad give them her medical history? Did he even have her medical history?

The next morning, Brook played her role. She woke up complaining of pains. She let out moans that woke up several of the other girls in her cabin. She even went so far as to make herself throw up when she was alone in the bathroom stall. Like Brook had planned, one of the counselors came rushing to her aid.

The older girl was worried that Brook was getting sick. The counselor sent her down to see the nurse, Virginia.

Brook hunched over and held her stomach. She took baby steps out of the bathroom toward the medical ward. The counselor did not see Brook's uncontainable smile.

"Lie down for a bit," said Virginia. "You'll be fine by this afternoon."

Brook looked as gloomy as possible. Her eyes were red from rubbing them before getting to the medical ward. She said it was because she was up all night with pains.

In a croaked voice, Brook tried to talk to Virginia about her diagnosis. "Maybe I should just go home. I don't feel right."

Virginia glared at Brook through her thick rimmed glasses. "I've seen these illnesses before. It'll pass. I'm sure it's just a twenty-four hour bug."

"This feels like something else," groaned Brook.

"I find it is best to go about your day," said Virginia. "Once you start moving around you'll start to feel better."

"Maybe it's allergies?" suggested Brook. "I feel itchy. I think I'm having a bad reaction to something in the air. I really should not be here."

Virginia smiled. She took Brook by the hand. Her skin was soft to the touch. "Brook, I know what is going on. You want to leave. I'm not a fool."

Brook lowered her head. She could not look the old nurse in the eye while caught in a lie.

"There is an adjustment period," said Virginia. "I know. You have to get past that. Pray to God. He will help you. We all will. That is what we are here for. You will find comfort and salvation here. It's only been two days. That is not nearly enough time to see what God can do."

Brook grumbled. Her plan had failed. Virginia put her arm around the defeated girl and gave her a gentle rub for comfort. Even in Brook's disappointment the embrace felt comforting. Without even wanting to Brook started crying.

"You can rest in one of the patient rooms if you like," said Virginia. "Take a breather and recollect yourself. It's going to be a good summer. You'll learn more about yourself than you ever thought possible. It starts with today."

Brook took Virginia up on her offer. She went in to the other room to lie down. Her scheming was exhausting. She thought it was a good time for a nap. There would be more time to figure out a way to get out of Psalm Springs.

Her next opportunity presented itself just later that afternoon. Pastor Robbins stopped by to check on Brook still in the medical ward. He was a surprise to her. When he walked in Brook was still asleep. She opened her eyes to see Robbins and Virginia smiling down on her.

"Good afternoon," said Pastor Robbins. "I hope you are feeling better."

Brook sat up in her bed. She nodded yes. "I'm starting to."

"That's great," said Virginia. She handed Brook a glass of water. "Here you go."

"Thank you," said Brook as she took the glass.

Virginia left without another word. She left Brook alone with Pastor Robbins. He remained standing bedside. Once the door was closed behind Virginia he began to speak.

"I understand you want to leave," he said. "I would encourage you not to."

Brook remained quiet. She wasn't sure how to respond.

"It's okay," assured Pastor Robbins. "This camp isn't for everybody. We welcome them. We always will. But that does not mean you have to stay."

"You mean I can go?" Brook asked.

"If you wish," said Robbins. "Your father enrolled you in the camp. I hope you don't mind I looked at your records before I stopped by. He says that you lost your way. You've lost faith in God. That's a shame. Really, just spending a little bit of time here can help.

You'll be shown the true power of God. It's breathtaking.

"If you don't then I can't actually stop you. It truly must be up to you if you want to accept God. We cannot force you. It does not work like that."

"Just like that, I can go?" Brook asked again. She was shocked at the turn of events.

"Yes," said Pastor Robbins. "I warn you though. Beyond the gates of our camp your sins will lead to your doom."

Brook rolled her eyes. She could not stand the hyperbole that church goers always gave her. Everything was hellfire and brimstone with those people.

"Thank you," she said. "I'll take my chances."

"I hope you find the answers you are looking for," said Pastor Robbins. "I will pray for you until then. Tomorrow, you and several others will be able to go. Please, enjoy the rest of your day. It was a pleasure meeting you."

"Same," said Brook.

Then Pastor Robbins left. Brook could not help but smile. She was on her way out.

The next day, Brook was surprised to see twenty other campers waiting at the gates to leave. She thought there would have been more. How could anybody possibly stand this camp? Brook thought they were idiots for believing all of this.

Brook stood quietly in the middle of the group. Shoulders and arms brushed up against her. Everybody was eager to go.

"Watch it," said a girl standing beside Brook.

"Sorry," Brook replied. Brook wasn't even sure if she was the one the girl was talking to. It was getting crowded in their area.

"Goddammit," yelled a guy toward the back. "Let's go already."

The rest of the crowd cheered on the request. The girl Brook had apologized to rolled her eyes.

"Now, is not the time to be an asshole," said the girl to herself. Brook looked over and saw her gently rocking in her shoes.

"Are you okay?" Brook asked.

The girl looked over. "I'm fine," she said. "It's just a little tight. I wish they'd open the gates too."

More yelling started to emerge from the crowd. The campers could not spend another minute at Psalm Springs.

"It's not going to make them move any faster," the girl said again.

"It's stupid," said Brook. "They brought us here

against our will to try and brainwash us. They should be yelled at."

"They didn't bring us here," said the girl. "Our parents brought us here. They are just doing their jobs. It's just a camp. We shouldn't be getting mad at them. They are letting us go."

Now, Brook rolled her eyes. She didn't want to admit the girl was right. "They still shouldn't even have this camp. Religion is a crutch. All it's done is caused wars over whose imaginary friend is better. They should not be celebrating it. We could be at a space camp or something."

"It's just a camp," said the girl. "People like different things. There's no reason to get mad about it."

The campers in the head of the group started to rattle the gates in front of them. Their patience was gone. It was time to leave.

Pastor Robbins walked toward the group. Two counselors accompanied him. He looked depressed. His eyes glanced at every single one of the campers.

"Good morning," he said. "I really hope some of you have reconsidered your decision. God does not want you to go.

"Do not carry your sins like trophies. You will not be able to take God's hand when your arms are full.

Proverbs 16:5, *everyone who is arrogant in heart is an abomination to the Lord; be assured, he will not go unpunished.*

"Once you are beyond these gates your judgment will be at hand. You have not atoned and God does not like sinners. You are not protected out there. When you die your soul will go to Hell along with your sins. God's power is great. He is to be feared and obeyed."

Brook could not believe what Pastor Robbins was saying. He was telling them that they were going to Hell.

"You go to Hell!" said somebody in the group. Everybody else started to laugh. Pastor Robbins shook his head. He could not get through to any of the campers.

Then just as they had hoped the gates began to open. The campers did not wait. As soon as the gate was open enough for one person they started to spill out of Psalm Springs.

The group spread out. Now that they were outside of the gates they felt free. They allowed space between each other. It was a relief for Brook and the girl she had been talking to.

"It's about time," Brook mumbled.

"That is much better," said the girl as she stretched

out her arms. Her body was less jittery now that she had room to breathe.

Once the last camper was out the gates started to close behind them. With a loud metal clang the gates closed and locked back up.

Brooked looked all around. She did not see any cars waiting for them. There was a whole fleet of vans that dropped off several of the campers. Where were they now to give them a ride home?

Pastor Robbins came up to the gate. "I will pray for you all during your time of judgment. I pray that I am wrong and God will see to it to spare your life and your soul for the time being. Sin is a difficult thing to defeat. May you be stronger in His eyes."

Then Robbins turned around and walked off with his counselors. The group of campers on the outside was left on their own.

"What the hell?" Brook said. "He just left us."

More concerns were heard from the group.

"Where do we go?"

"No cars?"

"How do we get out of here?"

"We're just going to have to walk," said the girl Brook had been talking to. She came to the front of the group to present herself. She was taking charge.

"We'll just have to walk to a main road. Somebody

will stop for us. We're not just a single hitchhiker. We're a big group. We'll be okay."

"Fuck those guys!"

"Yes, yes," responded the girl, reluctantly. "They're assholes. Now, listen please. Find a partner, a walking buddy. We're on a road, but these are still the woods and can be dangerous. Do not wander off. If we stick together we will be fine."

The group started their trek. Brook found herself partners with the girl that was leading them. Nobody talked much once they were moving. It was still early and all of their energy was concentrated on the hike.

The road through the woods was convoluted. It weaved through the trees with a natural flow. They made very little progress in their first half hour.

They turned around another bend, and the group stopped. The former campers in the back bumped into each other, unaware of the group's actions upfront.

Up ahead a figure stood in the middle of the road. The Avenger of Blood was an imposing sight. Its matted beard and leathery face stood out against the sunlight. A shiver went down Brook's spine.

"Who is that?"

"We should go another way."

"It must be a local."

The group did not move any further. The Avenger of Blood stayed in place. They were at an impasse.

Then Brook's partner stepped forward. She was the unofficial spokesperson for the group.

"Don't go over there," warned Brook. "I don't like this."

"He might be able to help," said the girl. "We need to try."

Brook's partner walked toward the Avenger of Blood. She waved at him and kept her other arm down and out. She did not want to scare off the stranger.

"Hello," she called out. "Can you help us? We're trying to get out of the woods. The faster the better."

Brook's partner kept walking forward as she talked. Then the Avenger of Blood began to approach her.

"We left the camp nearby, Psalm Springs. I'm sure you know it. They just kind of dumped us outside the gate. Have they done this before?"

As the Avenger of Blood got closer Brook could see more of the details of the man. Its face never changed. It was the same expression at every moment. She realized the man was wearing a mask.

"Come back here, now!" Brook screamed out.

Her partner got the same idea. She could see the hulking killer continue to walk closer to her. In its hand the blade of his spearhead glinted in the light.

The girl turned away to run. The group began to panic. None of them knew what to do. Brook remained still. She was ready to move if she needed to, but she did not know to where. She waited to see what was going to happen next.

Despite the girl rushing back to the group the Avenger of Blood kept up with her. Its stride was long and fast. A simple walk for the Avenger of Blood was a staggering jog for the girl.

Brook gave her partner an embrace when she reached the group. It did not stop the Avenger of Blood.

The behemoth crashed into the group of campers. Its spearhead went directly for Brook's walking partner. The blade dove into her spine. She screamed out, but it was cut off by her dying whimper.

More screams echoed out into the woods. Many campers tried to run, but they only made it as far as the next camper beside them. They tumbled to the ground tripping over each other.

The Avenger of Blood began the Lord's judgment. Every swipe of the spearhead struck another camper. Blood spilled out to the dirt. Bodies began to litter the road.

Brook fell to the ground with her partner's body. It

was then she realized she never even learned her name. This girl died trying to help the rest of them. Brook was not going to die like that. She was not going to die as just another camper.

Run.

Run was the only thing going through Brook's mind. She had to escape. The Avenger of Blood was going after somebody else. She could run. She could run into the woods and disappear.

There were more screams as the Avenger of Blood caught other sinners at the end of his blade.

Brook forced herself up. She got to her feet. There was no more time to waste.

Run.

She ran off. She ran into the woods. Every tree was a blur. Branches struck her across the face, but she did not feel any one of them. Brook dared not look back. She was afraid that if she did then she would see the Avenger of Blood hot on her tail. If she just kept moving forward then she could never get caught.

Finally, she ran out of breath. Brook braced up against a tree. She breathed in deeply to her burning lungs. She looked out from where she had come. There was nothing. She was alone.

The screams were gone. Brook had no idea how many others survived, if any. Was there any way to meet up with them?

This was not what she asked for. She wanted to leave the camp. She wanted to go home. She did not want to be attacked by a maniac in a mask.

Psalm Springs had a killer. Brook could hardly believe it. They were so desperate to get people to stay they hired a murderer to kill anybody that would try to leave. This camp was filled with monsters.

Her legs hurt. Her feet ached to be left alone. Then the rest of Brook's body followed suit. But there was nothing else to do except keep moving.

The road in the woods was disorienting. She had no idea where she was in relation to the camp or any of the main roads that lead there.

With no other decision for her, Brook continued on. She turned back around and began to head out in the direction she was running originally, away from the massacre.

But she was not free.

The Avenger of Blood was out in the distance. He had gotten ahead of her. Brook stumbled back. She did not want to go back the way she came. There had to be another path nearby. It was the only way the Avenger of Blood could have gotten there so fast. While she was running around trees the killer was walking freely along a road.

Brook turned and ran. The Avenger of Blood followed chase. Every time Brook turned around to see, the Avenger of Blood was getting closer.

He never got tired. He never needed to rest.

The trees all looked the same. Brook ran as fast as she could with her legs begging to stop. She never ran like this before. She could not keep it up forever. She needed to find a way to get away from the Avenger of Blood.

There was a slope out to the left. Brook looked over. A river cut through the woods at the bottom of the ravine. She slid down the small slope. The last few yards she started to tumble. There was no time to recover. Brook got to her feet and stepped into the water.

The river was cold. Her toes curled up to try and stay warm. Behind her Brook could see the Avenger of Blood at the top of the hill. He looked down on her.

There was no time to lose. Brook jumped into the river. She submerged to get completely covered and try to adjust to the water's icy touch. Pins and needles prickled her skin. Her body shuddered as it dealt with the sudden rush of cold sensation.

The river started to take her away, but Brook kicked back to the surface. The air was cool against her wet skin. She clung for every breath she could take. The woods were moving by her. She was being carried away by the current. Back up the river she could see the Avenger of Blood standing by the shore.

The pursuer then stepped into the river.

Brook panicked. The Avenger of Blood was not going to stop. She swam as hard as she could to reach the shore on the other side of the river. Once she touched ground again she pushed herself up and farther out of the water.

The shore and the woods were welcoming. Brook took a second to catch her breath. The Avenger of Blood was nowhere to be seen. He had disappeared into the river. Brook hoped the bastard drowned in the current.

After a few steps forward she heard water splashing against the river. Brook shook her head in wide eyed disbelief. The Avenger of Blood emerged from under the surface. He was not bothered by the force of the river at all.

Run.

She was not going to give up. She could survive this. There was a way out. Brook knew it. If only there was a way she could take a minute to think of a new plan. The Avenger of Blood was on top of her every second.

The killer was relentless. He was never out of sight of Brook. She ran as fast as she could, but he followed her with ease. The trees could not hide her. This was the Avenger of Blood's domain.

As Brook ran, dread started to fill her heart. A new obstacle was waiting for her.

A metal rod fence stretched out through the woods as far as she could see. She was running into a dead end.

Brook turned to her right to see if there was any end in sight. She ran along the fence looking for anything that would help. The bars were too close together. She could not squeeze through them. Behind her the Avenger of Blood was close by.

Then she saw the door. The gated door was covered in vines. Brook nearly missed it. For the first time since starting the chase she stopped for more than a few seconds.

The door was locked in place. She fumbled with the handle to get it open. Rust and grime held a tight grip on the door.

Brook was panicking. The Avenger of Blood continued to get closer. With every step the mighty follower was getting bigger. Brook pulled harder on the lock. The killer's breathing was deafening in her ears. He was nearly on top of her.

The Avenger of Blood was only yards away now. His blade was raised above his head. Judgment was going to be swift.

She heard a screeching of metal. The lock pried loose and the door swung open. Brook dashed inside. She pulled the gate closed behind her. The bars vibrated from the force.

Brook fell to the ground. That was it. Her energy was gone. She rolled on to her back. Looking up she saw the Avenger of Blood staring back at her.

For the first time she saw his eyes. They were glazed over. The pupils were dull. Even then she could tell the Avenger of Blood was looking right at her.

Brook waited. She could not move. She waited for the Avenger of Blood to burst through the gate and make his final move.

He never did.

The two continued their glares. Then the Avenger of Blood turned away. Just like that he began to walk back into the woods. Brook listened to his footsteps. Each one was a stomp that trailed through the woods.

Soon that was all she could hear. Then he was gone. Brook was truly alone.

She had made it back into the security of Psalm Springs.

Brook stuck close to the fence. She was only at the camp for a few days, but where she was now looked very different. The trees and the foliage looked unkempt. She walked along the fence line for an hour. She moved slowly. Her adrenaline was wearing off. Every little cut that she received while running through the bush was begging to get noticed. She was in worse condition than she thought.

In the distance, Brook could hear a low mechanical humming. Her heart began to race faster. She was reaching some kind of sign of civilization. A new gateway was visible along the fence.

Just like before the gate had not been used in years and was difficult to open. Brook was thankful she was not being chased. She was able to take her time and get the lock open with little drama.

Going through the gate was like entering an entirely different world. The sun shone brighter on the greener grass. The noise was coming from several generators that were connected to the rest of the camp.

Brook was careful to close the gate behind her. Then she covered it up with some of the vines that were overgrowing along the fence. She did not want anybody to know how she got back in. The less people knew about her the better.

She had to do everything she could to erase her tracks because she knew she was going to have to get help. Her vision was getting blurry. Any quick move caused her to become dizzy.

Brook made her way to the medical ward. She remembered how nice Virginia was. Brook could only hope that she was still just as nice and forgiving. None of them wanted Brook to leave. Brook was relying on that still being true.

She stumbled into the medical ward. A counselor that was behind the front desk rushed over to Brook. The counselor called out for Virginia to come help her with the injured girl.

"Oh dear," said Virginia as she came from the hallway. "Brook, what are you doing here?"

Brook mumbled words that nobody understood.

"I prayed that you would come back," said Virginia as she took Brook toward one of the patient rooms. "I prayed for you all to come back. God picked you."

Brook was tended to. Her wounds were disinfected and bandaged up. She was given plenty of water and a full stomach. Every minute Brook was at the medical ward she thought the door would come bursting open. Somebody would be coming to get her. She just knew it. The Avenger of Blood would find her or Pastor Robbins would throw her back out beyond the fence.

That moment never came. The next day, Virginia said Brook was allowed to go back out to the camp. She would be fine. There were no major injuries.

"You've been given a second chance to bring God into your heart. He believes in you," said Virginia before Brook left for the rest of the camp. "I'm sorry you had to go through what you did, but that is the true power of God.

"1 Corinthians 10:9-11, *we should not test the Lord, as some of them did- and were killed by snakes. And do not grumble, as some of them did- and were killed by the destroying angel. These things happened to them as examples and were written down as warnings for us, on whom the fulfillment of the ages has come.*

"You might not understand it, but He is cleansing the world of sin and preparing our souls for Heaven. You are stronger now for bearing witness. Cherish it. He cherishes you."

Brook was free to go. She started the next day simply walking around the camp. Nobody was stopping her. Nobody was surprised or concerned that she was still alive.

With her newfound freedom Brook decided to take

action. She knew she couldn't walk out of there, but she knew she could not stay at Psalm Springs.

First, she wanted to get out of sight. Everywhere she went there were campers with Bibles in their hands or counselors praising the word of God. Brook couldn't stand it.

The next day she returned to the gate leading to the abandoned part of the camp. It was early in the morning. Not too many other campers were out yet. The gate had not been tampered with. The vines Brook had placed on the door were still there.

She went to the other side then waited. She had to be sure the area was really forgotten. She sat under a tree a few yards away from the fence. Brook had gathered some fruit from the cafeteria before she left. She was going to make sure the gate remained unused.

Brook went undisturbed the entire day. None of the counselors came her way. Nobody came looking for her.

The next day was the same thing. Brook's suspicions were correct. The area she found was really abandoned. It was closed off from the rest of the camp. Brook was alone out there.

The third day of being at the abandoned section Brook decided to wander around. She followed the fence line in the opposite direction from when she had arrived.

There was very little in an actual path. Brook had to step through bushes and branches that cut wildly against her legs. She stayed hidden in the tree line just in case anybody could see her through the fence.

The fence curved away from the rest of Psalm Springs. Brook followed the fence with her back to the rest of the camp.

As she continued her path she stopped in her tracks. There was another gate.

Brook's heart jumped a beat. Where did this exit lead?

Hesitantly, Brook approached the new area. She kept low to the ground. Her legs were ready to run at a moment's notice. A new gate meant another entrance for the Avenger of Blood.

Brook continued to look in every direction. There was no sign of the Avenger of Blood. Then she looked out to the open woods. Details started to pop out at her.

It was more than woods. She caught the sight of a Jesus statue poking its head out of the grass. The Virgin Mary had her arms open around hundreds of weeds. Several crosses started to reveal themselves. Brook was looking at a cemetery.

The more she looked at it the more she saw.

Headstones were scattered around the area. She could not count how many wooden crosses were staked in the ground. None of the names were legible. They were old. The elements had erased the names of the dead from time. The dead were damned to be forgotten.

Brook dared not go further. She couldn't bear to think about how many people had died at the camp.

She returned to the main section of Psalm Springs. There had been enough snooping for the day. She needed to rest and figure out what to do next about her situation.

Unfortunately for Brook, there was not much time for rest. The next day was the first Sunday for the campers and everybody was called down to the sermon hill.

Brook sat in the back at the top of the hill. She did not want to be seen not paying attention. When Pastor Robbins starting talking again about how God was so great, Brook wanted to scream out what had happened to her. She wanted to revel in their hypocrisy.

Then Erika was dragged out.

Erika was screaming as loud as she could. She needed help. She was pleading for any of the campers to come save her. Nobody moved.

The counselors began to carry Erika to the opening gates. Brook sat straight up. She knew what was out there. She knew what was waiting for Erika.

The Avenger of Blood returned from the woods. His footsteps preceded his appearance. Brook ducked down out of sight. She was afraid the Avenger of Blood would see her and decide that she would not get away this time.

From between the people in front of Brook, she watched as Erika was attacked and then dragged away by the killer in the woods.

Brook started seeing flashes of the first attack when she was with the other campers leaving the area. They cried out for help and nobody came. She remembered her partner that she never got the name of. The girl was on her own.

Then Brook decided that was not going to happen anymore. There would be somebody to help. Brook would be there to help.

There was no time to waste. Brook ran off from the hill. There was still hope. The grand gate at the bottom of the hill was on the same side as the cemetery.

Brook ran to the generators. There was nobody watching. They were all at the sermon. As fast as she could, Brook ran through the abandoned camp toward the second gate of the fence. She had to help Erika. She was the only one that would.

Out of breath, Brook reached the edge of the perimeter. She was worried she was going to be too late, but when she arrived Brook could hear the wails of Erika.

Brook looked out and there she was in the middle of the cemetery. Erika was on the ground. Her bloody figure lay on top of a pile of stones. The Avenger of Blood was nowhere to be found.

This was her moment. Brook had to decide. She could still turn back. She could pretend like this never happened. She had to survive too.

Then she stepped forward. The gate creaked open. Brook was outside of the fenced area in just two short steps. There was no way left to go but forward.

Erika writhed in pain. Her clothes were stained red. The stones below her dripped of blood from her wound. Closer, Brook could see that Erika had been placed on a pile of stones formed to a giant cross.

Brook charged up to her. Erika screamed at the sudden entrance.

"Shhh, shhhh, it's okay," said Brook. "I can help you."

Erika continued to scream. She swatted Brook

away.

"I'm here to help you," said Brook. "My name is Brook. I can get you out of here."

Finally, Brook had to cover Erika's mouth with her hand. It did little good, but Erika eventually got the message to quiet down.

Brook held Erika's head firmly. She stared at the girl.

"Where is he?" Brook asked.

Erika shook her head. She had no idea.

"Can you get up?" Brook asked.

Erika looked down at her leg. It was bleeding and already starting to swell.

"I'll help you up," said Brook. She put Erika's arm over her shoulder. Hastily, she started to lift Erika up to her feet. Erika screamed out in pain again.

"You're gonna have to deal with it," said Brook. "I can't carry you. We have to move fast. It's just over here. Past the fence. You can make it."

They hobbled together past headstones of former campers lost to the sins of damnation. Each one gave Brook the extra boost needed to take another step further. She was not going to be like the others. She was not going to die for somebody else's truth.

Another scream erupted from Erika. Brook turned back to see what she was scared of. The Avenger of

Blood was back. He stood across the cemetery from them. The foreboding breathing returned.

"Move!" Brook ordered.

They limped faster through the weeds. The Avenger of Blood was on the move. He was charging for the two girls.

Ten feet.

Five feet.

Brook and Erika were almost there. She never looked back, but she could hear the footsteps of the Avenger of Blood. He was gaining on them.

They were right at the fence. Dead leaves signaled the Avenger of Blood's presence. He was right on top of them.

Erika tripped over a small rock on the ground at the entrance of the fence. She did not know it was there. The door was wide open. Erika's body collapsed on the ground taking Brook with her.

Brook reached out with desperation. She grabbed the gate and swung it closed with her momentum. It slammed shut as she fell to the ground inside the perimeter.

They hit the dirt hard. Brook tumbled over to see their attacker. The Avenger of Blood stood only a few feet from them. The killer was still. It looked at the two girls with curious eyes, shifting its head back and forth.

They were back in the fenced perimeter. The Avenger of Blood would not cross the line. Brook was silently relieved. She did not stop though.

Brook returned to her feet. She grabbed hold of Erika and started to drag her away from the fence and the Avenger of Blood. The angel of death watched as the two girls disappeared deeper into the abandoned camp.

Brook got Erika back up to her feet. They walked together slowly through the wooded area. It was growing less dense. They were able to see more.

Up ahead, Brook saw the first structure since being in the abandoned area. It was an old bathhouse similar to the ones they had in the rest of the camp. The building looked decrepit. Part of the roof was caved in. It smelled of piss and rot. They went inside anyway.

Brook laid Erika down against the wall. Her leg was doing worse since the run. Brook took the moment to finally catch her breath. A smile couldn't help but creep across her face. She was alive. Still.

"Thank you," said Erika.

"You're welcome," replied Brook. "How are you?"

"Not good," said Erika. She glared at Brook for

asking such a stupid question. "What do we do now?"

"I don't know," said Brook.

"You rescued me, and now you have no plan?"

"I wasn't thinking it through," said Brook. "I just thought I could save you. Fuck. I don't know what to do. We can't leave. That guy is out there."

"What if he finds us here?" Erika asked.

"I don't think he will," said Brook. "He won't go past the fence. It's some kind of rule."

"Are you sure?"

"He didn't follow us just now. He didn't follow me when I first got through the fence. What's he waiting for then?"

"So, now what?" Erika asked.

"We have to go back to the camp," said Brook.

"Hell no!" cursed Erika. "I am not going back there. Are you crazy? They tried to kill me."

"I went back. They let me go after that. I was welcomed back like I was just learning a lesson."

"Fuck that," said Erika. "I am not going back there. Especially not like this." Erika gestured at her leg. She could hardly walk.

"Fine," said Brook. "I will go back. I'll try to get you some food and some stuff for your leg. You can stay here, hidden."

"Then what?"

"Then we'll figure out how the hell to get out of here."

Brook returned to the everyday normality of Psalm Springs. Every day she went to class, Bible study, and laughed with the other campers. The classes were unbearable. Pastor Robbins talked about sin as if it was going to destroy the world.

She had been hurting nobody. She did not deserve to be thrown out to the lions for slaughter.

In the evening, she escaped to the hidden bathhouse to tend to Erika. Brook was able to smuggle her food and water from the cafeteria.

When Brook wasn't in class she spent her time wandering through the camp. She needed to know what the schedules were for all of the counselors and Pastor Robbins. They were the ones in charge and the only ones with keys to the area.

Brook's only way of escape was by a vehicle. She knew she could not outrun the killer out in the woods. She could try to sneak by without him noticing, but then she would be alone out in the woods. It was not a favorable situation.

Sometimes in the evenings Brook would wander through the abandoned part of the camp. There was only the second gate near the cemetery. She tried to avoid it as much as possible.

Weeks later in June, on one of her walks Brook stumbled onto the wretched cabin. The building was still intact, far better than the bathhouse Erika was staying at.

As she got closer Brook started to rethink her original opinion. The floors were stained with blood. She hoped it was an animal's blood. That would be slightly more comforting.

Every step creaked through the cabin. The inside looked identical to the ones in the Psalm Springs proper. Beds were thrown about the room. Under all the debris and dirt Brook could see signs of the previous tenants. Old books and pictures were molded to the floor.

This was once a part of the camp. Then something terrible happened.

Brook came into the center of the room when she heard a soft moaning sound. It startled her. The floorboards groaned under her feet. She tried to stay quiet to listen. It did not sound like the Avenger of Blood.

She listened closely to try to find the source of the noise. It sounded close. In the corner of her eye she saw another door. Brook quietly walked over to it. She did not want to disturb the maker of the noise or draw attention to herself.

The door was partially closed. Brook came up to it. The moaning was growing louder. She was getting closer.

Brook waited. Nothing was happening. Nobody knew she was there. Then she cracked the door wider and peeked in.

She was stunned to see another camper there. Hayden was nearly unconscious. His red hair was grungy. His skin was pail. He looked like a corpse waiting to happen.

Brook rushed over to him. She brought out her bottle of water and force fed Hayden some of it.

"Hello? Are you okay? Do you understand me?" she asked.

Hayden was non-responsive. He looked too fragile to carry on a conversation.

"My name is Brook," she said. "I'm going to take care of you."

Suddenly, the entire burden was on Brook. She now had two helpless and stubborn campers to look after. Hayden did not want to return to the camp, but he demanded a lot from it. Brook was constantly charging phone batteries and getting him all kinds of food. Every other day was an argument with him about the food she brought for him. She would tell him to go get it himself. Hayden would just shrug and go about playing whatever stupid game the phone had on it.

Erika was a different story. Brook did not want her returning to camp. Erika was ready to scream. She had every right to be furious. They had thrown her out as an example for the others. If Erika ever returned to the camp there would be hell to pay.

Brook was able to keep things together with the three of them. She never mentioned Erika to Hayden. He did not need to know.

Then Gabe and Justin came along.

Brook heard the commotion during the night. The counselors were out looking for the two of them. She saw them capture Justin and take him to the gates by the hill. Brook stuck to the shadows. She dared not interfere while the counselors and Pastor Robbins were preparing for judgment.

Then she watched as Gabe came around. Justin called out for him. He begged Gabe to help him, but Gabe kept his back turned. Brook could not believe he was not going to help. Brook had no other choice but to step in.

Bringing the two of them to the cabin added complications. She now had to trust the entire group.

If one was caught or returned to the camp they all risked capture.

Brook tried to play it smart. She knew Hayden would never leave. He did not care enough. She had to rely on Gabe. He was more than eager to leave the cabin. He and Justin were far from friends anymore.

Justin could not risk going back to the camp. The counselors knew what he looked like. They expected him to be dead.

Brook had Gabe doing much of her old routine. He came just in time. Many of the campers were starting to earn the trust of the counselors and Pastor Robbins. They were given more responsibility. Some of them even had keys and access to off limit parts of the camp. Brook wanted to keep an eye on who they were and what they did. Gabe offered a second pair of eyes to keep an eye on the entire operation.

Brook tried to get keys for herself. She asked to volunteer at several of the offices. Each one turned her down. Her reputation preceded her. The counselors knew Brook was one of the campers that left in the first week. That fact that she made it back did not help her. She was going to have to do more to earn the kind of trust that it took to get keys, and she was too busy keeping her head down to do that. Brook was going to have to rely on the deceit of others if she was going to get access to anything.

Her plan was coming together. Brook figured they could steal a set of keys during one of the classes. The counselor always kept them in her bag. A simple distraction would allow Brook the chance to grab them. They would be free of Psalm Springs by the next night fall. If that didn't work they could sneak into the main office through the window Hayden broke. Brook wanted as many plans as possible. She was not going to take any chances.

Then everything started to fall apart.

Gabe and Justin did not get along since the night Brook brought them to the cabin. Hayden did not help. He continued to push both of them into arguments and fights. It was Hayden's way of finding entertainment whenever Brook did not charge any batteries.

First, Gabe never returned from an errand at the main camp. Brook and Justin went out to find him. They had to split up. Brook needed to find Gabe. If he did anything brash her whole operation could crumble. They had to find him before the counselors did.

She sent Justin back toward the entrance of the main camp to look around. Her area was deeper in the abandoned campsite. She knew the area better than

Justin.

Brook started by checking out the area near the entrance at the generators. She thought Gabe might have tried to find his way back to the camp, but gotten lost. He had only been that way once, she believed.

When Brook returned to the cabin later that day she discovered Justin had never returned. Brook was forced to go back out there and continue the search, this time for both Gabe and Justin.

"Gabe! Gabe! Justin!" she called out for hours. There was never any reply. The day was ending and Brook was running out of time. If she didn't find Gabe or Justin before dusk then she would have to give up and try again tomorrow. It would do her no good to look in the dark.

She had one last shot at finding them before nightfall. Brook headed directly to the cemetery. Her new worry was that one of them found the exit and tried to leave. She warned them about the Avenger of Blood, but he was something you had to see for yourself.

Brook stayed by the fence line. The sun was almost down. The trees cast huge shadows over the graveyard. Somewhere in the dark Brook could hear the sounds of shuffling against the dead leaves. Brook looked out and her stomach dropped. The gate to the fence was open. The door swung lightly in the wind.

Brook held her breath for a better listen. The sound she heard was becoming clearer. It was not the fateful footsteps of the Avenger of Blood. It was something else. It sounded like something dragging across the ground.

"Gabe? Justin?" Brook whispered into the night. She did not want to yell. She feared it would alert the killer.

"Guys? Is that you?"

The sound stopped. The woods became dead silent.

Brook tried to adjust to the low light. Hidden in the shadows across the cemetery was the familiar yellow shirt of Psalm Springs.

"Who's out there?" Brook asked.

Without realizing it, Brook stepped out beyond the fenced perimeter. Her desire to get a closer look at the camper was more powerful than her desire for protection.

She was so focused on the other side of the cemetery she was not paying attention to the path in front of her. Brook tripped over something hidden in the leaves. Her palms took the brunt of the fall. Pain echoed through her wrists.

Brook looked at what she had tripped over. It was Justin. His dead body stared back at her with terror frozen eyes. His throat had been slit.

Brook shuffled away from the body. Justin must have wandered out past the fence earlier. He did not listen to Brook, and now he was dead.

She was disoriented. The night was growing darker. The fence disappeared into the trees. She could not tell which way to go to return to the camp area.

More noise came from behind her. She looked over. The other camper was coming toward her with a shovel in hand. It was too dark to see who it was.

Then suddenly the camper stopped. Brook got up to one knee. Before she could get a good look at the person he turned around. The guy was sprinting away like he had seen a ghost.

Brook got back to her feet and dusted herself off. She had to get back to the fence line. Her search was over. Justin was dead, Gabe was still missing and it looked like the camp was covering it up.

Then she was grabbed from behind.

The smell of decay filled her nostrils as a hand covered her mouth.

The camper did not run because of her. He ran because the Avenger of Blood was behind her.

One arm held tightly to her. The other was raised high in the air, blade in hand.

She did not hesitate. Instinct kicked in. She bit down hard on the Avenger of Blood's hand. Flesh and blood tore away into her mouth.

The hand released Brook. She tumbled forward. The Avenger of Blood stepped forward to grab her again, but Brook did not stop moving. Leaves and dirt flew into the air as Brook got traction and started to run.

She had to circle around the Avenger of Blood. She had to run the opposite direction as the camper. That was the way back to the abandoned camp ground.

The Avenger of Blood stood motionless as Brook made her escape. She was in such a rush that she almost hit the fence. Her banged up hands took another hit against the metal bars. Then Brook felt her way to the opening. With one final push she threw herself across the fence line. The door clanged shut behind her. Once again she was safe from the final judgment of the Avenger of Blood.

Tears, both mournful and joyous, came rushing out of her. Brook's plan was at jeopardy, but she was still alive.

She could still taste the Avenger of Blood in her mouth. It was a taste that would not go away.

Brook was going to have to come up with a new

plan. She was going to have to figure out a way to stop the Avenger of Blood. She knew now that she could hurt it.

Gabe never returned. Brook assumed he was dead, but she had to prepare for the worst. Gabe could have turned on her and the rest of the group. He could have given up Justin and the counselors could be on their way to the cabin.

She warned Hayden to disappear for a couple of days until she was sure nobody was coming for her. He merely shrugged her off. He wasn't going anywhere.

Brook left the cabin and went into hiding with Erika at the bathhouse. She never told Gabe or Justin about it. They had a chance of not being discovered there.

After a few days, everything started to go back to normal. Brook lingered around the camp. She was relieved when none of the counselors were after her. There was no search going on. It was just a regular day in Psalm Springs.

Nobody came around to the cabin. Every day Brook came to check on the place Hayden was just a little more pissed off. He was hungry. He was bored. And it was all Brook's fault.

Now, Brook had to rebuild her plan from scratch. She was once again left without allies that would return to the main camp. Her network was growing thinner by the day.

She always listened in on conversations and tried to discern who was likely to help her. Anybody that showed a lack of interest in the Bible or bitched about wanting to go home Brook kept a note of. As the summer rolled into the end of July, her list grew shorter. People were crossed off when she started to hear them praise God and enjoy reading the Bible over and over again.

Then Brook stumbled onto another rumor. Word was going around about Cora. She was caught having sex with one of the boys. They were calling her a slut and many proclaimed she should be thrown out beyond the gates.

Brook could not stand to listen to the other campers talk like that. Cora did not deserve that. As she got more details about the incident involving Cora a new plan began to form in Brook's head.

Cora was found drunk and high. It meant she had access to contraband. Brook wanted to know how that was possible. She needed the connections.

When Brook felt the coast was clear she made her move. In the cover of night Brook snuck into the medical ward and found Cora's room. She startled the fragile girl.

With some convincing Brook was able to get Cora to come with her. Cora looked in bad shape, and it sounded like the medical ward was doing her no good. Brook remembered the first time she came there. Virginia had immediately dismissed her. The old nurse could help, but Brook worried that she relied too much on the power of God instead of modern medicine.

Brook was forced to bring Cora to the bathhouse with Erika. Cora was more delicate than she had thought. Brook did not know the whole story.

Erika was not thrilled. They just lost two people that knew about Brook's existence. If they lost Cora after showing her the cabin and the bathhouse all would be lost.

They let Cora rest the first night. Brook could use another day, but then they would need to get moving on a new plan. Time was running out.

The three girls sat together by camp fire inside the bathhouse. The smoke wafted out into the night sky.

"Can you tell us what happened?" Brook asked.

Cora remained silent. She still looked weak, but Brook had to push her. She needed information.

"Please?" asked Brook. "I need to know what you have been doing. You were found drunk. There was a bottle of wine in the cabin and a bottle of pills. Where did you get them?"

Cora looked away. She could not look either girl in the eyes.

"What does it matter?" Cora asked.

"It matters because it might be a way out," said Brook. "I'm trying to get us out of here. I can't do it alone though. I need help. Robbins will not trust me with access to any of the buildings. You had a way to get items that were locked up. How did you do it?"

"She's fucking useless," said Erika, just loud enough for Cora to hear.

"Not now," said Brook. "She's not useless. She's hurt."

"We had parties," whispered Cora. Brook and Erika turned their attention to her. They leaned in to try to get every word Cora was saying.

"Morgan started them," said Cora. "He had a spot that you couldn't see from the camp. Hidden in the trees."

"Morgan has keys?" Brook asked.

"No… no, don't go to him," said Cora. "He… He…"

"What did Morgan do?"

Cora shook her head. She could not talk about it. The words she held back turned into tears.

"There were others," said Cora. "I don't remember. The last party, somebody brought the wine."

"You have to remember," said Brook. "Or I'm going to have to find Morgan."

"Please, don't," said Cora. "Do not bring him here."

"It was him wasn't it?" asked Erika. "He hurt you."

Cora dug her head into her arms and knees, and curled up into a ball. "Yes."

"Then he's the one that should be thrown out the gates," fumed Erika.

Brook rubbed her hands against her face. She needed to put everything together. Morgan was their only lead so far, but he was the one who raped Cora. Brook could not bring him into the circle. She refused.

"Neil," said Cora. "Neil could help."

"How?" Brook asked. She was relieved that Cora came up with a different name, but it was still one that brought Brook concern. She knew Neil. He was in several of her classes. He was never on her lists because he was always so gung ho about God and the camp.

In the past couple of weeks she noticed him more. At first, Brook thought Neil was working for the camp then she realized Neil was infatuated with her.

He was a lovesick puppy that followed Brook. He could never take his eyes off of her.

"He used to follow me around," said Cora. "He had a crush on me. I tried to use it to get stuff, but it didn't work. Even then he still couldn't get over me. When I started hanging out with Morgan we noticed Neil would watch from the distance. He never wanted to join us in the parties, but every now and then we would see him walk by or steal a glance our way. He knows who was at the party. He has some keys and knows others that do. He can help."

Brook was satisfied. She stopped with the questions and let Cora relax. There was a new lead and Brook was going to have to figure out how to exploit it.

There was only one thing Brook could do. She had to go straight up to Neil and confront him.

Several days passed. Brook stuck around to the camp and let Neil follow her around. She wanted to see what he did while following her. It was a game of cat and mouse, only it was a kitten following a rat.

Neil seemed harmless. Whenever Brook stopped Neil would stop around a group of campers to remain hidden. It never worked. The group never included him. Neil would just stand on the outside looking like he was a part of the whole.

Finally, Brook decided to make her move. She closed in on him. Neil panicked. Instead of running Neil froze. Brook was relieved. She did not want to have to chase him down.

"Hi," Neil said shyly. "What's up?"

"Cut the act," said Brook. "I know you've been following me."

"What?"

"I said enough," said Brook. "I need your help."

"Oh," said Neil. He was suddenly more curious. He leaned in close to Brook. Closer than what Brook was comfortable with. She could feel his breath on her face. "What do you need… sweetie?"

Brook let her annoyance slide. She had to play to her advantage. She placed her hand on Neil's arm. "I was hoping we could talk." Her voice got softer. Brook tried to be as gentle as she could.

"About what? I'm here for you. Are you having problems? We can be alone if you like," comforted Neil. Then he reached out and grabbed hold of Brook's shoulder. His arm was stiff and his grip was tight. Brook brought her own hand back in the hope that Neil would do the same.

"It's not just me that needs help," said Brook. "I'm with Cora. She also needs your help."

Neil's face soured. "She doesn't want my help."

"She was the one who told me about you," said Brook. "She said you were a great guy. She said I could rely on you."

She waited patiently while Neil thought about what Brook just told him. Then a smile came across his face.

"I will be your guys' light," said Neil. "Cora has had some problems and if you are with her then you must have some problems too. It was good that you are coming to me. I can help. God can help."

"No," said Brook. "I just need your help."

"It's all the same."

"You have to keep this a secret," said Brook. "Cora is scared. She doesn't want people to know about it. They are already talking about her enough."

"I know," said Neil. "That's why I want to help. I can redeem her."

"That's great," said Brook, insincerely.

"What do you need?" Neil asked.

"We need to get Cora to a hospital," said Brook.

"What about the medical ward?"

"It's not good enough," said Brook. "They don't have the resources to take care of her properly. We need to get her out of the camp."

"How do we do that?" Neil asked.

"We need one of the vans," said Brook. "Do you have access to the garage?"

"No," said Neil. "That was never my job."

"Do you know somebody that does?" Brook asked. She was getting impatient. Now that she knew Neil was only going to be a stepping stone she wanted to be done with the conversation.

"Yeah," said Neil. "Carl does, I think. I'll have to double check."

"Can you introduce me?" Brook asked. "If we can get his help then we can save Cora."

"I'll try and set it up. Give me a couple of days," said Neil.

"Thank you," said Brook. "And remember keep this a secret. The less people know the better. Cora will be very grateful. You'll be her hero, and mine."

A few days later, Brook's new plan started to come to fruition. Carl approached Brook. She was surprised at his confidence. He had no problem talking to her about her problem and how he could help.

Brook grew an instant liking to Carl. He was genuine, and his blonde hair and good looks were easy on the eyes.

"Brook, hey, wait up," waved Carl.

Brook stopped walking. She was shocked when Carl came up to her.

"How do you know me?" she asked.

"I've seen you around. Neil told me you needed my help," Carl said when he got close to Brook.

"Yeah," said Brook. "What did he tell you?"

"He said you needed access to the vans. I have that," said Carl. He jingled the keys in his pocket.

"You'll help us?" Brook asked.

Carl leaned in close to whisper to Brook. "Truth is I want out of here too. This place is nuts."

"Does Neil know that?"

"No," said Carl. "He's pretty naive about this whole place. He means well, but you know."

"Yeah, I get that," said Brook.

"When you get the van what will you do?" Carl asked.

"I plan on getting out of here," said Brook.

"Then count me in," said Carl.

"Good," said Brook. "I'll let you know when we are ready. I'm not ready to leave yet."

"You better hurry up then," said Carl. "The more time you waste the harder it will be to leave."

"I know," said Brook. "I'm going as fast as I can. There are complications."

"Fine," said Carl. "Just let me know."

"Why haven't you left yet?" Brook wondered.

"What?"

"You have the keys. You want to leave. Why haven't you done it then?"

"I guess I just needed a push. I was doing fine for a while, but things change. I have to get out of here now. The more people I have with me the better.

"Actually getting to the van will be the hardest part. It will take several people. There are counselors and receptionists in the main office building. I'm not stupid enough to try it on my own."

"Okay," said Brook. "I will let you know when I am ready. I just have to get a few things in order."

"I can't wait," said Carl.

Brook's complications came from Cora. She was getting worse. Her condition was not improving without any help from some medicine. It was Erika's suggestion that they get her back on her pills. It could help bring her back up and then they could wean her off. Erika was worried about the short term. They could not have Cora freaking out during their escape. They needed her ready.

Brook went out in search of Cora's remaining pills. They were left in her cabin. Once they got Cora back on her feet Brook planned on getting out of there.

There was only a few weeks left in the summer. The Night of the Tenth was looming.

When she got to the cabin she started riffling through Cora's belongings. There was not much. Cora said she had been basically kidnapped and brought to the camp. There was no opportunity to pack.

Then Brook saw Mindy. The poor girl was exiled to the back of the cabin. She was another doomed soul. Brook remembered Gabe talk about her. Mindy was desperate for attention. She wanted everybody to love her.

Brook could not turn away. She thought back to Carl's words. The more people the better if they were going to take one of the vans.

Mindy was brought to the cabin. Brook was able to keep her in the cabin which kept Erika's secret safe.

The pills were starting to help Cora. She was growing more comfortable and stable.

Brook's plan was coming together. She was now a group of six people. She thought that would be enough to secure one of the vans and they could all make their escape together. The killer in the woods would not be able to catch them.

Then once again everything turned to disaster.

First, Mindy disappeared. It wasn't like before with

Gabe and Justin. There was no fight. There was no reason for Mindy to leave. She was just gone one morning.

Then Hayden vanished. Brook returned to the cabin one day and for the first time since the beginning of the summer it was empty.

Brook had to go into lock down. She huddled in the bathhouse with Erika and Cora for several days. She sparingly went to the main camp. Only when their food and water was low or curfew did Brook dare show her face.

Finally, Brook knew her plan was done for. The locks were changed. All the keys that the volunteer campers had were useless. Carl was no longer her strongest ally. He became yet another burden relying on Brook's help to get out.

Mindy had given them up. Brook's own plan had backfired on her because she thought she could help Mindy.

The Night of the Tenth was just around the corner. Brook had no expectations for that night. The camp was warned that their judgment was going to be at hand.

Her only hope now was they could fight their way through the office and get to the garage. Their only chance was to do it on the last night of the camp, the

Night of the Tenth. Brook was counting on it being a busy time for everybody. She could use that to her advantage and sneak in to the garage to steal a van. It was the only way.

The Night of the Tenth was finally upon them. Fear and dread filled the air. Cora was unmanageable. Neither Brook nor Erika could get her to her feet.

It hurt Brook to admit it, but they had to leave her behind. She decided once they got the van they would come back around for her. It was the only way they would survive.

"We have to go," said Brook. They were now down to only three people once they joined with Carl. Brook hoped that was enough.

The camp was eerily quiet. Brook and Erika walked through the clear skies. The sun was setting and the moon was starting to shine. The girls were planning on meeting Carl at his cabin. Then they would make their charge for a van.

Most of the campers were in their cabins. The curfew was earlier than usual. Brook and Erik had to be careful not to get caught on their way to the cabin. If they were seen their plan would be in jeopardy.

Luckily, they made it without a hitch. Night took over. When they got to the cabin Brook looked through one of the windows. The cabin was empty. They circled around and entered through the backdoor.

"Carl?" Brook called out.

Footsteps shuffled around in the front room. Carl opened the door. He smiled with relief when he saw Brook.

"What took you so long?" he asked.

"We had to be careful," said Brook.

"Just one more person," said Carl. "That's it?"

"I've been having problems," said Brook. "We'll have to push through."

Carl looked at Erika. He examined her from top to bottom.

"Are you that girl from the first week? I thought you were dead."

"I got better," grumbled Erika.

"Where are the rest of your bunkmates?" Brook asked.

"They are at the chapel," said Carl. "They said you could wait there over night."

"Then we need to go," said Brook. "Do you still have the keys to the van?"

"Right!" exclaimed Carl. He felt around in his pockets for a quick second then gestured for Brook to wait a moment. He went back to his bed and dug through his drawers. After a little bit of searching he found the keys. Carl was proud and raised them up for display. "Here we go!"

"Then let's move," ordered Erika. "I've had it with this place."

They were interrupted by a scream cutting through the night. It carried all through the camp. Then it was followed by another and another. It was an endless echo of fresh cries for help.

The three of them stood in silence as they listened to the chorus of pain that was going through the camp.

"What the hell is going on?" Brook asked. Neither of the other two could answer.

They hurried out of the cabin to investigate. What was once a quiet camp now became a madhouse. Campers were running around the grounds in a panic. Some were running in one direction others were heading the opposite to see what was happening.

The screams were coming from one direction; away from the runners. It was toward the sermon hill. Brook could not resist. She had to know what was going on. The more information she had the better chance she had at escape. She had to know what she was up against.

Erika and Carl followed Brook toward the source

of the screams. They arrived at the hill. Torches were lit at the base. They could see the gates were wide open.

Brook's heart dropped. If the gates were open that meant the killer was free to roam. The Avenger of Blood was on the campsite.

Then she looked over and registered what was on the cross near the altar. Fear gripped her even tighter. She could not breathe. She could barely think.

Cora was crucified on the cross. Her skin was peeled off. Brook could only tell it was Cora by the color of her hair. The rest was blood and bone. Campers were swarming around the gruesome display.

The Avenger of Blood had been in the abandoned zone. How long had they known Brook and the others were out there? There was no going back. Brook needed to escape tonight or die trying. There was no longer any place to hide.

"We need to go now," said Brook.

The three of them changed directions and headed for the main office. More screams echoed into the night. As they made their way through the camp dead bodies started to pile up. The Avenger of Blood was making His judgment over the damned. Sinners would perish in Hell.

"Oh my God, look," said Erika. She pointed to

their right. Out in the distance they saw it.

The Avenger of Blood marched through a group of campers. His spearhead struck those with sin in their hearts. As the destroying angel walked through the crowd it left several alive. Those lucky few were covered in others' blood. They cowered on the ground fearful for their souls. They were God-fearing and praised the Lord for their lives.

"They can't do this," said Erika. "They have no right. God cannot make this kind of judgment."

"This is not God," said Brook. "It's just some crazy people. That is all."

"I don't care," said Erika. "They are doing it in God's name. We are dying because God does not approve. I don't approve of Him."

Erika started to walk off in another direction. She left Brook and Carl behind.

"Where are you going?" Brook asked. "The garage is this way." She pointed in the opposite direction.

"I'm going to stop this," said Erika.

"We have to stick together," said Brook.

"Then I'll catch up to you," said Erika. "Just get the van."

Brook could not stop her. Erika went off looking for revenge.

"We can't do this with just two of us," said Carl.

"We will have to," said Brook.

Brook and Carl returned to their main goal. They continued on their mission to the garage at the main office. Their path kept to the sides of the cabins and the tree line. They wanted to keep their backs to safety and their eyes on the camp.

After a few minutes, the office building was in their sights. There was just one final run and they would be safe inside. Then Brook heard her name being called out. She looked over. Neil was coming up to them.

"Brook! Brook!" Neil cried out. "Brook! I have been looking for you all over the place. I'm so glad to see you okay."

"What are you doing?" Brook asked Neil when he was closer.

"I wanted to help," said Neil. "I saw Carl get struck down by the Avenger of Blood earlier. The church was hit first."

"What do you mean Carl was struck down? He's right here," said Brook. She pointed at Carl.

Neil looked confused. He looked at Brook then over at Carl. Carl grimaced.

"That's not Carl," said Neil.

Brook looked over at the camper she assumed was Carl. His contagious smile was gone. He glared at Neil.

"That's Morgan," revealed Neil.

"Morgan?" Brook repeated. She remembered that was the name Cora said who hurt her. It was the name Gabe had said got him into his mess. Brook writhed in her skin. She had been helping him.

"Damn it, Neil, why couldn't you have kept your mouth shut," said Morgan.

"What the fuck are you doing?" Brook asked.

"I'm trying to get out of here," said Morgan. "I'm not dying here. I will not be killed by God."

"You hurt Cora," said Brook. "You're the reason she is dead now."

"No," said Morgan. "I just fucked her. She's the reason she's dead. She couldn't handle her life. She deserved to die."

"And you don't?"

"I'm a survivor," said Morgan. "I suggest you come with me. My offer is still open. We can still get out of here, Brook. I have the keys to the van. We just need to break inside."

"You did rape her," Neil said. "You told me you didn't."

· "I lied," said Morgan. "You fucking idiot, what is it going to take for you to realize that people use you. Nobody actually wants to be around you."

"That's not true," said Neil.

"Brook?" said Morgan. "Do you want him around?"

"He can stay," said Brook.

"Really? Was that before or after we were making our way to the van without him? He helped you find me. Didn't that deserve a ticket out of here? Or were you just using him?"

Brook kept quiet. She did not want to answer.

"Brook, I thought you needed my help. I was going to save you," said Neil.

"I did need your help," said Brook. "I got it. Thank you."

"I saw you in the cemetery," said Morgan. "You fought off the Avenger of Blood with real bravery. I knew from that moment that I had to know more. I wanted you on my side. Little Neil here, fell in love with you because I wanted him to follow you. It was adorable. We were all just using him."

"No. No!" screamed Neil. "It wasn't like that." He covered his ears to protect himself from what Morgan was saying.

"I'm not going with you," said Brook. "I'll find another way out."

"What are you going to do? There is nowhere to run. You can't walk out of here. It's my way or Hell."

As their conversation was going on none of them noticed the fourth presence approaching. The

Avenger of Blood was ready for his newest judgments.

The Left Hand of God stood over the three campers. Fresh blood covered its already grungy robe. There was no place to run. Its eyes were set on the three of them.

"Holy shit," muttered Morgan.

Neil dropped to the fetal position.

Brook stood her ground. She wasn't going to hide anymore. She was going to beat the killer before her.

"Neil, you have to get up," said Brook. "You have to get up and get out of here. Run as fast and as far as you can. Get out of here."

Neil would not budge. He was scared stiff.

"You don't have to tell me twice," said Morgan. He ran off into the shadows of the trees.

"Morgan! Morgan!" Brook called out. She did not want to lose him. He had the keys. But Brook could not leave Neil behind.

The Avenger of Blood was closing in. Brook got down to talk to Neil face to face.

"Please, run, Neil. You have to get out of here."

Neil shook his head. He was not going anywhere.

"I wanted to be with you," he said. "I wanted you to want me like any good boyfriend. Was that so wrong? Everybody always looked so happy. That's all I wanted. I just wanted to be desired like everyone else."

"You can still have that, Neil," said Brook. "But you have to get up and get out of here."

"No," said Neil again. This time he stood up to his feet. Brook was right beside him. Neither was going to run. The Avenger of Blood was only yards away now.

It stopped in its path then looked at the two of them. Its head tilted back and forth as it gazed at each of them.

"I'll get judged first," said Neil. "You should go. You are not ready."

"Neil, do not go up there," said Brook. "This isn't God. He will kill you."

"I will survive this," said Neil. "I have seen others pass the judgment. I will as well."

Neil stepped forward. Brook grabbed his arm, but he shook it off. He was determined to be judged like everybody else.

"Do not do this!" Brook screamed. "There is no such thing as God. He is not real. That is just a man in a mask. He will kill us all!"

Neil was not listening. He approached the Avenger of Blood with a smile on his face. The Avenger of Blood breathed down on top of Neil. They stood toe to toe.

Nothing happened.

Neil's smile grew wider. He turned around to face Brook with his arms opened wide.

"See!" celebrated Neil. "I can do it! I can be like everybody else. I am saved!"

Neil was so consumed in his victory he did not see the Avenger of Blood raise his spearhead. The blade dangled over Neil's head.

Brook cried out. "Neil, watch out!"

Then she charged to him.

The blade of the spearhead dropped down. Brook collided with Neil just as the Avenger of Blood pierced into Neil's neck.

Blood gushed out of his jugular. Brook tackled Neil to the ground. In a second, she was covered in Neil's blood. The spearhead was caught inside his neck. It was stuck in the fresh wound.

Brook looked into the fading eyes of Neil. Confusion and fear washed over his pale face.

He tried to talk, but he was too weak. Blood drooled out of his mouth. Then he died in Brook's arms.

The Avenger of Blood did not move. He stood over Brook and the fallen Neil. His breathing was deafening. Brook could not stand it. Why was the killer alive but Neil wasn't? This wasn't justice; not to Brook.

She grabbed the spearhead from Neil's neck and yanked it out. There was no pause. She turned around and rushed the Avenger of Blood.

Brook drove the blade into his chest. Then again. And again.

The spearhead went in and out of the Avenger of Blood's body. She hit the chest, the face, the arms, and legs; everywhere she could reach on the behemoth standing before her.

Then the breathing stopped. The Avenger of Blood crashed to the ground. Brook lost all of her strength. The spearhead was lodged in the Avenger of Blood's chest. It fell with him to the earth.

Brook collapsed on the ground. Two dead bodies surrounded her. For the first time the entire summer she started to cry. Her nightmare was over.

She mourned for Neil. In the end, he did save her. Brook just wished there was a way to repay him, but he was dead and that was it.

Brook still had to escape. The killer was gone, but they were still stuck in the middle of nowhere without a vehicle. Morgan was out there somewhere with the keys to the van. Brook figured she could head to the garage. If Morgan was serious about making his escape she could cut him off there. He would not know Brook had killed the Avenger of Blood. He would still be running in the shadows.

Brook struggled to get back to her feet. She could only get to one knee. All of her energy was spent. She needed a second wind. There was still a lot to do. Erika was out there somewhere. She needed to find her.

Then the breathing returned.

All of Brook's thoughts ended. She heard the breathing coming from behind her. It was the familiar sound of someone breathing through a mask.

Brook turned around. The Avenger of Blood was moving. Its hand reached out and grabbed hold of the spearhead pierced in its chest. It pulled the blade out and gripped it tight.

Then the Avenger of Blood sat up. Brook could not move. She was afraid. There were over a dozen stab wounds on the Avenger of Blood. That was before Brook lost count. He was dead.

The Avenger of Blood stood up to its feet. It looked down on Brook. She could not rise. She was stuck on her knees. The power of God was holding her down.

Her lips started to move. No sound came out but words were forming. She was praying.

Brook was praying to God. She had just killed the man standing over her. She knew of no other answer.

The Avenger of Blood raised its blade over its head. It was ready for His judgment.

In that last second, for the first time in Brook's life, she believed.

Wrath

Erika hated her summer.

She was forced to Psalm Springs by her parents. They insisted she go or be thrown out of the house. They told Erika she was not the same since her best friend's death the previous year. This was her chance to get right with God. If she could not do that then she had no right to be living under their roof, a house of God.

Erika hated the way the others were excited to be at Psalm Springs. There was nothing to be excited about. She only saw the ugly side of God and wanted nothing to do with it. God did not cherish their world. He let his people suffer. There was nothing to celebrate.

When Erika expressed that fact she was banished from Psalm Springs. She was left to be slain by the Avenger of Blood. There was no love in that action.

Her escape only fueled the flame of her hatred. Brook tried as hard as she could to get as many people as she could to safety. Erika watched her fail time and time again as the others fell to the power of the Lord.

It was the last night of the camp. The Night of the Tenth had begun. The Avenger of Blood walked through the camp handing out His judgment on all the sinners of Psalm Springs.

Sin had festered all summer. It spread amongst the campers like the plague. Like any sickness it only needed a few carriers before it became a pandemic.

Now, Erika could not stand back as the Avenger of Blood continued on its path of annihilation. She stood in the middle of a bloodbath and she remembered why she turned her back on God to begin with. He was a vengeful God, and Erika was made in His image.

Brook and who she thought was Carl were left behind. They could find a van without her. Erika had a different idea. She wanted to stop all the madness once and for all. Psalm Springs was allowing the deaths of hundreds of campers.

She began following the trail of dead and mutilated campers. Their bodies were sprawled across the grass around all of the cabins. Some were still alive. Their weeping could be heard underneath the screaming out in the distance.

Erika walked past several campers on their knees praying. She did not care if she disturbed them. They should not be praying to God anyway. He was not worthy.

"Get out of here!" she yelled at the campers on the ground. They looked up at her through bloody faces. Then they looked back down to the ground and their praying intensified.

Erika would have called them out by name, but she knew known of them. She was at the camp for only a week, even less if she didn't count the days she was taken away and locked up. None of these people around her were her friends. They were victims just like her, only they did not realize it.

Lights were on in many of the cabins. Erika could see inside through the windows. Girls and boys waited patiently for their time to be judged. Some were more dignified than others. There were groups huddled in the far corner of the room offering comfort to each other. One cabin was asleep.

As Erika turned the corner around one of the cabins she saw it. The Avenger of Blood was nearby. Its footsteps drummed in place with her breathing. It got closer with every breath she took.

This was the time. She was going to have to fight.

There was no more running. No more hiding. She was not afraid. She was angry.

Erika burst from around the cabin. She rushed forward and ran straight into open air.

The Avenger of Blood was gone. Erika looked around. The door to the cabin was wide open. Light poured out into the night. The monster was walking toward a group of girls sitting inside. They were each at their bedside praying. The Avenger of Blood walked down the center of the room; its fatal spearhead leaving drips of blood as it walked.

Erika attacked. She ran as fast as she could directly toward the Avenger of Blood. With full force she smashed into the monster's legs and lower back. The Avenger of Blood stumbled while Erika crashed to the ground.

Gasps were given all around the cabin. The girls looked at Erika in shock and fear. The Avenger of Blood was still standing. It turned around to look at its assailant.

Erika shuffled around to look at the Avenger of Blood. Colliding with it felt like slamming into a brick wall. Her arm was numb and it felt like she twisted her ankle.

That still did not stop her.

"Do you want to try to kill me again?" she screamed

at the Avenger of Blood.

There was no reply from the silent killer. Instead, Mindy spoke up from the group of girls.

"Erika? How? What are you doing?" Mindy asked.

Erika was stunned to see Mindy. She was so calm about the situation. Death was right at their door.

"I'm saving you," said Erika.

"God will save us," said Mindy. "The Avenger of Blood will not harm us. He is here to protect us."

All eyes were on Erika now. The girls stared at her with curiosity. The Avenger of Blood looked down on her. Its dead eyes placed judgment on Erika.

"We are safe," said Mindy. "I will pray for your soul." Then Mindy returned to her bedside and continued praying. The rest of the girls followed her example.

Erika slid backwards on the floor. The Avenger of Blood took a step forward toward her. She slid back again. Again, the Avenger of Blood stepped forward.

Erika was not going to beg for her life. She was not going to pray to be spared. God was a cruel being. Only a cruel god would allow its people to wallow in pain and anguish through their lives and then be sent to damnation for eternity because they did not have the strength to live up to His ideals.

Her best friend was dead. There was no reason that

Erika could see for it. Then everybody told her God had a plan. If this was God's plan then Erika hated it. It meant that God's plan was for her to suffer. That was not a god Erika was willing to follow.

The Avenger of Blood lunged forward. Erika scrambled to her feet. She was quicker than her would be murderer.

When Erika stood up a sharp pain ran through her right leg. She had re-aggravated her injury from the beginning of the summer. The Avenger of Blood was now in between her and the front door. Erika began to stumble through the cabin to the back.

She was moving at a slower pace now. The Avenger of Blood could easily keep up with her. Erika hurried for the door with her hobbled foot. She needed to regroup before attacking the Avenger of Blood again.

Then Mindy rushed to the back door. She stood right in front of it blocking the exit for Erika.

"Move!" Erika demanded.

"You must face your judgment, Erika," said Mindy. "He comes for us all eventually."

"Then I have time to wait," said Erika.

"You have struck out against God," said Mindy. "Your actions have consequences. Sinners must be punished. It is the only way the righteous will get into

Heaven."

The Avenger of Blood was getting closer. Erika could hear its footsteps grow louder. Its breathing kept a hollow rhythm. She could not stop. She could not let Mindy be the end of her.

Then Erika grabbed hold of Mindy's hair and slammed Mindy's head into the door. There was a crack as Mindy's skull broke away pieces of wood and paint. Blood was left on the spot where Mindy made impact.

She fell to the ground. Pieces of hair stayed in Erika's hand after she let go. Mindy convulsed in the corner of the room. Erika hurried to force the door open. Mindy's dying body was wedged between the door and the wall.

Erika rushed out of the cabin. The space felt free. Looking back she could see the Avenger of Blood was exiting the cabin. It was still following her.

Ignoring the pain, Erika ran and hopped out into the darkness. She needed to get as much room from her and the Avenger of Blood that she could.

Erika was going to need help to bring down the Avenger of Blood. She thought she could regroup with Brook and Carl. Together they could kill the monster. They were headed toward the main office and the garage.

Then Erika had another idea. Pastor Robbins was at the main office. He would be easier to kill.

Pastor Robbins was the leader of it all. He was the first one that told Erika she needed to forgive God for his actions. It was not her place to judge the Almighty's actions. It was above her understanding he told her. They were not the ones to question God. They were only meant to follow in His footsteps.

The main office was out in the distance. Erika stumbled several times on her way there. Every time she looked back. She was alone. The Avenger of Blood disappeared. It was no longer following her.

The screaming resounded in the near distance. Erika assumed there was somebody of more interest than her at the moment. She took the moment to rest against a tree. Her leg throbbed with pain.

Branches were scattered all around the ground. Erika grabbed hold of one nearly four feet long. She used it to stand back up. The dead branch was still strong enough to hold her weight. She had to keep moving. The Avenger of Blood could return at any time. There was no telling how many more campers there were that still needed to be judged.

Her journey was easier using the branch as a cane. The garage was on the other side of the building.

With every step the walk grew with agony.

Erika was planning on going through the garage. Brook and Carl should have been there by now. They could let her in and she could infiltrate the main office from within.

Screams were still off in the distance. The Avenger of Blood was circling the main office.

Erika got to the door of the garage. She used her stick to knock on the door. It echoed into the building several times.

There was still nothing behind her. The sight was clear. Then the door opened. Erika was relieved. She nearly fell through the doorway getting inside. Luckily, Morgan was there to catch her.

"Carl," she said to Morgan. "You guys made it."

"Just me," he said. "Brook didn't make it."

Erika dropped her head. "I'm sorry. What happened?"

"She saw somebody she wanted to try to save," said Morgan. "She wasn't fast enough. I told her not to go."

"Thank you for waiting for me," said Erika. She limped further into the garage. There were a dozen vans parked side by side. One van was running and had its lights on.

Erika looked around the room. She saw the

doorway to the rest of the main office building.

"Will you wait for me a little longer?" Erika asked.

"What? Why? Let's go," said Morgan.

"I have one more thing I have to do," said Erika.

"We can't wait forever. That thing is coming for us," argued Morgan.

"Then go without me," said Erika. "Are there keys to another van? I'll drive myself out of here."

"What is taking so long?" said Chrissy. She was standing in the back of the van at the open sliding door.

Erika looked over and glared at the unfamiliar girl. She was not a part of the plan.

"Who is that?" Erika asked.

"Who are you?" Chrissy asked Erika.

"What's going on?" asked Alissa as she joined her friend, Chrissy, in the doorway of the van.

"Where the hell did they come from?" Erika asked Morgan.

"They needed a way out," said Morgan. "I said I could offer them one."

"How do you know we can trust them?" Erika fumed.

"It's fine. I know them," he said.

"I don't care," said Erika. "I don't know you. I just had to fight past a number of girls that would throw me out to the fucking killer without a second thought. They are no different." Erika pointed at the two newcomers accusingly.

"Morgan, can we just leave already?" Chrissy asked.

Erika turned her attention back to Morgan. Her eyes were red with fury.

"Morgan?" Erika asked. "I thought your name was Carl."

Morgan's demeanor changed. He no longer looked defensive and foolish. His shoulders dropped down like a weight had lifted off. The final lie was exposed and he was free.

"Just get in the car," said Morgan. "I'm tired of this shit. I'm leaving. Thanks for nothing. I got in here all by myself. This whole camp is going down in flames. Nobody bothered to watch the garage. I guess I over prepared."

"You're Morgan," Erika said. "You're the one who hurt Cora."

"I did fuck all to her," said Morgan. "She was just a whiny bitch. All she ever did was get people to give her things. Just because she had breasts did not mean she could have anything she wanted. Fuck her."

"Let's go!" yelled Chrissy.

"Shut up!" Erika yelled back.

"You're not going anywhere," Erika said to Morgan.

"You don't deserve to leave."

"I am not dying here," said Morgan. "All the shit I've had to put up with this summer. I had my fun, and it's not going to end now."

Morgan turned away and headed towards the car. He was done talking to Erika.

"Finally," said Alissa. "We need to go. Is she coming?"

Erika was furious. She was not going to let Morgan leave. She swung her walking stick wide and low. It struck Morgan across the back of the knees. He crumbled to the floor.

"I told you, you are not getting out of here," yelled Erika. She slammed the branch down again onto Morgan's back.

He cried out in pain. Erika did not stop. She pinned Morgan to the floor. Her entire weight pressed down on his chest. His arms were pinned down. He could not move. He could not escape.

Erika began pummeling Morgan with her fists. She struck his face with her left then her right. He begged her to stop in between punches, but Erika was not going to listen. She was going to give Morgan what he deserved.

Chrissy and Alissa ran out from the van to try to stop Erika. When they got close Erika stopped for a moment from hitting Morgan to pick up her stick. She growled at the girls.

"Stay away!"

Chrissy and Alissa kept their distance. They pleaded with Erika to let Morgan go and they could all get out of there. They were still being hunted by a killer on the loose.

"Stop it!" they yelled. "We need to leave."

Erika grew angrier with every punch she threw. Morgan was no longer defending himself. His face was becoming a bloody mess.

Then the girls screamed even louder.

Erika looked up from her beat down. The doorway to the garage was open and the Avenger of Blood stood in its path. Blood and slash marks covered the Avenger of Blood all across its upper body. Erika could tell it had been in a fight.

She stood up from the defeated Morgan. The van was close by. She knew she could make it before the Avenger of Blood caught her.

"Get in the van," she ordered the two girls.

There was nobody left but her. Cora was dead. Brook was dead. The summer was over.

She kneeled back down and started feeling for Morgan's keys in his pockets. Morgan groaned in pain as Erika began digging for them. She was not gentle about it. The Avenger of Blood was walking forward into the garage. Then she got a hold of them.

Erika moved as fast as she could with her injured leg to the van. Chrissy and Alissa were already waiting for her. They trembled in the back of the van. Their eyes never left the Avenger of Blood.

Erika started the engine. The Avenger of Blood was still a distance away. She locked all the doors. They were safe for the moment, but she did not know how to open the garage door.

Erika looked all over for a remote control. There was nothing on the sun visor. It wasn't in the glove compartment. She realized they were still trapped inside the building with the monster.

"Let's go, let's go, let's go, let's go," said Chrissy.

"Hold on," yelled back Erika. The rest of her thought was cut off by the sound of breaking glass.

The Avenger of Blood broke through one of the side windows of the van. Its arm reached inside the van with its spearhead. Chrissy and Alissa screamed at the top of their lungs. They dived down to the ground to avoid getting cut by the blade.

She put the car into gear. Erika jerked the van forward several feet. It sent the Avenger of Blood reeling to the ground.

The remote to the garage door was nowhere to be

found. Erika adjusted. She moved the van around and placed it facing directly at the closed garage door.

The Avenger of Blood was getting back to its feet. This time the behemoth looked directly at Erika. She could hear its heavy breathing.

Erika waited. She did not take her foot off of the brake. Her exit was close, but she could not make a run for it yet. There was still something she had to do.

The Avenger of Blood started to come around to the front of the van. It was making its way to Erika in the driver's seat.

Then Erika put her foot on the gas. The van charged forward.

The tires screech from the sudden acceleration. The van hit the Avenger of Blood head on. Erika felt the impact then the rough ride as the van drove over the monster.

Her speed did not stop. She did not look back. That impact was satisfying enough. The van continued forward and collided with the garage door.

Sparks erupted from the hit as the garage door scraped against the van. And just like that they were outside. Erika was one step closer to freedom.

She tried to keep the van steady, but the collision was too much for her. The van swerved to the side. Erika overcorrected. The van went swerving in the other direction.

Then gravity grabbed hold. Erika felt her stomach jump to her throat. Chrissy and Alissa screamed louder than ever.

The van toppled over and slid across the ground. Erika jumbled around in her seat. She didn't even realize she had put on her seatbelt.

Broken glass sprayed everywhere. Erika's entire body was in pain. She hung in her seat tangled in her seatbelt.

The plan had fallen apart. Everything that Brook was working toward just ended in one desperate attempt to flee.

Erika struggled, but she finally freed herself from her restraints. She had to fight through the pain to climb out of the sideways van. She did not bother to check on Chrissy or Alissa. When she reached the outside she fell out over the side. The ground was an unwelcome break to her fall.

Her only solace was that it was over. She ran over the Avenger of Blood. He would not be walking anytime soon.

"That is enough!" interrupted a new voice. Pastor Robbins and several counselors in green were outside of the garage.

The counselors moved fast. Erika was hurt. She

did not have the strength to fight back. Her stick was still in the garage.

When she looked over in that direction she saw two more counselors carrying Morgan outside toward them.

"Let him die!" Erika yelled out. "He deserves to die!"

"It is not your place to judge the lives of others, Erika," said Pastor Robbins. "Only those without sin may cast the first stone."

"He raped Cora. He's been lying to us all. He deserves to die," screamed Erika.

"That will be for the Lord to decide," said Robbins.

The counselors rounded up all of the campers. Erika was held down by two counselors, while the other two got Chrissy and Alissa out of the van. They were badly hurt. Chrissy was holding her arm. It had been broken. Pastor Robbins came to watch over them. They were too afraid to run away.

"There is nothing to be afraid of," said Pastor Robbins. "Unless there is sin in your heart. I warned you at the beginning of the summer that you should not wear your sin like a badge of honor. It is not a badge. It is an anchor."

"This is crazy," said Erika. "This is evil."

"Watch your tongue," said Pastor Robbins. "Evil is

letting the world fester in its own filth. Evil is bringing the good hearted down to the pits of Hell. God is not evil. It is you Erika that is evil. It is the sinners that come to Psalm Springs. They are evil.

"They disobey their creator and savior. This world was never meant to be their playground. We were created to serve the Lord. Then and only then will he love us like we deserve."

"We are innocent. We haven't done anything," defended Erika.

"Haven't you?" questioned Pastor Robbins. "You spoke out against God. You planted the seed of distrust in all the minds of many of the sinners here. I have failed this summer because you had a vendetta against God.

"And all the others that have fallen tonight. What of them? I'll tell you. They are thieves, liars, deviants, heathens, sluts. They spread diseases, corrupt others around them, and they enjoy it. When you are told about the word of God then there is no further excuse. You need to become His faithful servant or be damned to Hell. That is the way of life."

"Now," finished Pastor Robins. "It is time for our judgment."

They were all lined up. The counselors held Erika in place. She could not escape. Morgan was nearly unconscious. He was in no condition to run.

"Ezekiel 37:5-6, *this is what the Sovereign Lord says to these bones: I will make breath enter you, and you will come to life. I will attach tendons to you and make flesh come upon you and cover you with skin; I will put breath in you, and you will come to life. Then you will know that I am the Lord*," preached Pastor Robbins.

Erika turned at the sound of rubble moving. Pieces of scrap metal were tossed aside. Erika watched in stunned fashion as the Avenger of Blood was walking through the destruction of the wreck. She hit it with the van and it had not died. What was it going to take to stop the monster?

"You cannot kill an instrument of God," said Robbins.

The Avenger of Blood first passed Pastor Robbins. Its blade was still.

Then it reached Chrissy and Alissa. The two girls cowered in front of the behemoth.

"Please, please, please," they whispered together.

Two hacks of the spearhead later the two girls fell to the ground dead.

"Noooo!" screamed Erika. She tried once again to free herself, but the counselors were too strong.

"Deceived by sin," said Pastor Robbins. He was disappointed in his campers. Many of them had failed.

As Erika listened to Pastor Robbins she began to feel around on the ground. Her fingers felt the sharp edge of a small rock.

The Avenger of Blood stepped up to the beaten body of Morgan. The counselors placed him on the ground. Then they dropped to their knees before the power of God.

"Don't you dare let him live," scolded Erika. "If you let him live then you better make sure you kill me this time because I am coming for him and then the rest of you."

The spearhead stayed at the side of the Avenger of Blood. It did not raise it up for a killing blow.

"You son of a bitch," cursed Erika. "He is a sinner. He is the worst of us. Kill him!"

Then the Avenger of Blood stomped down on Morgan's head. His skull was crushed under the weight of the mighty killer.

Erika reveled in seeing Morgan die. Cora was not perfect, and Erika barely liked her, but Morgan had no right to touch her. Her thirst for vengeance was being filled.

Now, she waited. The Avenger of Blood approached her and the counselors holding her down. They released her.

The Avenger of Blood stood before her, and Erika

stood up to face the Left Hand of God. Her hand held tightly to her new weapon.

"Wait!" came another interruption from the darkness.

Erika looked over. Brook was emerging from the shadows. Erika was surprised to see her unharmed. Morgan told her she was dead.

"Don't kill her," said Brook. She walked straight up to Erika and the Avenger of Blood. There was no fear in her step.

"She can still be saved," said Brook. She was talking to the Avenger of Blood. When she got to the two of them Brook stood in between the confrontation.

"What's going on, Brook? What are you doing?" Erika asked.

"I'm saving you," said Brook.

"It's going to kill us."

"No," said Brook. "Not if you believe."

Erika grabbed a hold of Brook's shoulder and turned her around.

"What is going on?" Erika asked again.

"I've seen the truth," said Brook. "I get it now. This is God. This is the power that we were meant to see. You cannot turn your back from that. It is awesome. There is no escaping it."

"Will you listen to yourself," said Erika. "This isn't you."

"I stabbed it. I killed it and it stood right back up," said Brook. "It breathes eternal life. That is the power of God."

"This is bullshit," said Erika. "I'm not following that thing. I don't care how powerful it is. I will not bow down to it!"

"You have to find the forgiveness in your heart," said Brook. "We are the same, Erika. We've both been putting our hatred on this camp. I let it go. You can, too. If you can find it in your heart to let go of your anger then God can save you."

"We are not the same," said Erika. "You hated the people here. You just hated the sheep that followed the shepherd. I hate the shepherd."

"Don't do this, Erika," warned Brook. "It does not have to end here. You can get through this."

"It does for me," said Erika. "I will not be judged by God for he is not my god."

Then Erika drove the rock in her hand directly into her throat.

"No!" Brook screamed. Brook grabbed hold of Erika before she could hit the ground.

Blood flowed out of the wound in her neck. Erika's once yellow shirt was staining red.

The pain irradiated all across her body then it began to dull. Erika felt herself begin to slip away. She looked up at Brook begging to save her life. She watched the Avenger of Blood begin to walk away.

Erika had beaten it.

We'll See You Next Year

It was the beginning of a brand new year at Psalm Springs. All the new campers with happy faces filled the area. The counselors were excited to spread the love and power of God.

Volunteer campers were huddled outside the special care facility at Psalm Springs. They were listening to their counselor talk about their duties while helping out.

Many of their patients could not tend to themselves. Some of them were old and had to be helped getting around. There were babies that needed to be watched. Others were their because of injuries and could no longer live a normal functioning life.

"This is one of my favorite patients," said the counselor. "She was a camper just like you and me at one time. Things went tragic though. She thought violence was the only answer and tried to take her own life. They tried to help her, but her injuries were very severe. She is lucky to be alive. I prayed for her every night. I still do. God saw to it to spare her. She still has the chance to forgive the hatred in her heart.

"She needs to be fed, changed, and washed throughout the day. While you are with her I recommend keeping her entertained. Please, read to her or tell her about your day. Her body no longer works properly, but that does not mean her mind doesn't. We're on the Book of John, right now. You can continue from there for her."

The campers nodded as they listened to Brook give her instructions. Erika could not move. Her major loss of blood destroyed functions in her body. She was paralyzed throughout.

Everyday Brook came to her to take care of her. It was just like before when they first met. Brook was the survivor, the girl that never gave up, and Erika was the girl destined to live in Hell.

Hebrews 10: 26-31

If we deliberately keep on sinning after we have received the knowledge of the truth, no sacrifice for sins is left, but only a fearful expectation of judgment and of raging rife that will consume the enemies of God. Anyone who rejected the Law of Moses died without mercy on the testimony of two or three witnesses. How much more severely do you think a man deserves to be punished who has trampled the Son of God under foot, who has treated as an unholy thing the blood of the covenant that sanctified him, and who has insulted the Spirit of grace? "It is mine to avenge, I will repay," and again, "The Lord will judge his people." It is a dreadful thing to fall into the hands of the living God.

For updates on future projects by
Dane G. Kroll
please visit

facebook.com/danegkroll

or

follow @DaneGKroll on Twitter

Dane G. Kroll is also the writer of the kaiju series *Realm of Goryo* and fantasy series *Eluan Falls*.

Made in the USA
San Bernardino, CA
20 June 2015